FROM PLAYING FIELD to BATTLEFIELD

Great Athletes Who Served in World War II

Rob Newell

Naval Institute Press
Annapolis, Maryland

Naval Institute Press
291 Wood Road
Annapolis, MD 21402

Library of Congress Cataloging-in-Publication Data

Newell, Rob, 1963–
  From playing field to battlefield : great athletes who served in World War II / Rob Newell.
     p. cm.
  Includes bibliographical references and index.
  ISBN 1-59114-620-8 (alk. paper)
  1. World War, 1939–1945—United States—Biography. 2. United States—Armed Forces—Biography. 3. Professional athletes—United States—Biography. I. Title.
  D769.N48 2006
  940.54'173092—dc22
                                                  2005037959

Printed in the United States of America on acid-free paper ♾

13 12 11 10 09 08 07 06   9 8 7 6 5 4 3 2

First printing

From
PLAYING FIELD
to
BATTLEFIELD

For all who place service to others above themselves

CONTENTS

ACKNOWLEDGMENTS

Much has been written about the unselfishness and generosity of what many say has been America's greatest generation. After conducting dozens of interviews with the men highlighted in this book, I believe those characterizations are right on the mark. Almost to the man, the former players and coaches I was privileged to speak with for *From Playing Field to Battlefield* could not have been more generous with their time. In many instances they welcomed me into their own homes and patiently answered questions I'm sure they've been asked many times before, usually ending with, "Anything else I can do for you, young man?" before they walked me to the door or concluded our phone conversations. They were humble, honest, and good-natured about their athletic careers and their experiences in the military, and I thank them again for sharing their stories with me.

In the instances where those profiled had already passed away, I tried to speak with family members, friends, or former teammates to get a more personal perspective. For example, Dom DiMaggio and Bobby Doerr graciously spoke about their friend and former teammate Ted Williams; Tom Landry Jr. spoke eloquently about his father, as did former players Charlie Waters and Larry Cole; Red Frye and Erwin Prasse gave up part of their afternoons to talk about their teammate Nile Kinnick; and Pete Wright spoke generously about his uncle, Jack Lummus. There are numerous others not mentioned here. I sincerely thank them all for their invaluable insights. In many cases, those I spoke with also had been in the military during World War II, and their own stories of service and sacrifice were both humbling and extraordinary.

There is one story in particular, told to me by Dr. Tom Brown, a U.S. Navy surgeon, that is not included in the book but that I will always remember. Brown was a friend of Jack Lummus, the Marine Corps platoon commander and former New York Giants receiver who was posthumously awarded the

Congressional Medal of Honor for his heroism during the Battle of Iwo Jima. Brown was also on Iwo Jima, working feverishly to help hundreds of Marines wounded during that bloody battle, including Lummus. He was sharing his memories of Lummus when I asked him how difficult it was—with the intense fighting taking place all around him—to do his medical work on the Marines.

He paused for a few seconds and then said, "Well, let me tell you something. That first night, I was laying down in this shallow ditch I'd dug for myself, and I was afraid. But then I remember looking up to the sky. It was a beautiful night, lots of stars, and I remember telling myself, 'There's a reason you're here. There are people who need you. You need to get a hold of yourself.' And after that, I was much more at peace."

Others I spoke with had similar stories. I thank them all for sharing them with me.

The research libraries at the baseball, basketball, and pro football halls of fame were an invaluable resource. Whenever I called, whomever I spoke with always seemed to have the answer or statistic right at their fingertips, and they were always willing to promptly e-mail it to me to ensure I had the proper reference. The same holds true for the sports information and alumni offices at the University of Iowa, the University of Michigan, and Notre Dame, Stanford, and Baylor Universities, all of which were extremely helpful in locating and connecting me with former players. I was also fortunate to have access to the National Defense University's top-notch library. Its professional research staff, led by José Torres, was tremendously helpful. During the past few years I've also relearned how important public libraries are as an information resource for our communities and young people. To all the librarians who patiently guide and introduce people to books and new knowledge every day, thank you.

Finally and most importantly, a special thank-you to my family—Mary, Mary Kate, Sally, Robby, and Timmy—for their encouragement, enthusiasm, and most of all good humor throughout this project. I love you all very much.

From
PLAYING FIELD
to
BATTLEFIELD

INTRODUCTION

"Be it enacted by the Senate and House of Representatives of the United States of America . . . the Congress hereby declares that it is imperative to increase and train the personnel of the armed forces of the United States . . . and that in a free society the obligations and privileges of military training and service should be shared generally in accordance with a fair and just system of selective compulsory military training and service."

> —U.S. Congress, Selective Training and Service Act,
> September 16, 1940

"As to the players themselves, I know you agree with me that individual players who are of active military or naval age should go, without question, into the services."

> —President Franklin Delano Roosevelt to
> Baseball Commissioner Kenesaw Landis,
> February 1942

When Congress passed the Selective Training and Service Act in September of 1940, requiring every man between the ages of twenty-one and thirty-six to register for military service, the sports landscape in America was much different than it is today. Baseball was truly the national pastime, the game Americans felt the most passionate about, followed by college football, boxing, and horse racing. The National Football League (NFL), although nearly twenty years old, had yet to generate widespread appeal, and the National Basketball Association (NBA) was still nine years from even being born. With the start of the National Collegiate Athletic Association (NCAA) tournament in 1939, college basketball was just beginning to register in the national sports consciousness. But as different as the sports scene looked in 1940, there was no question that sports mattered to Americans—a lot. Since the early 1920s, when the first radio broadcasts had allowed people to share in the feats of athletes such as Jack Dempsey, Red Grange, and most of all Babe Ruth, sports had become an increasingly important part of the country's social fabric.

"They united America and bound Americans to each other as other aspects of national life had not," said writer and historian David Halberstam. "They offered a common thread, and in time a common obsession. Americans who did not know each other found community and commonality by talking of their mutual sports heroes."[1]

Even during the Depression years of the 1930s, when one out of every four Americans lost their jobs and thousands of banks failed, sports continued to be a popular escape for a country struggling to regain the promise and prosperity that had seemed so limitless just a decade earlier. Instead of Jack Dempsey, Babe Ruth, and Red Grange, it was now names like Joe Louis, Joe DiMaggio, and Sammy Baugh that graced sports pages and movie newsreels across the United States.

By 1941 America's passion for sports—fueled by a recovering economy and one of baseball's greatest seasons—had never been higher. But in one day— December 7, 1941—everything changed. Suddenly, to both fans and players, the Japanese attack on Pearl Harbor made sports seem very inconsequential.

"Like a lot of people, I really thought we were in serious trouble," recalled Cleveland Indians pitching great Bob Feller when asked how he felt when he heard the news about Pearl Harbor. "The British were getting beaten up, and the war effort now just seemed more important than anything else."[2]

Up until then, Congress's passage of the Selective Service Act had not had much impact on either college or professional sports. While college athletes twenty-one and over had registered as required, the law contained a provision that gave all university students a deferment from the draft until July of 1941. It also contained provisions to defer service for the majority of men with families and for those "found to be physically, mentally, or morally deficient or defective." Hank Greenberg, the Detroit Tigers' star first baseman, had been the most well-known professional athlete to join the service prior to December 7. Troubled by the increasing reports of Jews being persecuted by Hitler's Nazi regime and sent to concentration camps in Europe, Greenberg left the Tigers nineteen games into the 1941 season to join the army. He completed his training on December 5, 1941, and was discharged, but when he heard the news of Pearl Harbor he immediately reenlisted, this time serving as an officer in the Army Air Corps. "I have not been called back," he explained. "I am going back of my own accord. Baseball is out the window as far as I'm concerned. I don't know if I'll ever return to baseball."[3]

Greenberg's actions reflected the overall sentiment of the country. Congress dropped the draft age to eighteen, but thousands of young men chose to voluntarily enter one of the services rather than wait to be drafted. Every aspect of American society was affected, and sports were no exception. The NFL championship game between the Chicago Bears and New York Giants was played as scheduled on December 14, but only 13,300 fans showed up to watch the Bears beat the Giants 31–7. The New Year's Day Rose Bowl game matching Oregon State and Duke University was moved to the Duke campus in Durham, North Carolina, for fear that a large public gathering on the West Coast might be considered too easy a target for another Japanese attack. And major league baseball, with spring training just a few months away, began giving serious consideration to canceling its season. Commissioner Kenesaw Landis felt it wouldn't be appropriate for baseball, or any other sport for that matter, to continue while American soldiers were fighting and dying in Europe and the Pacific. His comments sparked a nationwide debate, and since baseball was the leader of the sports world, it was widely believed that whatever baseball did, other sports would follow. Aware of the significance of his decision, Landis wrote a letter to President Franklin Roosevelt asking for direction. "Baseball is about to adopt schedules, sign players, make vast commitments, go to training camps," he wrote. "What do you want us to do? If you believe we ought to close down for the duration of the war, we are ready to do so immediately. If you feel we ought to continue, we would be delighted to do so. We await your order."

After giving it some thought, Roosevelt responded to Landis with what has become known as the "green light" letter. "I honestly feel that it would be best for the country to keep baseball going," wrote Roosevelt. "There will be fewer people unemployed and everybody will work longer hours and harder than ever before. And that means that they ought to have a chance for recreation and for taking their minds off their work even more than before."

"Here is another way of looking at it," he continued. "These players are a recreational asset to at least 20,000,000 of their fellow citizens—and that in my judgment is thoroughly worthwhile." He did add that he felt those players who were qualified should leave the game and serve in the military. "As to the players themselves," wrote Roosevelt. "I know you agree with me that individual players who are of active military or naval age should go, without question, into the services. Even if the actual quality of the teams is lowered by the greater use of older players, this will not dampen the popularity of the sport."[4]

Baseball went on, but as the war continued its impact on the game was significant. Major league rosters steadily deteriorated as more and more players left to serve. The game's biggest names—Bob Feller, Ted Williams, and Joe DiMaggio—all enlisted. Eventually, 340 major leaguers and another 3,000 minor leaguers would serve. Some players, like DiMaggio, Pee Wee Reese, and Phil Rizzuto, spent the better part of their war years playing in exhibition games to entertain the troops, or serving as physical training instructors. But others saw combat. Feller, who voluntarily enlisted the day after Pearl Harbor, spent two years aboard the USS *Alabama* in the South Pacific as a chief petty officer in charge of one of the ship's 40-millimeter gun mounts. Warren Spahn, the game's all-time winningest left-handed pitcher, had just begun his major league career when the war started. He joined the army and fought throughout Europe with the 276th Combat Engineers, eventually earning a battlefield commission. Ralph Houk, who returned from the war to play for and later manage the Yankees, fought in the Battle of the Bulge, earning Silver and Bronze Stars as well as the Purple Heart. And a young minor league catcher named Lawrence "Yogi" Berra, not even seventeen at the war's beginning, served on navy rocket boats and was there off the coast of Normandy when U.S. and allied forces stormed into Europe on D-day.

The major leagues continued to play a regular schedule throughout the war, calling back older players who were long since retired and in several instances bringing up promising teenagers to keep the game going. (Joe Nuxhall was fifteen when the Cincinnati Reds put him into their starting rotation. "Probably two weeks prior to that, I was pitching against 7th, 8th and 9th-graders," he would recall. "All of a sudden, I look up and there's Stan Musial."[5]) However, the minor leagues were hit especially hard. In 1940 there were 314 minor league teams in 43 different leagues. Just three years later, that number was down to 62 teams in just 9 leagues.[6] When minor league owner Spencer Abbot lost his third starting second baseman to the army, he wondered if it might be time to shut his team down for the remainder of the war. "They must be gonna fight this damn war around second base," he said in frustration.[7]

Those baseball players who, for whatever reason, had been deferred from serving by their local draft boards came under increasing scrutiny and public criticism as the war progressed. Prior to the 1945 season, James Byrnes, head of the war mobilization effort for the Roosevelt administration, went as far as directing Gen. Lewis Hershey, chief of the Selective Service, to reexamine the draft status of all athletes. "Byrnes openly questioned how men with major disabilities could perform so superbly as athletes and yet be unfit for military service, or unable to find employment in war factories." The review resulted in dozens of additional players being drafted, which meant the further depletion of major and minor league rosters.[8]

Because of its enormous popularity, baseball was the sport most visibly affected by the war, but it certainly wasn't the only one. By 1941, college football had a devout following in many parts of the country. When college players began leaving their schools in big numbers in the summer of 1942, the rosters of college teams changed regularly as hundreds of players—now military trainees—were sent to new universities for specialized training. Elroy "Crazy Legs" Hirsch, an all-American halfback at the University of Wisconsin in 1942, joined the Marines and was one of several Badgers sent to Big 10 rival University of Michigan for officer training. Borrowing the name of President Roosevelt's prewar program to assist Great Britain, their new Michigan teammates referred to them as the "lend lease" Badgers. Hirsch's new surroundings didn't prevent him from also being an all-American for the Wolverines. Alex Agassi, an all-American guard for the University of Illinois in 1942, joined the Marines and spent the 1943 season playing for Purdue while attending their officer training program.[9]

Every Heisman Trophy winner from 1939 to 1944 served. Tom Harmon, Michigan's great running back and the 1940 Heisman winner, enlisted in the Army Air Corps. While on a training mission in 1943, his plane went down in a tropical storm over Dutch Guiana (now Suriname) in South America. Armed with a machete and a compass, he survived by hacking his way through fifty miles of jungle. Later in the year, he was shot down by Japanese Zeros in a dogfight over China but survived thanks to the help of the Chinese underground. "If you didn't have religion before the war, you did then," Harmon would later write in his book *Pilots Also Pray.*[10]

Iowa's legendary halfback—and the 1939 Heisman winner—Nile Kinnick put on hold a budding career in law and politics to join the navy in 1941. "Every man whom I have admired in history has willingly and courageously served in his country's armed forces in times of danger," wrote Kinnick in a letter to his family. "It is not only a duty, but an honor, to follow their examples as best I know how. May God give me the courage and ability to so conduct myself in every situation that my country, my family and my friends will be proud of me."[11]

While flying his F-4F Wildcat in a training mission over the Caribbean in June of 1943, Kinnick was tragically killed when his plane's engines failed, sending him crashing into the water. "Offhand, it is hard to think of any good quality which Nile Kinnick did not possess in abundance," were the words from newspapers throughout Iowa. "And now he is gone forever, and his dreams with him."

While the war shuffled the rosters of college football teams, it nearly forced the still-struggling NFL to shut down completely. With the military draft scooping up would-be professionals from the college ranks, as well as its current draft-age players, the league struggled to find enough players to field competitive teams that were worth watching. Like baseball, they survived by playing men who were overage and deferred from the draft, but some teams did fold. In 1943 the Cleveland Rams suspended their operations for the season, and the Pittsburgh Steelers merged with the Philadelphia Eagles to form the Phil-Pitt Steagles. When Philadelphia decided to go it alone for the 1944 season, the Steelers merged with the Chicago Cardinals. And in 1945 the old Brooklyn Dodgers (referred to as the "Tigers" for the 1944 season) merged with the Boston Yanks. By the end of the war, 638 professional football players had served in the armed forces. Twenty-one of them died in combat.[12]

Byron "Whizzer" White, the former all-American halfback from Colorado and future Supreme Court justice, returned from a year at Oxford to lead the NFL in rushing in 1940 as a member of the Detroit Lions. He joined the navy in 1942 and saw combat serving aboard destroyers in the South Pacific. Future Hall of Fame quarterbacks Sid Luckman and Otto Graham both served—Luckman in the merchant marines and Graham in the navy. And two NFL players, the Lions' Maurice Britt and the Giants' Jack Lummus, were awarded the Congressional Medal of Honor: Britt for his heroic actions during an intense battle against the Germans in Italy, and Lummus for his courage leading a Marine Corps platoon during the Battle of Iwo Jima.[13]

Despite facing a withering barrage of Japanese fire, Lummus single-handedly attacked several Japanese positions, allowing his platoon to break through Japanese lines. "Dearest Sis," Lummus had written his sister on his way to Iwo Jima. "It's been a long time since you heard from your long legged brother. . . . I needn't explain why I haven't written. . . . Our outfit is aboard ship and going into combat—just where I can't say . . . don't get excited if there is a delay because I'll write the first chance I get when we are ashore. There will be lots of work to be done before we have everything secured and little time for writing. . . . Take good care of yourself and say an extra prayer for your bud."[14] Although Maurice Britt would heal from his wounds and go on to become the lieutenant governor of Arkansas, Jack Lummus died from the injuries he suffered on Iwo Jima.

When World War II began, basketball—specifically, college basketball—was just beginning to develop a national following. The National Invitational Tournament (NIT) and the NCAA's own end-of-the-season tournament were creating new interest in the game. Although the war didn't halt the sport's rise in popularity, its impact was even more pronounced than it had been on college football. Instead of plugging holes in the line or backfield, basketball coaches adjusted to entire starting lineups leaving to join the service. In 1943 the University of Illinois had assembled the most dominant team in the country, going undefeated in the Big 10 and posting an overall record of 17–1. Their starting lineup of Andy Phillip, Ken Menke, Art Mathisen, Jack Smiley, and Gene Vance was known as the "Whiz Kids" and seemed a lock for the national championship. But on March 1, just before the start of the NCAA tournament, all five players left school for the military, abruptly ending the Fighting Illinis' tournament plans. Wyoming won the NCAA championship, but right after the tournament, they too lost their best players to the military, including Player of the Year Kenny Sailors, who enlisted in the Marines. At the other extreme, in 1944 Dartmouth made it all the way to the NCAA championship game after Bob Gale from Cornell, Larry Leggatt from New York University, and Dick McGuire of St. John's transferred there for officer training. They lost to Utah in overtime, and shortly after, the three left their new school for the navy.[15]

Professional basketball, meanwhile, was still trying to establish itself. Comprised of a hodgepodge of teams mostly from the Midwest, it was widely viewed as dull and uninspiring compared to the more fast-paced college game. Called the National Basketball League (NBL), its thirteen teams existed on shoestring budgets, representing small cities such as Sheboygan, Wisconsin; Akron, Ohio; and Fort Wayne, Indiana. To speed up games, the league abolished the rule requiring a jump ball after each basket, but other changes that had led to the growing popularity of college basketball—specifically, more fast breaks and the one-handed jump shot—had yet to be widely incorporated into the conservative NBL. As a result, pro games were low-scoring, rough-and-tumble affairs, played in gymnasiums where the number of empty seats usually outnumbered the fans. So when the war hit, its impact on the already fragile NBL was significant.

Several teams immediately lost their best players, and by the start of the 1943 season, teams in Akron and Indianapolis were forced to fold. The Chicago Bruins were also headed out of business until the Chicago-based Studebaker Car Company decided to step in and sponsor the team. The company had been converted to build military vehicles, exempting its employees, which now included the members of the basketball team, from the draft, because they were working in a war-related industry. Studebaker's sponsorship enabled Chicago to continue fielding a team, but by the beginning of the 1943–1944 season, there were only three other teams left in the NBL for them to play against.[16]

At that time, basketball's best player—college or pro—was Hank Luisetti. A three-time all-American at Stanford, and college basketball's all-time scoring leader, Luisetti had revolutionized the game with his running one-handed jump shots and flashy ball-handling. Married with a young daughter, he was working and playing for Oklahoma's Phillips Petroleum Company when the war began. His family responsibilities warranted a deferment from the draft, but Luisetti joined the navy in 1943 and served for the duration of the war as a physical training officer.

"My father came to San Francisco from Italy just after the 1906 earthquake," he said in explaining his reason for wanting to serve. "He was a very quiet man, and he worked in restaurants from six in the morning until ten at night. He was grateful for the opportunities this country gave him. When I was growing up he told me, 'This country's been good to us. If you get a chance, do something in return.'"[17]

John Wooden, himself a three-time all-American guard at Purdue, was teaching English and coaching basketball and baseball at Central High School in South Bend, Indiana, when the war started. After graduating from Purdue in 1932, he'd supplemented his eighteen-hundred-dollar-a-year teaching salary by playing professional basketball on the weekends for fifty dollars a game with the Indianapolis Kautskys. He enlisted in the navy and was called to active duty in February of 1943, receiving orders to be the fitness officer aboard the USS *Franklin*, which was deployed to the South Pacific. But just before shipping out, he came down with acute appendicitis.

"Since Navy regulations [at the time] say you can't go to sea for a minimum of thirty days after certain types of surgery, my orders to Franklin were rewritten," said Wooden. "I was reassigned to Iowa Pre-Flight, and a friend of mine from Purdue, Freddie Stalcup, replaced me on the Franklin."[18]

Several months later, Stalcup was killed when a kamikaze plowed into his battle station on one of the *Franklin's* gun mounts. Wooden, who would be discharged from the navy in 1945 and go on to coach UCLA to ten national championships, never forgot his friend or the realization that if not for his emergency appendectomy, it might have been him at that battle station.

Of course, baseball, football, and basketball were not the only sports to lose athletes to the war. Professional boxing, whose widespread popularity in 1941 was surpassed only by baseball, essentially came to a halt because so many fighters were in the service. "Five of eight titles were put on hold because Americans serving in the military were the champions and couldn't take time off to train or fight." Joe Louis, the heavyweight champion since 1937, enlisted in the army in 1942 and spent the duration of his service traveling around the world, visiting troops and participating in boxing exhibitions to raise money for the war effort. Billy Conn, Tony Zale, and Sugar Ray Robinson, as well as former champions Jack Dempsey and Gene Tunney all enlisted. And one future champion, a young Italian from Brockton, Massachusetts, named Rocco Marchegiano joined the army, serving with the 150th Combat Engineers in the European campaign following the allies' D-day invasion. He planned on becoming a baseball player when he returned home, but when a tryout with the Red Sox didn't work out, he turned to boxing, hoping to build on some of the boxing experience he'd gotten in the army. Six years later, and now known as Rocky Marciano, he knocked out Jersey Joe Walcott to win the heavyweight championship. When he retired in 1956, he'd still never lost a fight, his record a perfect 49–0.[19]

Golfers Slammin' Sammy Snead, Ben Hogan, and the legendary Bobby Jones all served, as did Lloyd Mangrum. Mangrum was injured at the Battle of the Bulge, but in 1946 he came home and beat Vic Ghezzi and Byron Nelson in a two-hole playoff to win the U.S. Open. And in tennis, top players like Bobby Riggs, Art Larsen, and Jack Kramer all put their careers on hold to enlist in the military.[20]

By the time World War II finally ended with the surrender of the Japanese on September 2, 1945, more than 16 million Americans had served their country in the armed forces. It had been a truly national effort, with men and women, young and old, putting their lives and careers on hold to enlist, not just because their country had asked them to, but also because they believed in their hearts that it was simply the right thing to do. Whatever their profession—doctor, teacher, lawyer, factory worker, student, laborer, or professional athlete—all were asked to share in the responsibility of answering their country's call to service. As the Washington Senators' star shortstop Cecil Travis would later say, "Everyone who was able was supposed to go in. Whether you were a baseball player . . . shouldn't and didn't have anything to do with it at all."[21]

It was a time in America when service truly mattered most. The pages that follow are profiles of some of the professional and college athletes who served in the military during the war. Some of the names you will undoubtedly recognize: baseball players such as Ted Williams, Jerry Coleman, and Bob Feller, or coaches such as football's Tom Landry and basketball's Dr. Jack Ramsay. Others are less well-known men, such as Bert Shepard, Bill Tosheff, Mario Tonelli, and Forrest "Lefty" Brewer. Although their notoriety and athletic and life accomplishments are as diverse as the personalities of the men themselves, they all have one thing in common: their experiences in the military profoundly influenced the course of their lives. Some, like baseball's Brewer and football's Jack Lummus and Nile Kinnick, made the supreme sacrifice, leaving friends and family forever wondering what might have been. Others would return with their perspectives of the world—and even more significantly, of themselves—forever changed, keenly aware that they were fortunate to have made it home, and determined, like the rest of their generation, to get on with the rest of their lives.

In the end, perhaps that is why the war years were truly such a unique time in the history of American sports. They were a time when, despite their unquestioned popularity and celebrity, the athletes themselves understood that something much more important than the outcome of games and matches was at stake: that they had an obligation as Americans to join their peers and do their part. They understood that it was a time when service to their country truly mattered most.

CHAPTER 1

The Man in the Hat

"There was no question, really. If you didn't fight, there was a chance the country would be taken over by the Germans or the Japanese. We were fighting a war for our country and wanted to get into the service to help. Then, we were a country of patriots. If we hadn't been, there's no telling what might have happened."

—Tom Landry

His image was in such stark contrast to his surroundings that if you didn't know him it would have been quite easy to wonder just what the stoic, sharply dressed gentleman in the gray fedora was doing among all the emotion and excess that exists on the sideline of an NFL football game. True, after twenty-nine seasons and five Super Bowl appearances as the head coach of the Dallas Cowboys—arguably the most popular team in America—it was difficult to imagine there was a person in the country who *didn't* recognize Tom Landry. But still, the contrasts were always startling.

While his younger coaching counterparts wore various outfits matching the colors of their team, Landry stuck to wearing a suit jacket, tie, and his trademark hat. In an environment where short tempers and emotional outbursts are the norm, Landry was always the picture of calm, rarely raising his voice and never using profanity. And in a sport increasingly dominated by chest-thumping, me-first athletes, Landry was about "team," demanding that his players, no matter how talented, set their egos aside and play within the framework of his disciplined system.

For the many millions of football fans who watched the Cowboys on all those Sunday afternoons, it was these contrasts that created the image of Landry as a cold and calculating "old-school" coach, who was emotionless, almost robotic, in the way he built and prepared his team to manufacture victory after victory. And there is truth in that image.

With a degree in industrial engineering, Landry was infamous for his analytical approach to the game. He would study films of an upcoming opponent for hours, dissecting their formations and plays to discern their weaknesses and then drafting his own game plans to exploit them. "It often seemed to me that he looked at football like a company production line," said D. D. Lewis, a Cowboy linebacker who played thirteen years for Landry. "He understood that there were certain controls you had to master . . . certain numbers you had to achieve . . . certain performance levels that needed to be maintained. And if that wasn't happening, you had to make changes."[1]

But year after year, with winning season piled upon winning season— twenty straight at one point—what all those fans, and even many of his players, didn't fully appreciate was that beneath the always-serious demeanor was the same kind of character that people such as NBC's Tom Brokaw would later capture to define an entire generation of Americans. They didn't see the humbleness, the countless small acts of kindness, and the unwavering value system centered on faith and family. And they didn't see Tom Landry the patriot—the World War II veteran who answered the call to military service, flying B-17 bombers from England in combat missions over Germany.

Tom Landry was all of those things. And like the generation from which he came, he shaped the lives of men in profound ways, teaching them how to succeed not just on the football field but also in life.

He was born and raised in Mission, Texas, a small town with a population of five thousand, nestled in the Rio Grande Valley in South Texas, just sixteen miles from the Mexico border. Like so many other towns of that size back then, it had a two-lane main street, Conway, lined with small, family-owned businesses—a barber shop, a few clothing stores, a grocery store, a movie theater, and of course the corner drugstore that doubled as a soda fountain, selling Cokes and malts. The Landry family lived in a small house a block from Conway Street. Ray Landry, Tom's father, was an auto mechanic, chief of the volunteer fire department, and Sunday school superintendent at the First United Methodist Church. Ruth Landry stayed home taking care of the four Landry children: Robert, Tommy, Ruthie, and Jack. During the Depression years, Tom recalls, his Mom fed and clothed all of them on $1.50 a day. "We never had a lot of anything, including privacy," said Landry in his autobiography. "All four of us kids shared a single attic bedroom that ran the full width of the house."[2]

He says Mission was like an extended family for the kids who grew up there. "Anyone you'd meet on the street knew who you were, where you lived, and often where you were heading," said Landry after he had become famous. "And while that meant privacy was at a premium and kids had a hard time getting into serious mischief, it proved to be good preparation for the kind of public life I've lived for more than forty years. I learned a sense of accountability early in life, accepting the fact that people were always watching—even when I wished they weren't."[3]

Sports—all of them—were just something he and his buddies did for the fun of it at whatever vacant lot or backyard was available. There was no formally organized Little League or Pop Warner football league. Their heroes weren't big-name athletes but the cowboys they'd see at the movie theater for a nickel on Saturday mornings—people like the Lone Ranger and Hopalong Cassidy. Tarzan was also a favorite.

"I knew little or nothing about organized professional sports," said Landry. "Once in a while I'd sit with the old black gentleman who shined shoes at the barber shop and listen to a radio broadcast of a New York Yankees game. Even in Mission we knew about the Yankees. But I couldn't have named a half-dozen big-league baseball teams. And I never knew there was such a thing as professional football."[4]

Landry did know about high school football, though. His older brother, Robert, played end for Mission High School, and as Landry moved into his high school years, he was eager to follow in his footsteps—perhaps too eager. When Bob Martin, then head coach of the junior varsity, held up the football and announced at the first practice that he needed a "smart, tough kid who will take this ball and initiate every play for our team," the freshman Landry immediately volunteered.[5]

"I believe I was tough, but I'm not sure how smart I was because that's how I became the 112-pound center of the Mission High School junior varsity football team," said Landry.[6]

But two years later, when Martin moved up to become the head varsity coach and needed a quarterback, he noticed that his once scrappy little junior varsity center was now 6'0", 170 pounds and could throw the football. "The kid had a good arm," recalled Martin. "He was growing tall, had some meat on him. I needed a quarterback and decided he'd be the one."[7]

It was 1940, and for the next two years Landry led single-A Mission High to district and South Texas regional championships, including a perfect

12–0 season in 1941—a season that was interrupted by the Japanese attack on Pearl Harbor.

Up until then, Landry says, the war had just been something he and his classmates occasionally heard their parents discuss, or saw in the newspapers. It seemed far away. "Honestly, until Pearl Harbor, I don't think we were all that aware about the war, what was happening overseas," he recalled. "I know personally, I wasn't. We were trying to win a championship in football and into school activities and just were not conscious of what was happening. That changed when Pearl Harbor was attacked."[8]

Landry's brother Robert immediately enlisted and began training to be a pilot with the Army Air Corps. Tom finished high school and, still just seventeen, accepted a football scholarship to the University of Texas. He was halfway through his first football season at Texas when his parents called with news that suddenly made the war hit home. Robert had been killed when the B-17 he was ferrying to England exploded in midair. Tom had been going through the typical freshman struggles, adjusting to more demanding academics and tougher competition on the football field, when he received the news. "I tried to shut it out by focusing on my classes and football," he said. "It didn't work, because they no longer mattered."

In November, a few months after his eighteenth birthday, Landry followed his brother's lead by enlisting in the army reserves and was accepted for pilot training with the Army Air Corps. He says although Robert's death accelerated his decision, he had always planned to serve. "There was no question, really," he said. "If you didn't fight, there was a chance the country would be taken over by the Germans or the Japanese. We were fighting a war for our country and wanted to get into the service to help. Then, we were a country of patriots. If we hadn't been, there's no telling what might have happened."[9]

He was called to active duty in February and immediately left school to begin pilot's training, stopping first at Shepherd's Field in Wichita Falls, Texas, for basic training and then Kelly Field in San Antonio for preflight training. It was during a stop at Eastern Oklahoma State College for additional classroom work that he had his first flying experience. Having never been in a plane before, Landry says he could hardly wait to take off. "We began to roll down that strip, engine whining, the plane gathering speed. The ground dropped away. Ten, twenty-five, fifty, a hundred . . . what a feeling to fly! But at 200 feet, everything went deathly silent." The plane's engine had died. "My heart began hammering in my chest. But my flight instructor never as much as flinched."[10]

The instructor quickly took the controls and glided the plane to a perfect landing in a cow pasture. After that initial harrowing experience, Landry says, the remainder of his flight training was easy. He earned his wings in Lubbock, Texas, and from there went to Sioux City, Iowa, to begin training as a copilot in the B-17 bomber. With machine gun mounts positioned around the plane to give it 360-degree coverage against enemy fighters, the B-17 was aptly nicknamed the "Flying Fortress" and had been flown extensively from England to strike deep into Germany. In the fall of 1944 the nineteen-year-old Landry, along with the rest of his ten-man crew, set sail for England aboard the *Queen Mary* to join the fight. They were assigned to the Eighth Air Force's 493rd Squadron in Ipswich, England, and were soon flying combat missions. By the fall of 1944 the once vaunted German Luftwaffe had been degraded, but the danger from antiaircraft guns on the ground was still very real. Flying into thick, dark clouds produced by hundreds of exploding flak rounds left a vivid and lasting impression on Landry.

"I can still picture the angry black cloud . . . as we approached our target that day," said Landry about their first combat mission. "And I remember the helpless, sinking fear I felt as we followed our squadron leader into the heart of that cloud. Nothing they had ever told us about during training prepared me for that experience. I could see the flak exploding all around us. And even though I couldn't really hear it over the roar of the giant B-17 engines, I could sometimes feel the shock vibrations through the plane."[11]

German factories, oil fields, and bridges were usually the assigned targets. The weather was often bad, and having enough fuel to make it back to Ipswich was always a concern. During one mission, Landry and his crew came within a minute or two of bailing out over enemy territory in the Netherlands when their plane's four engines suddenly died at once. After running through several restart procedures with no success, he and the plane's twenty-two-year-old pilot, Ken Saenz, concluded they had no other choice but to bail out.

Landry was making his way back to the bomb bay doors to jump when it occurred to him to try one last thing to restart the engines. He returned to the controls, pushed the fuel mixture knob all the way forward, and as he says, "nearly fell down when the engines roared back to life and the plane surged ahead. . . . Ken and I jumped back into our seats, pulled the plane out of its dive, and headed for home so close to the ground we had to zigzag to avoid the gunfire from the Germans in Amsterdam."[12]

That wasn't Landry's only close call. During another mission, he and his crew were tasked with bombing a German target in occupied Czechoslovakia, a long mission they knew might require more fuel then they had. Fortunately for them, the allies now controlled much of France, creating backup landing sites for crews that were low on gas. Sure enough, after successfully dropping their bombs, it became apparent they didn't have the fuel to make it back to Ipswich, so Landry and Saenz steered toward a backup landing field in France. But fog rolled in and became so thick they couldn't find the base.

"We finally dropped below the ceiling, nearly brushing the tree tops, our engines coughing and spitting on the fumes," remembered Landry. "We could see nothing but forests ahead. When a clearing suddenly opened up beneath us we dropped the plane and plowed a furrow through some farmer's land, hurtling toward a windbreak of trees at the far end of the field. We had no control and no steering as we slid between two trees that clipped off both wings."

Amazingly, when the plane finally came to a halt, the entire crew walked away from their crash landing uninjured. "We hiked out to the nearest road, hitched a ride from some allied soldiers to the nearby base, and flew back to Ipswich, where we were assigned another B-17."[13]

Twenty-five was the magic number for B-17 crews. It was the number of combat missions they were required to fly before they could be eligible to return home. It was estimated that pilots and crewmembers flying twenty-five missions had a 35 percent chance of survival. Landry flew thirty missions and lived. But many didn't. More than half of all Army Air Force casualties were suffered by the 8th Air Force. By war's end, forty-seven thousand men had been wounded and twenty-six thousand had been killed. In November 1945, six months after Germany's surrender and two months after Japan's surrender, Lt. Tom Landry received his discharge papers and headed back to Texas.

"At the time, I don't guess I stopped to seriously ponder my experience," said Landry. "Looking back now, I marvel at all that happened to me. War tested me, but I survived. And that experience gave me not only a broader perspective on life, but a confidence in myself I had never known before."[14]

In his own words, he had gone from being a "scared college freshman lost on his own university campus to a grizzled war veteran of 21." It was an experience that would help propel him to the enormous success he would soon enjoy as a football player and then later as a coach.

When he returned to the University of Texas in the spring of 1946, he discovered a campus that was much different than the one he'd left three years earlier. Thanks to the GI Bill, thousands of young men now had the opportunity to attend college who couldn't before the war. Enrollment at

Texas included a unique mix of veterans now in their mid- to upper twenties and eighteen-year-old teenagers right out of high school. "College was no longer just a place where kids went to grow up and find direction in life," said Landry. "The older students brought with them a seriousness, a maturity, and a sense of purpose that made for a unique era in college education and in college athletics as well."[15]

On the football field, Landry shook off his rustiness to become an all-Southwestern Conference fullback and cornerback on Texas teams that would win twenty-six games during his three years, including victories in the Sugar and Orange Bowls. The war years hadn't made Landry any speedier, and at 6'1", 185 pounds, he certainly wasn't physically imposing, but he was very smart, adamant in his preparation, and a fierce competitor.

"I remember when we first began checking on him," recalled Jack White, an assistant football coach for the All-American Football Conference's (AAFC) New York Yankees, the team that would eventually draft Landry. "I talked to Dutch Meyer [head coach] at Texas Christian University, and he said, 'He's a hoss. Landry's a hoss.'"[16]

"Tom could have played any position except guard or tackle," said Bully Gilstrap, a Texas assistant coach. "He studied and listened, and he knew all the assignments."[17]

Landry was a tremendous punter, and more than anything it was this talent that got him into professional football, first with the AFC's Yankees, and then, when the Yankees folded, with the New York Giants. He points to a game against the Cleveland Browns during his rookie season with the Yankees as a defining point in his development as a professional player and coach.

He had been inserted into the lineup to replace one of the starting defensive backs, and Cleveland's future Hall of Fame quarterback Otto Graham took advantage of his inexperience. All during the game, Mac Speedie, the Browns' wide receiver, got open against Landry, gaining more than two hundred receiving yards and setting the AFC single-game record. Landry sites that day as the most "embarrassing athletic performance of my life," but he also says it was one of the most important.

"I realized my own limitations. I conceded that it was impossible to succeed solely on skill, on emotion, or even on determination," said Landry. "Any success I ever attained would require the utmost in preparation and knowledge. I couldn't wait and react to my opponent. I had to know what he was going to do before he did it. With my 10.4 speed in the hundred, I could never cover a 9.6 receiver by running with him; but if I knew where he was going, I could be there when he arrived. That day in Cleveland was the starting point, the beginning of the challenge to really learn the game of football."[18]

And learn he did. Within two years—now playing for the Giants—he was widely recognized as one of the best defensive backs in the NFL, becoming an all-pro in 1954. "Most of us in those days just played the game," said Frank Gifford, the Giants Hall of Fame running back. "Not Tom. He studied it, studied everything. He put the same kind of discipline in the defense that the offense had. He had begun to create pro defense as we play it today. He had begun to give us keys . . . but you had to be disciplined. One time I remember I intercepted a pass. I'd just gone for the ball, but I was out of position. Tom didn't say nice play. He just said, 'Frank, you know you were out of position on that play.'"[19]

He was named the player-coach of the defense before the 1954 season, and in 1956 he retired as a player to become the Giants' full-time assistant coach. Landry ran the defense, and a young assistant named Vince Lombardi was hired after coaching at West Point to run the offense. "I hadn't planned on a coaching career at all," said Landry. "It just happened. I had my work during the off-season and planned to pursue a career in another profession when I retired as a player."[20]

With head coach Jim Lee letting his two young coaches run the show, the Giants won the NFL championship in 1956, then lost in overtime to the Johnny Unitas–led Baltimore Colts in the 1958 championship. By the time Unitas beat them again in 1959, Tom Landry was already regarded as somewhat of a defensive guru and, at thirty-five, the best young coach in the NFL. When the league decided to put an expansion team in Dallas for the 1960 season, Tom Landry, the native Texan, was the natural choice for the team's new general manager, Tex Schramm. It was a relationship that would last twenty-nine years and result in 270 wins, five Super Bowl appearances, and thirteen division titles.

Landry's Cowboy teams were renowned for their precision, their efficiency, and their innovation. It was the Cowboys who perfected the 4–3 defense, passing from the "shotgun," and an offense full of shifts and multiple formations. And it was Landry who became one of the first coaches to track the trends of opposing offenses and defenses. He was also one of the first to signal and shuttle plays in from the sideline.

"There were backdoor plays, fake punts and gadgetry that seemed even more startling because of their source," wrote Bill Minutaglio in *Sporting News*. "Opposing players, coaches and fans looked at the unemotional man in the hat and then looked at the consistent, controlled havoc he was unleashing on the field, and simply marveled."[21]

When asked what it was that made Landry so successful, his former players cite the usual traits attributed to people at the top of their professions—dedication, perseverance, discipline, and a commitment to excellence. They say they were never close to him during their playing days, that he purposely kept his distance and kept his relationship with them strictly professional. "Shoot, the first time I ever went into his office was to tell him I was retiring," laughs Larry Cole, who anchored the Cowboy defensive line from 1968 to 1980.[22]

"He never became good friends with us," says Charlie Waters, the Cowboys all-pro safety. "He felt it would affect him doing his job, and that was something that was really at the center of who he was—fulfilling your responsibility, doing your job."[23]

"I can remember one time," says Cole, "when Charlie overslept and was a little late for the afternoon practice. He showed up, and Coach asks, 'Charlie, why are you late?' Charlie explained that his alarm clock didn't go off. And Coach says, 'Well, you should have a backup alarm clock.' There were no excuses with Coach Landry."[24]

It was only after their playing careers had ended that they began to fully realize and appreciate the lessons Landry had taught them, the impact he had on their lives. "He always told us that our priorities should be faith, family, and then football," said Waters. "That's what he believed and lived by."[25]

"Come to work, suit-up, and show-up," added D. D. Lewis. "You do your duty, you don't take the easy route, and you face things head on."[26]

On February 12, 2000, Tom Landry passed away after a lengthy battle with leukemia, eleven years after coaching his last game for the Cowboys. At the funeral and memorial services in Dallas, his former players and coaches, along with hundreds of other friends and admirers, gathered to remember the man in the hat. They remembered not all the football victories and Cowboy glory, but things such as his lifelong involvement with the Fellowship of Christian Athletes, his forty-three years as a dedicated member of Highland Park United Methodist Church in Dallas, his frequent visits to Happy Hill Farm, a home for abandoned kids, and his countless other small acts of kindness that touched people's lives.

"Once I got older and my dad left the Cowboys, I really got to know him as a friend," said Tom Landry Jr. "I can't tell you how many times someone wrote me or came up to me and told me something my father had done for them, none of which he had ever talked about. What has always made an impression on me is that despite being as busy as he was, he always made the time to help others. He was consistent in his values, and as he became famous, that never changed. His priorities were God, family, and football, and he never got himself out of line with those."[27]

Perhaps more than any other, the one player who best exemplified the Dallas Cowboys of the 1970s and 1980s, the player who was most responsible for turning Coach Landry's vision and ingenuity into reality on the field, was quarterback Roger Staubach. He had come to the Cowboys in 1969 after completing four years of service in the navy following his graduation from the U.S. Naval Academy. Many felt it was Landry's own experience and success in returning to play football at Texas after three years in the army that led him to draft Staubach and have confidence that he wouldn't lose the talent that had led him to winning the Heisman Trophy in 1963.

During his playing days, there had been a healthy tension between the eventual Hall of Fame coach and his Hall of Fame quarterback. Staubach, the ultimate improviser, wanted the freedom to call his own plays rather than have Landry send them in from the sideline. Landry, of course, disagreed, and the two joked and bickered frequently about it, in the end agreeing only to disagree. Despite this regular friction, each had enormous respect for the other, and in the end, they would each ask the other to introduce them upon their entry in the Pro Football Hall of Fame.

At both the private and public services for Coach Landry, Roger Staubach rose and spoke eloquently and emotionally about Tom Landry, capturing for all what made the man in the hat so special. "Tom Landry had a decency about him that was unsurpassed," said Staubach. "He achieved great fame while not seeking it. Everyone knew he wasn't a phony. He just didn't put on airs, not ever. He did things for the right reasons. That's what his Christian religion taught him to do . . . the right thing, the things that helped others. Tom Landry was there for the people when they needed him. He was there for his country in World War II. He was there for his community, for his team, and most important, for his family.

"Coach Landry was able to keep things in perspective. He knew what was important in life, and he helped us understand that his road was the high road. He didn't dwell on defeat. He looked to the next play, the next game, the next season. He was our rock, our hope, our inspiration. He was our coach."[28]

CHAPTER 2

The Perfectionist

"Everybody tries to make a hero out of me over the Korea thing. I was no hero. There were maybe 75 pilots in our two squadrons and 99 percent of them did a better job than I did. But I liked flying. It was the second best thing that ever happened to me. If I hadn't had baseball to come back to I might have gone on being a Marine pilot."

—Ted Williams

It wouldn't be correct to say that Theodore Samuel Williams was a professional athlete who jumped at the opportunity to serve in the military. Twice his playing career was interrupted to serve in the U.S. Marine Corps—first from 1943 to 1945 in World War II, and then from 1952 to 1953 in Korea. Both times he was not overly enthusiastic about leaving a profession where he was being paid well and was arguably the best player—unquestionably the best hitter—in baseball.

When he entered the navy's Aviation Cadet program in the fall of 1942, he was coming off a season that saw him lead the American League in batting average, home runs, and runs batted in (RBI)—the rare "triple crown" of baseball. All of this followed a 1941 season that saw him become the first player since Bill Terry in 1930 to hit over .400. By the time he was recalled into the Marines, six games into the 1952 season, the then thirty-four-year-old Williams had already hit 324 home runs in his career, had a lifetime batting average of .346, and was making a league-leading salary of one hundred thousand dollars a year. When he first entered the major leagues in 1939, the brash and outspoken rookie had told teammates that he hoped one day people would see him on the street and say, "There goes Ted Williams, the greatest hitter to ever play the game." After ten seasons with the Boston Red Sox, he no longer had to hope. Many people already believed it was true.

It was with this record of success—and the financial rewards that came with it—that Williams twice left the Red Sox to become a United States Marine Corps fighter pilot. He was a hesitant warrior both times, but the experiences he would have and the unselfish, courageous manner in which he served defined his character in a way that baseball never could and solidified him in the eyes of many as one of the true American legends of the twentieth century.

In the early months of 1942, with the images of a burning Pearl Harbor still stoking Americans into a patriotic furor, not many people—particularly in New England—believed Ted Williams would *ever* enter the military, let alone serve with such distinction. As would be the case countless times throughout his nine-teen-year career, Williams was the topic of a very public debate, but this time the subject wasn't something he did on the field. It was his draft status.

With his parents divorced, Williams had been the sole provider for his mother for most of his three years in the big leagues. In November 1941 he had filled out the required paperwork to register for the draft, but because of the support he provided to his mother, he'd been classified 3-A by the draft board, meaning he would not immediately be drafted. But after the Japanese bombed Pearl Harbor, his draft status, along with that of thousands of other men who had previously been deferred, was reviewed again, and this time Williams was classified 1-A. If he did not voluntarily enlist, he would likely be drafted into the army within the next several months.

At the age of twenty-three Williams was spending the winter in Minnesota to be closer to his girlfriend. He had just signed his Red Sox contract for the 1942 season. He would make thirty thousand dollars a year—a significant raise from his 1941 salary—and the additional money had allowed him to set up several annuities for his mother, who still lived in Williams's hometown of San Diego, California. The Red Sox had also given him a five-thousand-dollar advance, which he was using to repair his mother's home.[1]

After learning his draft status had been reclassified to 1-A, Williams told a friend he was worried he would not be able to fulfill these financial obligations if he was immediately drafted. The friend recommended he consult with a selective service adviser. After reviewing William's case, the adviser, a man named Wendell Rogers, believed that because Williams was still providing the sole financial support for his mother, he should not have been reclassified to 1-A. Rogers took the case to the local appeals board, which promptly voted him down, 5–0.[2]

That was not the end of it, though. Rogers then took the case to the state's appeal agent in Minneapolis, who felt the case warranted further review by the presidential review board, which served as the final decision maker on all questions regarding an individual's draft classification. Three weeks later the decision was released—Williams was back to 3-A—but it set off a media firestorm in Boston, where Williams was already a lightning rod for newspaper reporters.

"Ted Williams Gets Draft Deferment" was the headline that blared from the front page of the morning edition of the *Boston Globe* on February 27, 1942. By the time the afternoon edition came out, one of the *Globe*'s reporters had already tracked down Williams in Minnesota. "'I Had Nothing to Do with Draft Deal'— Williams," was the *Globe*'s follow-up story. Essentially, the articles insinuated that Williams had received a deferment because of his baseball fame and that he was dodging his obligation to serve. A column in the *Boston Herald* several days later, urging Williams to enlist to avoid further public criticism, reflected the overall tone of the coverage. "God help any American youth dependent upon good will and public applause when the crowd begins to find its voice and hurl that yellow word, 'slacker,'" wrote Bill Cunningham. "Plenty of sons making just $16.50 a week and turning $10 of it over to also-dependent mothers have been taken, and are being taken. That's what gives the case its bite."[3]

Hearing the mounting controversy and criticism surrounding their client, Quaker Oats joined in by canceling the four-thousand-dollar contract they had with Williams to endorse their cereal. Williams, though, stood his ground. With other stars such as the Yankees' Joe DiMaggio and the Cardinals' Stan Musial set to play the 1942 season, along with teammates Dom DiMaggio, Bobby Doerr, and John Pesky, he felt he was being unfairly singled out. He was not against serving, but he had made commitments to his mother that he felt he could not break. Just prior to reporting to Sarasota, Florida, for the start of spring training, Williams announced his intention to play the 1942 season.

"While deferred from the draft in a 3-A classification, I made certain financial commitments," said Williams in a statement released to the media the first week in March. "I must carry through with them. Therefore, despite a strong urge to enter the service now, I have decided to play ball with the Red Sox this summer. That will enable me to fulfill my obligations to my family and make everything right all around."[4]

In recalling the controversy surrounding his longtime friend and teammate, Bobby Doerr says much of the media criticism was unfair. "In Boston back then there were so many papers. They all had to write something, and writing something critical helped them sell more newspapers. The truth was, Ted *was* supporting his mom and he should have been deferred."[5]

When the season started, the Red Sox—and to some extent Williams himself—were concerned about the fans' reaction toward him, but with a few minor exceptions those fears proved unwarranted. In the months leading up to the season, baseball commissioner Judge Kenesaw Landis had written to President Roosevelt asking him whether the season should be canceled. Before responding, Roosevelt had lunch with one of his secretaries whom he knew was a die-hard baseball fan. "Should he shut the game down?" he asked her. "'Never!' she told him. Americans needed to be able to cheer their favorite players and boo the umpire. Otherwise the tensions of war would simply be too great."[6] FDR agreed and in a letter he sent to Landis the next day told him he thought it would be "best for the country to keep baseball going."[7]

It was probably for this reason, more than any other, that the cheers for Williams far outweighed the boos during the first months of the 1942 season. "The nation, even its trainees and fighting forces, delighted in the image of normalcy and energy displayed on the ball field. It was a tonic, not an outrage, that the season continued and that the finer players were still on the field."[8]

Whatever criticism that remained surrounding his draft classification disappeared altogether in late May when Williams himself requested to be reclassified to 1-A so he could join the navy's aviation program. His decision stemmed from a tour he had received of a nearby naval air station during an off day the month before. Williams had been captivated by the planes and had applied for the program at the tour's conclusion.[9]

Saying he felt like his mother was now being taken care of, and thanking those who had supported his decision to wait to enlist, Williams said he was looking forward to the challenge of learning how to fly. "It's okay with me however it works out," he said. "I'm ready to go whenever they call me. I know now that I've done the right thing all the way through, and I'm sure tickled to death to get into this branch of the service. I'm not looking for any favors and I know I'll have to start from scratch."[10]

He didn't waste any time. After the midseason all-star game, he began taking four hours of navigation, physics, and mathematics courses three nights a week with other cadets whenever the Red Sox were in Boston for home games. With the controversy over his draft status behind him, Williams caught fire at the plate. Hitting .319 with nine home runs and thirty-seven RBIs before making his decision to enlist, he finished the season leading the league in average (.356), home runs (36), and RBIs (137) to win the triple crown.

Williams took immediately to flying, becoming so energized that he told reporters, "[I]f I can make a success of flying, I'd just as soon stay in the service—provided I could get a month off once in a while to go hunting." At Amherst College for the first phase of the training program, he and teammate

Johnny Pesky spent hours brushing up on math they hadn't seen, if ever, since their high school days. "You know how hard and long he practiced hitting?" Pesky told a reporter. "Well, he's bearing down much harder in this course than he ever did on his batting."[11]

While Pesky's lack of flying aptitude would eventually result in his being dropped out of the program, Williams progressed steadily through each phase—preflight training at Chapel Hill, North Carolina; basic flight training in Kokomo, Indiana; intermediate training in Pensacola, Florida; and finally operational, or advanced, flight training in Jacksonville, Florida. "It was absolutely different from anything I'd ever been through, and even the hairiest times were interesting," said Williams in his autobiography. "I damned near killed myself in Amherst. Two of us were flying Cubs and I didn't see some power lines across a river—we were flying upriver—and I just barely cleared at the last second."[12]

After earning his wings in May of 1944 in Pensacola, Williams and his fellow new pilots were given the choice of following either the fighter pilot or flight instructor curriculums to complete their training pipeline. Williams chose the flight instructor route, primarily because it would give him the additional flight time he felt he needed before going into combat.

"Everything about Ted was exemplary," recalls Bill Churchman, a fellow flight instructor in the same squadron with Williams in Pensacola. "He had great technique and was just an outstanding pilot—gunnery in particular."[13]

In Jacksonville to complete ten weeks of final combat training, he set the student aerial gunnery record before receiving his orders to San Francisco to pick up a ship. He was there when the war ended. "If you had your orders, though, they carried through—if you were scheduled to go to Siberia, you went to Siberia," said Williams. "They just didn't put a stop to things. I was in Honolulu when they finally froze me."[14]

He was discharged from the Marine Corps as a second lieutenant on January 12, 1946. During his final months in the military, as he watched other players such as the Tigers' Hank Greenberg and the Indians' Bob Feller return to their teams for parts of the 1945 season, Williams started to get the itch to play baseball again. Unlike other major leaguers, who had kept sharp by playing regularly for their base or unit's team, Williams had not played nearly as much. In Pensacola he had played briefly but admitted his heart wasn't in it. "I played lousy," he said later. "I was more interested in flying since it was going to be my job for the duration."[15]

But with the war over, he was now eager to return to his old profession, and his enthusiasm for flying had significantly waned. "Flying is all right in wartime, and I like it, but when I get out of this uniform I'm never going to fly again," said Williams.[16] No one would have predicted that seven years later, baseball's greatest hitter would be back in uniform and getting shot at in the skies over North Korea.

While many players returning from the war struggled to regain their pre-service form, Ted Williams was not one of them. In 1946, still in the prime of his career at the age of twenty-seven, he immediately picked up right where he left off, leading the Red Sox to the only World Series he would play in during his nineteen seasons, batting .342 with 38 home runs and 123 RBIs. The Red Sox would lose the series in seven games to Stan Musial's Cardinals, but it was a great return for Williams and other teammates who had also lost prime years to the war.

"The team came together and gelled in '46 just like we'd never left," says Dominic DiMaggio, the Red Sox's center fielder and one of Williams's closest friends. Like Williams, he had enlisted after the 1942 season and had spent the next three years as a PT boat commander in the navy, running supplies between Treasure Island and Alcatraz in San Francisco Bay.[17]

From 1946 to 1951, Williams would lead the league in batting average, RBIs, and home runs twice each, winning the triple crown for the second time in 1947 and narrowly missing winning it for a third time in 1949 when the Detroit Tigers' George Kell got two hits on the final day of the season to hit .345 to Williams's .343.

When war broke out on the Korean Peninsula in the summer of 1950, Williams, his name on the Marines' inactive reserve list, gave little thought about the possibility he might be recalled to active duty. He was thirty-one, and everyone suspected the conflict would be short in length and handled by the career military "regulars." If there was a need for recalls, the thinking was, they would—and should—come from the ranks of the active reserves and the draft, not from those who had already served in World War II. But as the 1951 season progressed and the conflict worsened, more pilots were needed to provide air support to the troops on the ground, and the military began plucking experienced World War II combat flyers from the inactive reserve ranks.

The thirty-three-year-old Williams knew his number was coming up. Remembering the controversy surrounding his draft status in 1942, he did not publicly complain about a program that was being widely criticized—even by his "friends" in the media—as unfair. "In my heart I was bitter about it, but I made up my mind I wasn't going to bellyache," said Williams. "I think if it's an emergency everybody goes. But Korea wasn't a declared war, it wasn't an all-out war. They should have let the professionals handle it. A lot of the professionals on duty for reserves didn't go."[18]

He played just six games of the 1952 season, hitting a farewell two-run homer on April 30 in his final at-bat against the Tigers' Dizzy Trout in the seventh inning. Before the game, the mayor of Boston, other city officials, and the Red Sox showered him with gifts at what was officially declared Ted Williams Day. Included was a memory book with signatures and well wishes from four hundred thousand Red Sox fans from across New England. After being serenaded by the capacity crowd with a somber rendition of "Auld Lang Syne," Williams—notorious for never tipping his cap to acknowledge the cheers of Red Sox fans, with whom he'd openly feuded during his years in Fenway Park—was visibly moved by the town's open display of affection for him. "This is the greatest day of my life. I'll always remember it," Williams told the crowd. "It is a day every ballplayer looks for, and one I thought I'd never have. I never thought when I came to the Red Sox fourteen years ago that they were such a wonderful organization. They've been wonderful to me."[19] At the age of thirty-four, Williams was headed back to war, and this time there wasn't much doubt that he would see combat.

Two weeks after the season ended, Capt. Ted Williams, U.S. Marine Corps, arrived at the air base in Willow Grove, Pennsylvania, for a six-week refresher course in flying an airplane. His flight instructor was his old squadron mate from Pensacola, Bill Churchman, who had been recalled and had already served a tour in Korea. "Ted hadn't flown an airplane since about 1946. Still, it only took him two or three hours sitting in the back seat before he got everything right—before he soloed," said Churchman. "We used to practice dog fighting. You go up to about 7,000 feet on collision courses about 1,000 feet apart and then you start scissoring and get up on the guy's tail. I said to Williams once [on the radio], 'Where the hell are you? I can't find you anywhere.' He says, 'Look in your goddamned mirror. I'm right behind you.' He was outstanding."[20]

It was Churchman who also convinced Williams that once he left Willow Grove for further training at Cherry Point, North Carolina, and at the air station in Roosevelt Roads, Puerto Rico, he should fly jets. As Williams writes, "He told me, 'Listen, if you can get jets, do it. If you take an SNV [the plane Williams had flown during WWII] into a target at 400 mph, you have to go out at 400 mph. You take a *jet* in, you're going 420, you release your bombs, you get the hell out of there at 500."[21]

That was enough to convince Williams, who had already been leaning in that direction. He signed up for jets and completed his training in the F-9F

Panther, arriving in Korea in January 1953 to fly with the 311th Marine Fighter Squadron.

Although Williams was often outspoken on the baseball field and could get on people's nerves with his never-ending oratories about the science of hitting, his teammates liked him. So did his squadron mates in Korea. Showing no deference to the Red Sox all-star, they called him "Bush Williams," as in "Bush League," and played practical jokes on him, once filling his bed with frozen orange juice cans. For his part, Williams fit right in. He took his turns as squadron duty officer, slept in the same cold, drafty huts, and flew whatever missions he was assigned. Those missions usually came down from the squadron's operations officer, a Marine Corps pilot named John Glenn.

"I'd guess probably half the missions that Ted flew in Korea he flew as my wingman," recalled the future astronaut and U.S. senator. "You get to know that guy pretty well. You fly as a two-person element. You're two people stuck together, and if you're going into combat, you fly together. We were doing a lot of close air support work, with napalms and bombs on the ground and rockets and so on."[22]

Williams flew thirty-nine combat missions in Korea, but it was his third mission, on February 16, 1953, that was his most memorable. "Our target was an encampment, a large troop concentration. We were nearing the target when I lost visual reference with the fellow in front of me," said Williams. "I swung out to pick him up and when I got back on target I was too low. We were supposed to be pretty low anyway, using daisy cutters that day, anti-personnel bombs that hit and spread out. But now *I* was a target for I don't know how many thousands of enemy soldiers in that encampment, and sure as hell I got hit with small arms fire. When I pulled up out of my run, all the red lights were on in the plane and the damn thing started to shake. The stick stiffened up and was shaking. I knew I had a hydraulic leak. Fuel warning light, fire warning light, there are so many lights on a jet that when anything serious goes wrong the lights almost blind you. I was in serious trouble."[23]

Glenn wasn't up there with him that day, but Marine Corps 2nd Lt. Larry Hawkins was. According to Hawkins, "I was coming up off the target after dropping my bombs, I was pulling up and heading west, toward the Yellow Sea. That's when I spotted this aircraft going towards the north/northwest and I said to myself, 'That guy's going in the wrong direction.' Then I spotted the puffs of smoke coming out. At first I thought it was just hydraulic fluid. So I flew up behind and checked him over. Then I flew up alongside and looked over at him, and he looked over at me and I still didn't know who it was."[24]

Williams's radio was out, so Hawkins communicated with him by hand signals, motioning for Williams to follow him. He led him to Suwon Air Force Base, an airfield just south of Seoul. "I set him up there and started circling," said Hawkins. "Then as we got down through the first circle, I gave him the 'wheels down' hand signal, which was a standard signal for that particular pattern. He put the wheels down and as soon as he dropped the gear, the damn wheel well doors blew open . . . and he broke on fire. So I hollered over the air, forgetting that he had no radio. I said, 'Eject! Eject!' Well, he didn't hear me, but he got the picture that something had gone wrong."

"I knew something bad was happening," said Williams. "All I cared about was getting on that deck. My approach was good and I'll never forget looking down and seeing a little Korean village near the field. With thirty feet of fire streaming from the plane, the villagers were running to beat hell. I pulled the emergency wheel latch, but only one wheel dropped down."

With sparks and fire streaming from the aircraft, Williams skidded some five thousand feet before coming to a stop at the end of the runway. "The canopy wouldn't open at first, then I hit the emergency ejector, and the fire was all around me, everything on fire except the cockpit. Boy, I just dove out, and kind of somersaulted, and I took my helmet and slammed it on the ground, I was so mad . . . I came back and looked at the plane later, and it was burned to a crisp."[25]

The next day, Lt. Col. Art Moran, Williams's commanding officer, met with him to gauge his psyche after the crash and to share the advice of fellow aviators who experienced problems in an airplane: "If you want to continue to fly, you'd better get right back in another one," Moran told him. "He agreed with that. I said, 'Well, let us know when you want to go again.' He said, 'What's wrong with now?'"

Moran told him to go see the operations officer. Shortly after Williams was launched, he got a call from a general asking him if he had "launched Williams." The general was not happy when Moran told him that he indeed had.

"Jesus Christ! Think of the publicity," he said.

"General, down here he's just another Marine Corps captain doing his job," responded Moran.[26]

While he was in Korea, Williams constantly fought colds. A severe case of pneumonia sent him out to a hospital ship off the coast for several weeks. In June 1953, with negotiations for a cease-fire gaining momentum and Williams battling a problem with his ears, he was sent to the States for treatment. He was discharged from the Marines on July 28, the day before the formal truce was signed between North and South Korea bringing the conflict to an end.

After initially being unsure whether he would be able to play again, Williams rejoined the Red Sox for the final two months of the season. Even with his return, the team could do no better then fourth place, but Williams demonstrated he still had his special gift. In ninety-one at-bats he hit thirteen home runs, drove in thirty-four, and had a batting average of .407. He would go on to play another seven seasons for the Red Sox. In 1958, at age thirty-nine, he narrowly missed batting .400 again, ending the season with a league-leading .388 average. In 1960, after once again hitting over .300 for the eighteenth of his nineteen seasons in the major leagues, he retired, hitting a home run on his final at-bat.

Those who played with Ted Williams or flew with him say what made him a great hitter was the same thing that made him a great pilot. "The thing about Ted was he had the smarts to go with this incredible inner strength," says Bobby Doerr. "Once he dedicated himself to do something, he was not afraid of the results. He had great courage and great strength."[27]

Bill Churchman explained it another way: "I remember one of the remarks I made at Cooperstown when Ted was inducted. I was trying to explain to Ted's guests his spirit of dedication, and how bright he is despite having very little formal education. What I have always said is that he'll conquer anything. If you were to say to Ted, 'We're going to give you two years off from your present duties, and we want you to become a Shakespearean scholar,' he'd be the best in the world. You could use that same theory in any field—computers, law, whatever. He'd master it."[28]

Ted Williams died on July 5, 2002. He was eighty-four. With 2,654 total hits and 521 home runs, it's not a stretch to assume he would have easily had more than 3,000 hits and close to 700 home runs—perhaps even challenging Babe Ruth's then all-time home run record of 714—if it were not for his five years in the military. However, he most certainly would not have enjoyed the same reputation.

And later in life his service was an open source of pride for him. "Any Marines in the crowd?" was a favorite question and icebreaker Williams frequently used to open speeches and talks. Perhaps John Glenn summed it up best when talking to fans about his former wingman during a special tribute to Williams at Fenway Park a few weeks after his death. "Who knows what would have happened with the record book if he had that time in baseball?" said Glenn. "[But] I don't think there was anyone prouder to be a Marine than Ted Williams."[29]

CHAPTER 3

Dr. Jack

"Much more serious matters than basketball were going on in the world at that time. The war was not going well for the United States in either Europe or the Pacific, and like most young men at the time, I felt a sense of duty to do my part."

—Dr. Jack Ramsay

It was the summer of 1977 when Dr. Jack Ramsay first decided he wanted to start competing in triathlons. As the story goes, the jogging craze had hit the Pacific Northwest, and Ramsay, then fifty-two and the head basketball coach of the NBA's Portland Trailblazers, wanted to take his fitness regimen to another level. Already an avid swimmer and runner, he immediately set about improving his "game." A friend connected him with a swimming coach, who helped refine his stroke, and Ramsay himself sought out a local high school track coach, who gave him pointers on distance running. By August he had entered and completed his first triathlon near Portland, Oregon, swimming 1.2 miles in 46 minutes, biking 22 miles in 1 hour and 20 minutes, and running 9 miles in 1 hour and 24 minutes.

Seeing how exhausted this new self-imposed challenge was making him, Ramsay's friends became a little worried. "I thought about making him quit," said Bucky Buckwalter at the time, then one of Ramsay's assistant coaches. "Then I realized you can't *make* Ramsay quit." Anything.

And quitting was the furthest thing from his mind anyway. "Now that I've done it," Ramsay said with his trademark zest for self-improvement, "I'd like to get my times down. Not that I think I could win it. But I know I could do a lot better. Maybe I *could* win one."[1]

It's a story that in many ways captures the essence of Jack Ramsay: who he is and how he has approached his life—full-bore, always taking a full cut at whatever's thrown his way. Like others in the coaching profession, he is blessed with a unique blend of talents that during his coaching days made him part teacher, part motivator, part disciplinarian, and part father figure. But what always separated Jack Ramsay from his peers was his intensity, his gift to see with remarkable clarity exactly what he wanted to accomplish, and his inexhaustible supply of enthusiasm and energy in turning that vision into reality.

"I loved playing for him because every game was so important," said Billy Cunningham, who played for Ramsay from 1968 to 1972 during his tenure as head coach of the Philadelphia 76ers. "You could see it in his eyes. You could feel it."[2]

Ramsay says it is an approach that grew from his tremendous passion for basketball. "Basketball was always huge to me," he says. But the intangibles, those special tools of the trade that helped him transfer the passion into player performance on the court—qualities such as leadership, discipline, communication, and toughness—Ramsay began developing those skills as a much younger man, and one of his early teachers was the U.S. Navy.

Ramsay was a senior at Upper Darby High School in Philadelphia when World War II started. A good student and the best player on the varsity basketball team, he says he felt an obligation to do his part. "I probably would have went right in [to the military], but when I graduated I was still seventeen," he recalls.[3]

He accepted a basketball scholarship to nearby St. Joseph's University instead, but less than a year later was back at the recruiter's office to join the navy. "My first choice was the Navy Air Corps, but when they learned I was allergic to pollen and got hay fever, they said, 'Sorry, we can't take you.'"[4] Instead they enrolled him in their V-12 officer candidate program and sent him to Villanova for two semesters, then on to Columbia University, where he received his commission as an ensign in December of 1944. Several months later he was in Florida for follow-on training when he heard the navy was looking for young officers to join their underwater demolition teams (UDTs). Created in 1943 to conduct underwater reconnaissance and remove obstacles for the island invasions taking place throughout the Pacific, the UDTs seemed like the opportunity Ramsay was looking for. "By the time I finished at Columbia, it looked like the tide was beginning to turn in the war," he said. "The invasion of Europe had happened, and it seemed like the Pacific was turning around. I was anxious to get into action and thought the UDTs would give me that chance."[5]

He was sent to Fort Pierce on the Florida coast and underwent two months of training in explosives and underwater reconnaissance, as well as rigorous physical conditioning. Each morning started on the beach with calisthenics and a mile swim in the ocean. "They pushed us hard," remembers Ramsay. "They'd wake us up at 2:00 AM for forced marches and constantly run us in and out of the ocean. We'd sprint into the water as far as we could go before we had to start swimming, come back out, and then do it again. The instructors were always yelling, 'Don't be last!'"[6]

Three hundred men started the training, but by the time the team—Underwater Demolition Team 30—was commissioned in July 1945, attrition had reduced that number to fourteen officers and one hundred enlisted. "It was really a great group of guys," recalls Ramsay. "We were all very young, but we had great instruction. Everybody understood what they had to do, and morale was very high. I loved it."[7]

At twenty-two, Bob Sweet was UDT-30's only chief petty officer and interacted regularly with the officers. "Oh, yeah," he replies when asked if he remembers nineteen-year-old Ensign Ramsay. "He was one of our platoon officers. Let me tell you, there was nothing slow about him. He was always on the go."[8]

"We all respected him," says Bob McKay, who would regularly go to Ramsay to organize softball games between the officers and the enlisted men. "He had a great personality. He was about the same age we [the enlisted] all were, but what was special about him was that he made us feel like he was one of us while at the same time keeping that separation, because he understood as an officer he had a role to play."[9]

After being commissioned in July, the team left Fort Pierce for Oceanside, California. Although UDT-30 had not been given their official orders, they all knew they were being positioned to board ships for the upcoming invasion of Japan. "Right before we left Fort Pierce, Lieutenant Commander Fowler, our commanding officer, called us all together," says McKay. "He said, 'We're giving you guys seven days off to go home, but you need to know, when you come back you're going to be in the big one.' And then I remember so clearly him saying, 'Guys, take a look at the person on each side of you. You need to know right now that only one of you is coming back.'"[10]

They joined twenty-nine other UDTs in California and in early August boarded ships in San Diego to begin heading west. But after being under way for just two days they were suddenly ordered to turn around. The atomic bomb had been dropped on Hiroshima. A week later the Japanese formally surrendered. "We were disappointed," says Ramsay. "The combat veterans on the other teams looked on the surrender as a blessing, but it was a tremendous letdown for our young group."[11]

With the war over, UDT-30 was deactivated. Although many team members were discharged, Ramsay's navy adventure continued for another eleven months. He was ordered to join USS *YP643*, an inter-island refrigerated cargo ship, at Kwajalein, a small island in the Southwest Pacific. With a crew of two officers and twenty-five enlisted, Ramsay was the third officer, but that quickly changed. In short succession, both the captain and executive officer received their discharges from the navy, and Ramsay, now twenty years old and with minimal shipboard experience, was placed in command. He says it was a little unnerving but that he had clearly benefited from his experience in the UDTs. "That really helped me. The UDTs were highly respected in the service, and fortunately for me a printout of my record had been sent to the ship before I got there. They knew I was coming and everyone gave me space," he recalls, laughing at the memory.[12]

To his surprise, he also discovered he had an innate touch when it came to driving the ship that further helped him gain the trust and confidence of the crew. "I guess the previous CO had not been good at it, but I really enjoyed the ship handling," he says. It was a good thing. Two months after assuming command, Ramsay was ordered to latch up with a convoy and sail *YP643* back to San Francisco, via Hawaii, for decommissioning—a thirty-two-hundred-mile voyage. The only problem was that the slowest convoy speed was ten knots and his ship's *top* speed was nine knots. If they couldn't keep up, they couldn't go. "There were no convoys listed for ships as slow as *YP643*," said Ramsay, "and I was well aware that the members of my crew, many of whom had been in the far Pacific for more than two years, were ready to gnaw on hawsers in their anxiety to get home."[13]

Ramsay decided to go to the ship's chief boatswain's mate, a career navy man, to see if there was anything they could do to gain the additional knots needed to join a convoy. "He listened carefully, than said that if we jettisoned all excess ballast and got the ship as light as possible, we could make ten knots. I agreed to try it, and the crew was ecstatic."[14]

After some cajoling with a harbormaster who threatened to send *YP643* to Eniwetok—"the barest and most forlorn of all the Marshall Islands"—if it couldn't keep up, Ramsay was given permission to join a convoy of landing craft headed back to the States. With so much ballast removed, he says, the ship floated like a cork and constantly vibrated from being pushed so hard but kept up . . . for a while.

At dawn on the fourth day, the chief boatswain knocked on Ramsay's cabin door and said, "Cap'n, you'd better come to the bridge." When he arrived and looked out to the horizon there wasn't another ship in sight. The convoy had changed course in the middle of the night and the mid-watch hadn't picked it up. "I was angry but didn't have time to waste reprimanding the people on duty," says Ramsay. "I got on the radio and called the convoy commander . . . he was not pleased to hear from me."

Ramsay responded to the "Where the hell are you, Captain?" by giving his position, and then awaited a reply. "He didn't respond for what seemed like an eternity . . . then agreed to slow the group's speed so that we could catch up. We were able to do that in another four hours and stayed with them the rest of the way to Pearl Harbor. They left Pearl two days later without us . . . and I couldn't blame them."[15]

After some needed repairs, the ship hooked up with another convoy and limped into San Francisco in June 1946 to finish the decommissioning process. "The ship had to be bone-dry and drained of fuel oil; and every bit of metal . . . had to be cleaned, greased, and rendered waterproof. It was a demanding task, but most of the ship's complement was ready for discharge when the job was completed, so they all gave it their full effort."[16]

Ramsay was ordered back to the Philadelphia Navy Yard, and on July 4, 1946, he was officially discharged. "The navy made me grow up," he says. "It was a great experience, and I gained a lot of maturity, which really helped when it came time for me to get on with the rest of my life."[17]

He returned to St. Joseph's and rediscovered his passion for basketball, starting each of the next three seasons at guard and captaining the team his senior year. A good student with a thirst for learning, Ramsay could have pursued any profession, but basketball was his passion. At St. Joseph's he had played against teams coached by some of the legends of college basketball, men such as Oklahoma A&M's Hank Iba, St. John's Joe Lapchick, and Nat Holman at the City College of New York. "The influence these men had on their teams fascinated me," says Ramsay. "Each team had its unique style that those outstanding coaches put in place. I wanted to have that experience with a team of my own. It was then that I decided on coaching as a profession."[18]

He began at the high school level, learning and developing his craft and teaching for six years at schools in Pennsylvania, then Delaware, before accepting an offer in 1955 to return to coach his alma mater. It was at St. Joseph's that Ramsay established his reputation for intensity. "We never got the great players at St. Joe's," says Jack McKinney, who played for Ramsay in high school and on Ramsay's first St. Joseph's team. "But Jack always did a great job getting 99 percent of the good player's potential out of him."[19]

In eleven years at St. Joe's Ramsay compiled a record of 234–72 and took his team to ten postseason tournaments. During his off-seasons, he worked on his doctorate in education at the nearby University of Pennsylvania, officially earning the title of "Dr. Jack" in 1963. He looks back on his years at St. Joseph's—as a student, athlete, coach, and administrator—with great fondness. "[Those years] were immensely fulfilling," says Ramsay, "and helped form me as a Christian person."[20]

In 1966, with Ramsay suffering from an edema on the retina of his right eye, his doctors advised that he take a sabbatical from the stresses of coaching. When Ramsay was offered the opportunity to jump to the pros as the general manager of the NBA's Philadelphia 76ers, he accepted. Professional basketball would be his life for the next twenty-one years.

In 1968 he returned to the coaching sidelines, leading the 76ers to the playoffs three times before moving to Buffalo to be the Braves' head coach from 1972 to 1976. While there, he had the opportunity to reconnect with Bob McKay, his old friend from UDT-30. At that time McKay was the recreation officer at Attica State Penitentiary in New York, and just before Christmas of 1975 he asked Ramsay if he would bring his team to the prison and conduct a practice for the inmates. Ramsay immediately accepted. "Even though he'd had all this success in coaching, he was still the same guy he was back in 1945," said McKay. "Very humble and modest. Just a great man."[21]

By the time he left Buffalo after the 1975–76 season to become the head coach of the Portland Trailblazers, Ramsay had a firm grasp of the pro game and a vision of how he believed it should be played. He just hadn't been able to find the right team to implement his vision. That changed in Portland. Inheriting a team that had not had a winning record or been to the playoffs in six years, he won the NBA championship his first year, beating a Philadelphia 76er team led by superstars Julius Erving, George McGinnis, and Doug Collins.

"What a wonderful team that was," said Bill Walton, the team's center and now an NBC broadcaster. "We became what Ramsay dreamed the game should be: fast breaks, teamwork, ball movement and pressure defense."[22] "[He] motivated players by staring into their souls," wrote Walton in his book, *Nothing But Net.* "He could do this by walking right up to you, stepping on your feet so you couldn't walk away, and then looking into your soul through your eyes. After a long, dramatic pause, he would say, 'Can you go . . . can you give me all you've got tonight? We need you.'"

Ramsay remained in Portland for ten years, leading the team to the playoffs nine times before concluding his coaching career in Indiana. The Pacers were young and talented, and the teaching challenge—as usual—appealed to Ramsay, but the team never came together. In November 1988 he was sitting in a hotel in Phoenix, getting ready to start his third season with the Pacers, when he decided it was time to call it quits. He was sixty-three and the NBA's oldest coach. "I'd had enough," he recalls. "I wasn't enjoying it all and was just ready for something else."[23]

For the next fourteen years, that something else would be broadcasting. And, not surprisingly, it is his energy, enthusiasm, and ability to communicate—the same qualities that helped him become the NBA's third all-time winningest coach—that have made him a successful, and very popular, broadcaster. At seventy-eight, he is an NBA analyst for ESPN and does the color commentary with play-by-play man Jim Durham on ESPN's "NBA Game of the Week."

During the off-season, he and his wife, Jean, who have been married for fifty-six years, split their time between homes in Naples, Florida, and Ocean City, New Jersey, enjoying the company of their five children and thirteen grandchildren. In addition to his work as a broadcaster, Ramsay is a regular contributor to the NBA section of ESPN.com, and in 2004 his book *Dr. Jack's Leadership Lessons from a Lifetime in Basketball* was published. It is a subject he is well versed in. "Leadership roles are thrust on most of us at one time or other in our lives," writes Ramsay, "but perhaps from an early age those destined to be leaders fill those roles more willingly than others."[24]

From leading a platoon in UDT-30 and commanding *YP643* as a twenty-year-old navy ensign to coaching a championship team in the NBA, Ramsay has lived a life of leadership. "Everything you do in life influences what you do in the future. I grew a great deal from my experiences in the navy, and they played a big part in developing my leadership style as a coach. Leaders have to be real. You've got to be who you are and not someone you're not."[25]

And perhaps in the end "real" is the word that continues to best describe Dr. Jack Ramsay. He still rises early every day, still hits the pool or ocean for a half-mile swim, followed by a mile-and-a-half run, and hits the weights after that. He doesn't hold as many basketball clinics as he once did, but when he does, he still gets right out on the floor with players who are now a quarter of his age. And they respond to him. His résumé and ESPN visibility certainly have had something to do with that, but when you're fifteen years removed from your last NBA head coaching job, those only take you so far.

The best reason for his success with players is that even as he approaches eighty, Dr. Jack Ramsay is still keeping it real.

Thanks to the Kindness of Strangers

"I often reflect back on what happened to me in the war. And I know for sure that I would never want to do that again. But I tell you one thing. It was such a great experience."

—Robert Chappuis

It's a humbling truth for so many World War II veterans—the knowledge and understanding that if it weren't for the selflessness of others, they would have never made it home, never become whomever it is they've turned out to be in the sixty years since the war's end. It's a truth Bob Chappuis came to grips with a long time ago, but every so often, he says, he still thinks about it. It's not so much the "who he turned out to be" part that occupies his thoughts. Although his life accomplishments are many, he's too humble and appreciative to dwell on those things. No, it's the people he thinks about—specifically, a group in small Asola, Italy (pop. 2,400), who in the winter and spring of 1945 risked their own lives to save those of Chappuis and two other young Americans who had parachuted into their town from a crashing B-25 bomber. It is a story, a real-life experience, that when you get down to its basics, is about courage, generosity, and above all, the kindness of strangers. And it left an imprint on Chappuis that has stayed with him throughout his life.

He was halfway through his freshman year at the University of Michigan when the United States entered World War II after the Japanese attack on Pearl Harbor. Although he'd joined the Enlisted Reserve Corps shortly thereafter, training as a B-25 radioman and gunner at Scott Field in Illinois during the summer of 1942, he wasn't sure he'd ever get into the war. Everything he was hearing led him to believe that he wouldn't be called to active duty until after he graduated. "That's what they were telling us at the time," recalls Chappuis. "That everyone in the ERC would be allowed to finish school."[1]

Frankly, the idea didn't bother him too much. He was doing well in his studies and had an excellent shot at becoming Michigan's starting left halfback once football season came around in the fall. A standout as a nonscholarship player on the freshman team, Chappuis had also done well his sophomore year as a substitute and role player on the varsity. Against Great Lakes, a navy team filled with professionals and college all-stars, Chappuis had started at left halfback in place of the injured Tom Kuzma and led the Wolverines to a stunning 9–0 upset victory. "He just came in, and it looked like he'd been playing his whole life," says former teammate Don Lund. "Right from the get-go, Chap had the ability to throw the ball, but he also had poise."[2]

Kuzma returned to the starting lineup, but Chappuis continued to make contributions throughout the season, leaving no doubt in the minds of his coach, Fritz Crisler, and teammates that he had a bright future. "He had really set himself up to do great things during his junior and senior seasons," remembers George Ceithmal, the senior quarterback on Michigan's 1942 team.[3]

But two months after the season ended, Chappuis's football future was suddenly put on indefinite hold when his reserve unit unexpectedly was called to active duty. Instead of finishing school in Ann Arbor, he was off to South Carolina to complete his training as a B-25 radioman and gunner. "I knew that eventually I was going to go on active duty," says Chappuis, "The general feeling about the war was that we all needed to get in and get it cleaned up. I just didn't think I'd go in as soon as I did."[4]

In November 1944 his B-25 crew was sent to Corsica, a small island off the western coast of Italy, to fly bombing missions in support of the allies' offensive against the Germans in Italy. "We flew a lot in the Italian Alps," says Chappuis, "bombing things like railroads and bridges to try and disrupt German communication lines."[5]

By February he'd already flown twenty missions when he was asked to be a substitute gunner with another crew assigned to block a tunnel used by German convoys. "Our job was to bomb the side of a mountain and create a landslide that would block the tunnel. We thought it was going to be a milk run," recalls Chappuis. "During the briefing we were told there wouldn't be any antiaircraft fire." The situation turned out to be just the opposite. As soon as they got close to the target, antiaircraft guns erupted, shooting up a withering barrage of flak that was so thick, the crew couldn't see their target and didn't drop their bombs on their first pass. "My first thought was, 'How'd they find out we were coming?'" says Chappuis, who was operating the waist guns on both sides of the plane.

They ignored the flak and made a second pass to release their bombs but this time took hits that damaged both engines on the aircraft. The pilot, figuring they stood a better chance if they could make it to the Adriatic Sea and ditch the plane in the water, ordered the crew to "lighten the load," and Chappuis began throwing everything out of the plane that wasn't bolted down. "Radios, our guns . . . everything!" says Chappuis. But shortly thereafter, another order came over his headset. "Pilot to crew, bail out!"

"There was a bail-out procedure you were supposed to follow where everyone went out in a certain order, with the tail gunner going first," says Chappuis, chuckling at the memory. "Well, because I was just filling in, I didn't know any of these guys, so I turn to the tail gunner and tell him to bail out, and he looks at me and says, 'No, *you* bail out!' We were so shook up, we didn't know what we were doing."[6]

The midair debate didn't last long, with the tail gunner deciding to go first, but when he jumped he got stuck in the hatch. With the plane losing altitude and his exit blocked, Chappuis's only choice was to try to kick the tail gunner loose in the only place his foot could hit—the man's face. It worked, and Chappuis quickly moved into position to jump. "You were supposed to get in the slipstream and kick away with both hands," he says, "then count to ten before pulling the rip cord. I didn't do that. I pulled the cord as soon as I jumped, and let me tell you, seeing the chute come out was a beautiful sight."

The euphoria ended when Chappuis remembered he was floating down into German territory. He landed in an olive grove near a road about twenty yards from where the plane's top-turret gunner, Jack Long, landed. The two of them quickly buried their parachutes and ran for cover behind a cement structure that allowed them to keep an eye out for anyone coming down the road. Unbeknownst to them, the Germans weren't the only ones looking for them. Italian partisans, an underground movement opposed to the German's occupation of Italy, had also seen them come down and were trying to find them before the Germans did.

One of them, searching on a bicycle, spotted the flak jacket Long had removed and hung on the cement wall. He stopped his bicycle in front of them, gave them the thumbs-up sign, and began speaking to them in Italian. "I didn't know what he was saying," recalls Chappuis, "but we knew that sooner or later we were going to have to take a chance."[7]

At the bicyclist's urging, they followed him to a nearby farmhouse, where they were joined by a third member of their crew, Art Kropp, the tail gunner whom Chappuis had helped dislodge from the plane earlier. They were served a meal of noodles and pig's liver and remained at the house overnight. Early in the evening, Germans came to the door looking for them, but the family hiding them denied they were there. In the morning they were each given a long cloak to put over their shoulders and were moved to the barn of another farmhouse, walking within ten feet of several German soldiers leaving another home. "They looked right at us," says Chappuis, "but nothing happened."

They avoided discovery again that day when the nine-year-old boy at the home ran into the barn, shouting, "Germans, Germans, Germans," and led them into the field, where they hid in a large corncrib as the Germans searched for them in the farmhouse and barn. They went undetected and remained at the farmhouse while Aldo Camucci, the local leader of the underground Italian resistance, worked to find them a safer place to stay.

At twenty-two, Camucci was the same age as the Americans. He knew where the German forces were, where the allies were advancing, and most of all, who could be trusted in town. "He was very shrewd," says Chappuis. "The first thing we asked him was if we could get back to our unit. In broken English, he said, 'I think not possible.' We then asked him if we could get to Switzerland, and he said, 'Possible. Seven days I return.'"[8]

True to his word, a week later a large, black sedan with a swastika on the door pulled in front of the farmhouse, and out jumped Camucci. The car belonged to the German commandant in charge of the local occupation force, whose Italian driver was loyal to the resistance. The driver had asked his unsuspecting German boss if he could use the car to run a quick errand in Asola. The errand was to pick up the three American fugitives and bring them not to Switzerland but to their next hideaway, a small ten-by-ten-foot upstairs room in the home of the Ugolini family. Located smack in the middle of the village and just a few doors down from the local German headquarters, it would turn out to be their home for the next three months.

Because of their close proximity to the enemy, Chappuis, Long, and Kropp never spoke above a whisper and never walked in front of the window. Mama Ugolini's work as a seamstress and Papa Ugolini's job as a butcher meant a steady stream of people coming in and out of the house each day—including Germans—which further helped them to avoid suspicion. But the tedium of spending their days cooped up in a small room and nights crammed side by side on two small beds quickly wore on the Americans. The Ugolinis' two daughters, twenty-three-year-old Gina and twenty-year-old Wally, did their best to try to alleviate the boredom, occasionally playing cards with the men when they brought them their meals, but they all became somewhat stir-crazy.

"The other two boys went a little wacky, and I guess I did too," said Chappuis. "I wanted to double up my fist and slug them so many times."[9]

To break the monotony, one night the Ugolinis decided to take the soldiers for a walk in the village. Dressed in the plain clothes of Italian peasants—with the exception of their GI boots—they spent an hour walking through the village, pretending to understand the constant Italian chatter coming from Mama Ugolini. "Whenever a German would pass," says Chappuis, "she would grab my arm affectionately and call me 'Roberto' as if I were a member of the family."[10]

But their closest call came one night when Gina's Italian fascist boyfriend made an unexpected visit. "The girls were serving us our dinner," recalls Chappuis. "He heard voices coming from the upstairs and came up and saw us. Gina walked down and he asked her who we were and what we were doing there. She told him the truth. He said he didn't have any choice but to turn us all in. Gina said, 'Go ahead. They will be taken prisoner, but my family will be shot.' He never turned us in, but I never wanted a relationship to succeed more."[11]

Mindful of the enormous risk the Ugolinis were making on their behalf, Chappuis says he asked numerous times why they didn't turn them loose. "No! You stay here," was always the response. "This is our way of telling the Nazis we don't like them. . . . Their courage in taking care of us at the risk of their own lives was just incredible."[12]

One night in May, Camucci unexpectedly burst into the Ugolinis's home with the news that Chappuis, Kropp, and Long had been waiting for. With the allies just miles away, the Germans had fled. "The town is ours!" he yelled. "Tonight, we dance all night!" "And by god we did," says Chappuis. "The seats were taken out of the village theater, and a band played at each end. Until then, only about seven people in the entire village knew we were there. They put us up on the stage, gave us flowers and cookies, and made us the guests of honor. The next day they had me raise the American flag from the steeple."[13]

A week later, Chappuis, Long, and Kropp said good-bye to Camucci and the Ugolinis to reunite with their units for the final months of the war. "I can only say that my farewell to those wonderful Italian people who saved my life was probably the most emotional experience I have ever had," said Chappuis when asked about the farewell. "Many tears were shed and many hugs were shared. I gave the Ugolinis a chit stating that their family had housed, fed, and cared for us for ninety days and in doing so sacrificed and exposed themselves to much danger. Therefore, if possible, they should be reimbursed for their efforts. I never knew if this happened."[14]

Chappuis, Long, and Kropp also said a final good-bye to one another. Chappuis never saw his fellow captives again. "One time I got a call from Jack, but it was just one of those things," said Chappuis. "We went our separate ways. Believe me," he says, laughing, "we saw enough of each other during those three months to last a lifetime."[15]

By the spring of 1946 Chappuis was out of the army and back in his hometown of Toledo, Ohio. Although he was eager to return to the University of Michigan, he was hesitant about playing football again. With so many former varsity players returning from the service (125 men went out for the Michigan varsity in 1946, including three former team captains from different years), Chappuis wasn't sure there was a spot for him. But he also wasn't sure he still had the desire to play. "I remember thinking, 'Who needs all the pressure of football on Saturdays?'" says Chappuis. "I didn't think I wanted to get myself all excited and lose sleep the night before games."[16]

Luckily for Michigan, he changed his mind. From his old position of left halfback, Chappuis became the focal point of head coach Fritz Crisler's multiple-formation offense, and the most valuable player on a team loaded with talent but slow to gel. "It was hard to get the chemistry right initially, because we had this mix of good players returning from the war and players from the '45 freshman team who were also very good," remembers Chalmers "Bump" Elliot, a Marine Corps second lieutenant who returned from the war to be Chappuis's backfield mate. "The coaching staff had a hard time determining playing time for everyone."[17]

Crisler solved the problem by making frequent substitutions and using separate units for offense and defense, both of which were unique strategies in that era of college football. But he also had another challenge—connecting with players who had changed significantly since he last coached them. Most were now in their midtwenties (Chappuis himself was twenty-four), and several were married. They were more serious, more mature, and according to Elliot, more "worldly" than when they had left Michigan two, or in some cases, three years earlier. "There was a definite change in that group, but it was a change that wasn't apparent on the outside. It was on the inside," recalls George Ceithmal, the senior quarterback and team captain of Michigan's 1942 team. Ceithmal had gone into the navy after graduation and piloted landing craft onto the beaches of Normandy on D-day. "They no longer needed the type of rev 'em up, 'let's go get 'em!' motivation that they did before, and it took awhile for Fritz to understand that."[18]

In the Wolverines' fifth game of the season—the homecoming game—Crisler's intense pregame preparations and speech completely backfired. Fumbling close to a dozen times, the Wolverines lost to an inferior Illinois team with a score of 13–9 to lower their record to 4–2. "We were too anxious and too overly motivated," says Chappuis. "He got us so fired up to play, we got tight and made all those turnovers."[19]

"From that point on, Fritz never gave them another pep talk," says Ceithmal. "He didn't have to. He understood that with that group their motivation came from within, and he really believed that was molded by their experience in the service."[20]

After that disheartening homecoming game, Michigan became a different team, outscoring its opponents 162–19 in four lopsided victories against Big Nine opponents Minnesota, Michigan State, Wisconsin, and archrival Ohio State—a 58–6 drubbing in Ann Arbor. Chappuis set the conference record for total offensive yards in a season, running and passing for 1,284 yards, and was also named to the all-conference team. The next year was even better. With the majority of the players back and now comfortable in the roles Crisler had carved out for them, the Wolverines went undefeated, beating Stanford 49–0 in the Rose Bowl to capture the national championship. "The '47 team was one of the great, great teams," remembers Don Lund. "They had this special combination of intelligence, deception, and poise, and no one felt like they were bigger than the team."[21]

Chappuis was their leader. In addition to breaking Michigan legend Tom Harmon's career record for total offensive yards, he was a consensus all-American and second to Notre Dame's Johnny Lujack in the Heisman Trophy voting. "Lujack deserved it," says Chappuis with typical humility. "He was a better player than I was."[22]

Lujack may have been a better runner, but Chappuis's all-around skills and his ability to throw the football resulted in an offer to play professionally for Branch Rickey's football Brooklyn Dodgers in the old All-American Football Conference. He accepted and played a year for Rickey and a year for the Chicago Hornets before leaving football behind for good to go into business and settle down with Ann, his wife.

Ann had enrolled at the University of Michigan in 1945 and met Chappuis when he returned in 1946. The two were married in 1949. "I've always said that the one really good thing that came out of the war was that I met Ann," he says. "That would not have happened if I hadn't gone into the service."

And none of it—the all-American years at Michigan, his successful career in business, his family of four children and nine grandchildren—would have happened if that small group of Italians in Asola hadn't risked their lives to save his. Over the years Chappuis never forgot that, and in 1974, twenty-nine years after he had left them to rejoin his unit for the remaining months of the war, he returned to Asola with Ann to once again say thank you.

They were all still there—the Ugolini family, Aldo Camucci, the driver of the long, black sedan, and others who had hid him from the searching Germans during those frightening first few days. As Camucci retraced their mutual adventure with Chappuis and Ann, one of those men, Oscar Sandrelli, went into his basement and returned with a package. "When I opened it, the tears came and I couldn't stop," says Chappuis. It was his flight jacket. During all those years, Sandrelli had saved it on the off chance that someday Chappuis would return.

The town had a big dinner for him, and Camucci spent a week driving Chappuis and Ann around the country. "At each place, I'd go to check out of the hotel and it would always be paid for," recalls Chappuis. "So I went to Ambra, Aldo's daughter, and said, 'Ambra, your dad is paying my bills, and I can't let him do that. I want to pay my own way.' She said, 'My father says you pay for the next hotel.' Well, the next day, I go to check out and my bill is paid again, so I tell Ambra and she says, 'Roberto, my father lies!'" Several years later Chappuis finally had an opportunity to return the favor when the Camucci family came to the United States and visited Chappuis in Indiana.

As he had been doing during the years before their last visit, Chappuis continues to correspond with the Ugolinis and Camucci. Mama and Papa Ugolini have passed on, and several years ago he received the sad news from Ambra that Aldo had passed away. "Roberto," she wrote, "it doesn't seem possible that it was almost 60 years ago that you and my father met each other. You were such beautiful young men."[23]

Chappuis himself is eighty-one now, and last year he and Ann left their longtime home in Fort Wayne, Indiana, to move to Ann Arbor, Michigan, to be closer to their children and grandchildren. He still keeps a close track on Michigan football. When this writer absentmindedly called Chappuis on the Saturday afternoon the Wolverines were playing Michigan State, he politely told me, "I'll be happy to talk to you, but right now I'm watching the game. Can you call me tomorrow?"

Every now and then, he says, he still finds himself thinking back to that February in 1945 when he unexpectedly found himself floating down to an uncertain fate. "I wonder if I were sitting in my living room and some Italian airmen fell out of the sky and into my backyard, what would I do? It bothers me," says Chappuis. "I would hope that given the same circumstance I would do what they did for me, but to be honest, I'm not sure I'd be that brave, but I hope so."[24]

CHAPTER 5
Still Serving Others

"I played in six World Series with the Yankees, but the thing I'm most proud of is my time in service. Those were the defining years of my life."

—Jerry Coleman

t's three-thirty in the afternoon, and although the first pitch won't take place for another three and half hours, seventy-nine-year-old Jerry Coleman is already at Qualcomm Stadium, home of the National League's San Diego Padres. Between now and then he'll tape his daily interview with Padres manager Bruce Bochy, kibitz with players during batting practice, and diligently prepare his scorecard for the game he'll be broadcasting later in the evening. It's the same routine he has been following since 1972 when then–team president Buzzie Bavasi hired Coleman to be the radio voice of the Padres. During the past thirty-one years, great players and great teams have come and gone in San Diego, but Coleman remains, calling 162 games a year with an old-school style and trademark "Colemanisms" that continue to bring smiles to generations of San Diego baseball fans. To them, he is the likable, always self-deprecating broadcaster who enthusiastically shouts, "You can hang a star on that one, baby!" on great plays by Padres players, and who every now and then will blurt out phrases that draw comparisons to another master of the malapropism, former teammate Yogi Berra.

But because he loathes talking about himself, and specifically his pre-broadcasting life, what many of the thousands who listen to him don't know is that there is much more to the life of Gerald Francis Coleman than his time in the San Diego broadcast booth. They aren't aware they are listening to a former Marine Corps fighter pilot who flew combat missions in World War

II and the Korean War. They aren't aware they are listening to the only former major league baseball player to see combat in two wars.

When he started his senior year in high school in 1941, combat was the last thing on Coleman's mind. A native Californian who grew up in San Francisco, he had a combined basketball-baseball scholarship offer from the University of Southern California. "And then the Japanese had to go and ruin it," he says jokingly, referring to December 7, 1941. It changed everything.

"In the spring of my of my senior year in high school," he recalls, "the principal gathered all the boys in the senior class in the auditorium to hear about different military options. We were all talking and asking each other what branch of the service we thought we'd enter. All of a sudden, in walked these two naval aviators, whose gold wings were about like THAT [spreading his arms for emphasis], and I just thought, that's it! That's what I want to do."[1]

The only problem was that he was still seventeen and wouldn't turn the required eighteen until the following September. Convinced that flying was the only option for him, he went ahead and accepted a contract from the New York Yankees to play baseball with their farm team in Wellsville, New York, during the summer. He played well, earning a reputation as a graceful middle infielder and solid hitter, but as soon as he turned eighteen, in September, he was back in San Francisco filling out his application for the Naval Aviation Cadet program.

"I almost didn't get in!" he says. "The head guy who gave the final approval looked at my high school transcripts and said, 'Son, do you know it costs three hundred thousand dollars to train a naval aviator? If I take you, you're going to wash out and cost the government thousands of dollars.' I remember saying, 'Sir, I can do it. I'm not dumb. I just didn't apply myself as much as I should have.' I guess I convinced him, because he approved me."[2]

Coleman's instincts about his ability to fly an airplane proved correct. He completed the various stages of his flight training in Colorado, North Carolina, and Texas without a problem, earning his wings on April 1, 1944, at the Naval Air Station in Corpus Christi, Texas. "I loved the feel [of flying]," says Coleman. "The formation flying, the acrobatics, the gunnery . . . I enjoyed all of that."

It was during advanced training in Texas that pilots chose what branch of the service they wanted to enter. Coleman picked the Marines and headed off to Jacksonville, Florida, as a first lieutenant to spend a few months learning the nuances of flying the SBD Dauntless dive bomber. "I remember my biggest concern going through training was that the war would end before I got there," says Coleman.

It didn't. In the summer of 1944 he boarded a troop ship in California as a replacement pilot bound for the island of Guadalcanal in the Solomon Islands. For the next ten months he flew fifty-seven combat missions with VMSB-341, "The Torrid Turtles," doing close air support for army and marine forces fighting on Guadalcanal and in the Philippines. He was nineteen; his gunner was eighteen. "Geez, you talk about some green peas!" he says, laughing at the memory. "If the Japanese knew we were in the war, they wouldn't have surrendered, for god's sake. I look at it now, and I think we must have been nuts. But you know, that's just the way it was back then, everything was accelerated. I certainly wasn't the only nineteen-year-old up there."

In July 1945, Coleman, who had qualified to fly off of aircraft carriers, returned to the United States along with other pilots to form the squadrons that would fly off of carriers in support of the planned amphibious invasion of mainland Japan. They were preparing for that mission when atomic bombs were dropped on Hiroshima and Nagasaki, bringing the war to an end. In January 1946, three years and three months after his entry into the military, the now twenty-one-year-old Marine Corps captain was transferred to the inactive reserve list and released from the military.

Although he hadn't picked up a glove in years and was unsure if he could even play anymore, Coleman was still the baseball property of the New York Yankees. "I really didn't know what else I could do, so I decided to give it [baseball] a try again," says Coleman.

It was the right decision. Playing primarily shortstop and third base, he moved up quickly in the Yankees farm system. He was called up briefly to the major leagues in 1948 before becoming the starting second baseman in 1949 on a Yankee team that went 97–57 and included World War II veterans Yogi Berra, Phil Rizzuto, and an aging Joe DiMaggio in center field. The team, under the leadership of first-year manager Casey Stengel, defeated the Brooklyn Dodgers in five games to win the World Series. It would be the first of five consecutive World Series championships for the Yankees, and Coleman was named American League Rookie of the Year.

"Jerry was a great defensive second baseman," says Irv Noren, a former teammate of Coleman's and an outfielder on two of those Yankee championship teams. "There weren't too many who could turn the double play like he could. Billy Martin and Gil McDougal were also on a few of those teams that won championships, but neither of them was as good defensively at second base as Jerry."[3]

Coleman followed up his 1949 season with an even better one in 1950, making the all-star team and being named most valuable player (MVP) of the Yankees' World Series sweep of the Philadelphia Phillies. "We had a lot of good players," says Coleman when asked what made the Yankees so dominant during those years. "The big thing was that nobody really cared about records. Winning was the whole thing. There was no second place in New York."[4] Noren gives a lot of credit to manager Casey Stengel. "I've always felt he was ahead of his time," he says. And he was certainly very colorful. "I remember someone once asking him how he kept us all working together as a team," recalls Noren. "He said, 'The key is keeping the 50 percent of the guys who don't like me away from the 50 percent of the guys who are undecided.'"[5]

Coleman had another solid season in 1951, hitting .249 as the Yankees defeated the New York Giants for their third consecutive World Series title. But while he was back in the San Francisco Bay area for the off-season, he received a call from a marine major who was stationed at nearby Alameda, asking him to come see him.

The Korean War was in its eighteenth month, and unbeknownst to Coleman, the Marines were badly in need of pilots. "The Marine Corps, and all of the military services, had drawn down significantly at the end of World War II and was practically undermanned when the Korean War broke out," says Bob Aguilina, historian at the Marine Corps History Museum in Washington, D.C.[6] When North Korean troops invaded South Korea on June 25, 1950, the commandant of the Marines had immediately committed a Marine Corps air wing and a marine division to the battle, expecting that with the help of more than forty-one different U.N. (United Nations) countries, the war would quickly come to an end. Eighteen months later, there was no end in sight, and the Marines needed pilots to replace those who had been flying since the war's beginning.

Coleman drove over to Alameda as requested and was caught completely off guard when the major asked him what he thought about going back into the service. "I told him, 'Well, to tell you the truth, I hadn't thought *anything* about it,'" remembers Coleman. The major told him about the shortage of pilots and outlined the Corps' intention to recall World War II veterans from the inactive list. "We're going to have to get you," he told him.

Coleman was no longer the nineteen-year-old "green pea" who had feared the end of the war before he got a chance to take his own shots. He was twenty-seven, married with two young children, and at the peak of his professional baseball career. But his response was the same as it had been back in 1942—"I'll go." "It was December of 1951, and the only thing I asked was for them to take me right away. They had said they needed me for eighteen months of active duty, and I thought if I left right away I wouldn't miss two full seasons with the Yankees."[7]

The New York papers quickly got wind of the plan to recall Coleman (as well as the Boston Red Sox's Ted Williams), and columnists decried what they perceived to be the unfairness of the military reaching down to pull someone who had already done more then his share in World War II. "Why . . . should young men who have done their stint be forced to step in the middle of their own reconstruction problems and begin the life of a warrior all over again, especially—and this is the main point—when there are millions of others available who have yet seen no service at all," wrote Joe Williams in the *New York Times.*[8]

Coleman, though, never hesitated and never complained. "Speaking only for myself, the reason seems simple enough," he told reporters. "For an experienced flyer it takes only about two months to get back in the harness. Starting with a youngster who has never flown before, it would take about two years before he would be ready for combat duty."[9]

"It really wasn't a case of the Marine Corps picking on people like Coleman," adds Aguilina. "They just really needed the specific skills they [World War II pilots] offered to try and stem the North Koreans' advance into South Korea."[10]

Despite his request to leave "right away," Coleman ended up playing the first eleven games of the 1952 season for the Yankees, collecting seventeen hits in forty-two at-bats for a sizzling .405 batting average before leaving the team on April 30. Because he hadn't flown a plane since November 1945, his first stop was refresher training at Los Alamitos Naval Air Station in California, where he spent a month flying single-engine, two-seater training planes to reacquaint himself with being in the cockpit. From there, he and a group of fellow pilots reported to El Toro Marine Air Base to begin training on the aircraft they would fly while on active duty.

"Right at the beginning we were all lined up and asked what we wanted to do," Coleman remembers. "Everyone wanted to be an instructor, but when they got to me they just said, 'You're going to be in VMA-323.' I wasn't given a choice. Looking back, I can see the reason for that. If they would have allowed myself and Ted Williams to be instructors, the Marines would have faced all sorts of criticism about letting baseball players avoid combat."[11]

There were two jet squadrons at El Toro and one squadron of F-4U Corsairs, a propeller-driven strike-bomber. Coleman was assigned to the VMA-323 "Death Rattlers" and began learning to fly the Corsair. He arrived in Korea in January of 1953, and by the end of the month had already flown his first combat missions, destroying railroad bridges in North Korea. The New York papers willingly carried stories of the popular Coleman's early combat success in their newspapers. "Coleman Bats 1,000 in Korea," "Jerry Coleman Hits Red Span 1st Time at Bat," and "Coleman Wrecks Commie Bridge" were the headlines. "It felt like old times flying with the marines again," said Coleman after his first mission.[12]

But as the weeks and months wore on, Coleman realized that combat as a twenty-eight-year-old was a different experience than it had been seven, eight, and nine years earlier. The flying was similar. As in World War II, Coleman was once again bombing and strafing targets in support of ground troops, but this time he found himself much more aware of his own mortality. "Back then I just thought it was normal stuff. You know, it was like being on a team . . . we were all sent out . . . sometimes some guys didn't come back. But you were young enough and dumb enough to think that everyone else would go before you. In Korea, we were all older, and flying out to missions I'd think, well, this just might be the time, this might be the one."[13]

And the reality was, there were several missions that came very close to being "the one" for Coleman in Korea. He barely avoided a midair collision while landing, and then a few weeks later the motor on his Corsair failed on take-off. His plane, outfitted with three one-thousand-pound bombs, flipped upside down, breaking the bombs loose and sending them bouncing down the runway. Miraculously, the bombs didn't detonate, and although the runway was damaged, Coleman, along with his quick wit, escaped unharmed. "I tried to land it on its back," he cracked, "but they're [the Corsairs] not made that way!"[14]

Several months after that incident, he and his roommate, Max Harper, the father of five children, were making a bombing run on a North Korean factory. Coleman followed him into the target, but then watched in horror as Harper's Corsair never pulled out of its dive, crashing instead directly into the center of the factory.

In June of 1953, after eight months and sixty-three combat missions in Korea, Maj. Gen. Claire Megee, the marine air wing commander of Coleman's squadron, took him out of the cockpit. "Jerry's got the heart of a lion and he's done a bang-up job for us," said Megee when the decision was announced, "but he's flown his share. And he's had three shattering experiences since he came to us. I decided I owed it to him to keep him on the ground for a while. He'd never have asked it. He's not that kind."[15]

Coleman was serving as the air wing's intelligence officer when the United Nations and North Korea signed an armistice agreement on July 27, 1953, bringing the war to an end. Less then a month later, he was on his way home. Including his time in World War II, Coleman had earned two Distinguished Flying Crosses, thirteen Air Medals, and three Navy Unit Citations during nearly five years of active-duty military service. He had actually been in the Marine Corps longer then he had been in the major leagues.

After stopping in San Francisco just long enough to see his family and receive his formal discharge from the Marines, Coleman rejoined the Yankees on August 29 for the remaining four weeks of the 1953 season. Two weeks later, 48,492 fans came to Yankee Stadium for "Gerald Coleman Day" to formally welcome him home.

In attendance to help honor Coleman was Adm. William "Bull" Halsey, whom Coleman had flown for in World War II, as well as the then-current commandant of the Marine Corps, Gen. Lemuel Shepherd. He was showered with gifts, and several pilots he'd served with did a flyover of Yankee Stadium, but it's the phone call he received a few hours before the game that will forever dominate Coleman's memory of that day. The call was from the wife of Max Harper, his roommate and close friend whom he'd seen go down in Korea.

Coleman's voice still goes hoarse with emotion recalling the conversation. "A lot of guys who'd been listed as missing were being located in Korean prison camps, and Max's wife was looking for confirmation. I was put in the position of having to tell her, 'Your husband is dead. I saw it.'"[16]

With that call on his mind, he thanked the fans and Yankee management for their kindness but said the day also belonged to the returned prisoners of war and those "who went to Korea for us and never came home. This is their day too," he said.[17]

When he had left the Yankees for Korea in April 1952, Coleman had fully expected to be able to pick up right where he had left off once he returned. "I thought, well, I'll get these two years out of the way and come back, but when I did I was never as good again," he says.

After watching the Yankees' 1953 World Series victory over the Brooklyn Dodgers from the bench, he returned as the team's starting second baseman in 1954, but a batting average of just .217 eventually resulted in his splitting time with Gil McDougal. Injuries kept him out of all but a fourth of the 1955 season, and after two years as primarily a utility infielder for the 1956 and 1957 seasons, he accepted an offer from the Yankees to be their assistant personnel director. "Bobby Richardson was coming on, and in fact, they wanted him to be the second baseman in 1957, but he wasn't quite ready," says Coleman. "I asked what would happen to me if I didn't take the personnel job, and they told me I probably would be traded. I had a wife and two children, and I didn't want to move."[18]

He spent two years placing minor league prospects in the Yankees' farm system and another two working with the Van Heusen Shirt Company. It was while he was working in Van Heusen's sales department that Bill McPhail, then-director of CBS Radio and Television, asked him to join Pee Wee Reese and Dizzy Dean in the weekly Saturday broadcast of baseball's "Game of the Week," beginning what has turned into a forty-three-year-and-counting career in radio broadcasting.

After teaming with former teammate Phil Rizzuto and Hall of Fame broadcaster Red Barber from 1963 to 1969 to broadcast the Yankee games, Coleman and his family headed back to their native California, where he worked several years broadcasting sports for KTLA Television in Los Angeles. He was doing that, along with broadcasts for the ABC Radio Network, when the Padres hired him in the winter of 1971. He and his family have been in San Diego ever since. "I've been very, very lucky," says Coleman about his long tenure with the Padres. "I know if I offered my job up, there'd be five thousand people stampeding for it."

He has always shied away from talking about his experiences as a Yankee—and a Marine—on the air, says Ted Lightner, his broadcasting partner of twenty-five years. "He's always told me regarding his experiences in World War II and Korea that the heroes were the guys who didn't come home," says Lightner. "He feels very strongly that just because he's on the radio, people shouldn't talk about him and what he did." Every now and then Lightner will do it anyway, as he says, "just to remind people that this is an amazing man."[19]

But while Coleman is reticent about his military service on the air, he is effusive in recognizing—off the air—the impact it had on his life. "I played in six World Series with the Yankees, but the thing that I'm most proud of is my time in the service," says Coleman. "Those were the defining years of my life. Nothing else came close to it. To me, the two things that are central in your life are your family and your country. I mean, I may sound like a Boy Scout, but frankly what else is there? What if we didn't have this country? Heck, I'd go tomorrow if they'd [the military] take me."

It's less than thirty minutes away now from the first pitch at Qualcomm Stadium between the Padres and the visiting Arizona Diamondbacks. The stadium is filling up in the lower box seats, and a Padres representative with a group from one of the club's sponsors pokes her head into the broadcast booth and asks Jerry if they could get a picture with him. She already knows the answer. "Suuurrre," he replies cheerfully. "Not a problem, not a problem at all."

His broadcast producer of ten years, Dave Marcus, says he can't remember Coleman ever saying *no* to anything. "He's the most accommodating and unselfish person I've ever known," he says. "In the ten years I've worked with him, I've learned a lot about how to treat other people."[20] The organization's admiration for him also extends to the field. "Other than my own father I can't imagine a man I'd admire more," says Padres manager Bruce Bochy, whose own father was a sergeant in the army.[21]

Coleman settles into his chair next to Lightner in the broadcasting booth. At seventy-nine, he is still just as vibrant, just as excitable, and loves the game just as much as when he began doing the broadcasts at age forty-eight. And although it takes him a little longer now to walk from the field to his broadcast booth high above home plate, his 6'1" frame is still lean, and his gait is that of an athlete.

The game begins, and Coleman and Lightner begin the comfortable, colorful banter of two men who know each other well and have worked together for a long time. In between pitches, the snippets of conversation between the two range from how they occupied the hours before arriving at the stadium to a wide range of trivia . . . usually having nothing to do with baseball, but always ending up with laughter. "Jerry's voice is Padre baseball," says Lightner. "It's entertaining and it's fun."

In the top of second inning, Padres third baseman Sean Burroughs makes a diving stop of a ground ball and throws the runner out at first. "You can hang a star on that one, baby!" shouts Coleman, and Dan Marcus, the producer, hangs a gold star out of the booth. For those who know him, it's a "Colemanism" that also applies to Jerry Coleman's own life.

CHAPTER 6

The Pioneer's Champion

"I matured a great deal in the military, both physically and emotionally. I also really learned when to keep my mouth shut . . . which for me has never been easy."

—Bill Tosheff

The living room in seventy-six-year-old Bill Tosheff's eighteenth-floor downtown San Diego apartment resembles the office of an overworked and underpaid graduate school research assistant. There are files, newspaper clippings, and recently received faxes, as well as a wall lined with an assortment of basketball books and encyclopedias. Although it's quiet now, the phone rings frequently during the day with calls from men who once graced the hardwood courts of professional basketball.

They're in their mid- to late seventies now. Some are calling just to shoot the bull and swap stories with the man everyone simply calls "Tosh." Others are calling in hopes of getting his help in obtaining a pension from the National Basketball Association. Since becoming president of the Pre-1965 NBA Players Association, Tosheff has launched a one-man crusade to obtain pensions for an estimated fifty or so players—almost all of whom are World War II veterans—from the pioneer era of the NBA, from 1949 to 1955.

He's had some success. Nine of these basketball pioneers have received benefits totaling more than a million dollars. To do it, he's gone one-on-one with the mega-rich NBA, accusing and cajoling, doing whatever it takes to get commissioner David Stern and his league of twentysomething millionaires to recognize the contributions of the very players who "set the table" for those playing in the NBA today.

"I admire the hell out of him for it," says Bud Palmer, a three-year player with the New York Knicks and a recent beneficiary of Tosheff's crusade. Last year, after receiving a retroactive lump-sum payment of $148,000 from the NBA, Palmer began getting a monthly pension of $1,200—more than fifty years after he had played his last game for the Knicks. "I would never have gotten it without Tosh."[1]

For those who know him best, Tosheff's determination and tenacity in support of those who were once his peers in professional basketball is not surprising. "When it comes to things he's passionate about, Dad has never done things halfway," says his thirty-six-year-old son, Alex. "He's just always been like that."[2] It is that statement—the knowing words of a son about his father—that perhaps best characterizes the life of William "Tosh" Tosheff.

A native of one of the most ethnically diverse neighborhoods in Gary, Indiana, he and his group of Yugoslavian and Macedonian buddies grew up doing the two things all guys from Gary did—playing sports and working in the steel mills. "We were highly competitive and did just about everything together. Whatever sport was in season, that's what we played," says Tosheff.[3]

His dad had a tailor shop right in the middle of the city's black section, and young Bill learned at an early age how to relate to people from a wide range of cultures and backgrounds. "Including hookers!" says the always colorful and never politically correct Tosheff. "There were about thirty whorehouses right around the area, and the prostitutes always brought their clothes into the tailor shop."

He attended Gary's Froebel High School and quickly became a four-sport star, captaining the football and basketball teams, pitching and playing shortstop for the baseball team, and setting a state record in the broad jump for the track team. Heading into his junior year, he was fast becoming one of the best athletes in the state when he heard about an opportunity to fly with the Royal Canadian Air Force. "Since the beginning of the war, we'd been hearing about the damage the German Luftwaffe was doing in Europe," recalls Tosheff. "When I heard about people going over to England to fly with the RCAF, I thought, 'Man, I want to do that.'"

Despite passing the flight physical and written exam, his request was turned down when the Canadian government put a moratorium on noncitizens joining their military. Undeterred, he waited a year and in the fall of 1944 joined the U.S. Army Air Corps at the age of seventeen, spending the next year and a half learning to fly the B-17 bomber. "The war against Germany was actually winding down by the time I finished all my flight training," Tosheff recalls, "but I just wanted to contribute."

He spent his final year in the army flying supplies around the Aleutian Islands for the 54th Troop Carry Squadron based out of Anchorage, Alaska, and returned home in December 1946. After turning down a minor league contract with the Chicago Cubs, he entered Indiana University (IU) in the summer of 1947 and a year later was a standout on both the basketball and baseball teams. In his senior year, he captained the "Hurryin' Hoosiers" to a 19–3 record and number five national ranking, earning all–Big Ten honors as well as being named to several all-American teams. A favorite of coach Branch McCracken, he was quick, an excellent passer, and an outstanding long-range, two-handed set shooter. "Tosh was the unquestioned leader of the team," recalls his former teammate Dale Vieau. "I remember the Illinois game. We lost 63–58 in a real heartbreaker, and Tosh played great. Anyway, he's walking off the court and this Illinois fan is just really giving him the business. Next thing I know, Tosh turns around and just decks him."[4]

"The military really accelerated my maturity," says Tosheff as he speaks about his days at Indiana. "Most of my teammates were eighteen or nineteen years old, and by the time I was a senior, I was twenty-four. They knew I was the leader, and I wanted to be the leader. All McCracken had to do was get on me a little and everyone else immediately fell in line."[5]

It was during his years at IU that he also cemented his reputation for being somewhat of a free spirit. "He always used to tell me and my brothers how he would take the dean of the university's daughter up in a biplane and buzz the football players while they were practicing," says his son Alex. "Well, you know, we would always say, 'Suuure, right Dad, whatever you say.' None of us ever really believed him. So a few years ago, I go with my dad back to Indiana for his fiftieth-year reunion, and some guy comes up to me and says, 'Oh, your dad was such a character in college! He used to take the dean's daughter up in a biplane and buzz the football field.' I started believing more of his stories after that."[6]

When he graduated from Indiana in 1951, the NBA was still in its infancy, having just been formed with the merger of the National Basketball League and the Basketball Association of America in 1949. Tosheff was drafted by the Indianapolis Olympians, and in his first year averaged nine points and four assists per game, earning co–rookie of the year honors with Mel Hutchins of the Tri-Cities Blackhawks. "There was great camaraderie among the players in those early years of the NBA," says Tosheff. "We traveled mostly by train and were much more approachable to people than players are today. I also think we cared more about each other."[7]

No one was getting rich. Tosheff's salary in his rookie year was forty-five hundred dollars, and six thousand in his second year. The majority of the players had been in the military, and they played for one reason—they loved the game. And back then, he says, the game was played on the floor. "Today, it's all above the rim," says Tosheff. "We weren't even allowed to dunk the ball. I say take the slam dunk away for one night and let's see what happens. Shaq wouldn't be scoring 30 or 40 [points] a night. And another thing—we didn't carry the ball! We weren't allowed to do what [Allen] Iverson does . . . carrying the ball around, crossing over this way and that. What is that? We had to have our hand on top of the ball!" he says, raising his voice.[8]

After his second year with the Olympians, the team was disbanded and Tosheff's rights were obtained by the Milwaukee Hawks. He had a solid third season in Milwaukee, leading the team in assists and minutes played, but when he returned from playing winter baseball in South America to sign his contract for the fourth season, they asked him to take a fifteen-hundred-dollar pay cut, bringing his salary back down to forty-five hundred. "I felt like it was an insult," he recalls.

As he was mulling it over, Tosheff, who would have turned twenty-nine that season, remembers wondering for the first time if all the travel, cold gyms, and the physical toll taken on his body each season was worth it for just a couple thousand dollars. "I'm not sure why the thought came into my mind, but I remember asking myself, 'How am I ever going to get out of my chair at fifty if I keep playing?'"[9] He turned the contract down, told the Hawks to put him on the voluntary retired list, and headed back down to South America to finish the winter baseball season. His professional basketball-playing days were over.

He spent the next three years pitching in the minor leagues for the Cleveland Indians and Milwaukee Braves organizations, rising as high as AAA in the American Association before deciding that it was finally time to get on with the rest of his life. Echoing the feelings of probably every professional baseball player who has reached the rung on the minor league ladder just below the majors, Tosheff says he should have made it to the big show. "During spring training I remember beating the Yankees, the Detroit Tigers. But my problem was that by the time I got up to AAA, I was old at thirty."

Although his three years in the military had helped put him physically and mentally ahead of his teammates in college, in professional baseball it had put him behind. To major league scouts and coaches, Tosheff's best years as a pitcher had already passed. When baseball's 1957 minor league season came to an end, he packed up his car, returned to Indiana University to earn his MBA in real estate and finance and embarked on a business career that eventually took him to Irvine, California, where for more than twenty years he was a successful general contractor.

He never stopped staying in touch, though, with his pals from the NBA's earlier years, or others who he'd met during his time in professional sports. Dr. Vince Ruscelli met Tosh in 1955 during Ruscelli's first year playing basketball for Tyler Junior College in Corpus Christi, Texas. "It was his off-season from baseball, and Tosh had stopped by the gym and volunteered to help with the team," says Ruscelli. "Because he obviously knew so much about basketball, he ended up being the head coach." Ruscelli says although it was for just one season, Tosh had a major influence on his life. "He gave me more confidence in myself and instilled a desire to achieve," he says. "Everyone has those accidental encounters in their life with people who end up having a major impact. For me, Tosh was one of those people." Although nearly fifty years have passed since that one season, Ruscelli says Tosh has always stayed in touch with him, checking up on him every now and then, asking how his family is, how his kids are doing.[10] "People just connect with him," says son Alex.

One of Bud Palmer's favorite Tosh stories is the time he visited him in San Diego. "We went for a walk on the boardwalk and every ten yards it was, 'Hey, Tosh, how ya doin'?' immediately followed by a ten-minute conversation. We never got anywhere!"[11]

When the Pre-1965 NBA Players Association needed a president in 1990, Tosh was the easy choice. Obtaining pensions for those NBA pioneers who helped jump-start the league in 1949 quickly became important to him. True to form, he is intensely passionate about it. "I just feel it's an injustice to the guys I played with that so many of them aren't covered by the league's pension plan," says Tosheff.[12]

Some are. In 1988 Commissioner David Stern, along with the NBA Player's Association, approved the extension of pension benefits to the pre-1965 pioneers who had played a minimum of five years in the league. They made the deal with a group of Hall of Fame old-timers that included Bob Cousy, Dolph Schayes, George Mikan, and Red Holzman. Tosheff says it was a bad deal. "That group agreed to the five-year playing minimum despite knowing that for all post-1965 players the minimum number of years played was only three. That's a double standard right there. They also agreed, as part of the deal with Commissioner Stern, that they would not go public with it. They wouldn't go to the media. Why? Because the league didn't want anyone to know! They didn't want to have to pay out any more benefits then they had to."[13]

An amendment to allow players to count their years of service in World War II and the Korean War toward their five is also flawed, says Tosheff, because it requires those years to immediately precede or follow a player's time in the NBA. The combination must be concurrent, which disqualifies players such as Tosheff and others who served, came home to attend or finish school, and then went into the pros. "When I heard all that I just said, 'Hey, there's something wrong here.' I felt someone had to do something about it."

Since then he has worked tirelessly to persuade the NBA to change the rules and to try to identify those pioneers who are eligible but don't know they qualify. In other words, to do the things Tosheff does now. "I go through the players' records, look at what years they were in college and what years they played in the NBA to see if they might have had some military experience in between," he says. He even personally calls the military records archives in St. Louis to get a copy of a former player's discharge papers. Once he has all the information and documentation he needs, he submits a package to the NBA. Right now he estimates there are fifty-four three- and four-year players from the pioneer era who are not receiving a penny for their contributions to getting the NBA off the ground and running. "That's unconscionable to me," says Tosheff. "It would take about $5 million total to take care of this group. We estimate about $650,000 annually. That's chump change for the NBA today. They could sell T-shirts and make more money than that in a year! But Stern won't do it."[14]

In the summer of 1998 Tosheff's crusade made it all the way to Congress, where he and a group of former players testified before the subcommittee on employer-employee relations about their plight. Although they received widespread support for their cause, their presence before the committee didn't result in any movement by the NBA. A statement provided by the league's lawyer at the subcommittee hearing outlined the NBA's position on the issue:

We continue to believe that the 5-season eligibility requirement represents an entirely fair mechanism for identifying and rewarding that group of individuals who made a truly significant contribution to the early years of the NBA. While it is understandable that those with only three years of service would like to receive money from the plan (as would presumably, those with two years or even one year of service), the NBA and the Players Association had to establish some standard of eligibility for this unprecedented benefit. That standard we established was five years of service.[15]

Tosheff fights on, researching cases and lobbying the NBA Player's Association to support his cause. He has established a trust fund on behalf of those pioneer players who are not eligible for pensions, and to their credit, the NBA has contributed to this fund. Some pioneers have also made contributions. Tosheff, with the approval of the association's board of directors, periodically sends out checks to those players who are most in need. And there are quite a few of them. "Many went on to successful careers in business or other professions," says Dr. Neil Isaacs, a former English professor at the University of Maryland, who, with Tosheff's considerable help, wrote the book *Vintage NBA: The Pioneer Era, 1946–1956.* A portion of all the proceeds from the book's sales goes into the Pre-1965 NBA Players Association trust fund. "An equal number, though, have really struggled. They gave the best years of their lives to basketball, and when they left the game, they didn't have anything else going for them."[16]

One of those is John Ezersky. Ezersky grew up playing basketball in New York City and was one of the first players on the East Coast to abandon the two-handed set shot and begin shooting with one hand like the players of today. From 1943 to 1945 he served in the army's 747th Tank Battalion. He landed on Omaha Beach on D-day and for the next ten months fought his way across Europe to Germany. "All I can say is thank God Mr. Truman came along," he says with a laugh. "He saved my life. When the bomb dropped, we were in Belgium training to go into Japan."[17]

Ezersky had been one of the best players in New York City before the war, playing for Power Memorial Academy, as well as several top Amateur Athletic Union (AAU) teams. When he was discharged from the army, he was immediately picked up for the 1946 season by the New York Gothams, a semipro team. He went on to play two years in the National Basketball League and Basketball Association of America before those two leagues merged to become the NBA. Ezersky then played two years in the NBA with the Boston Celtics and Baltimore Bullets, giving him a total of four professional seasons, as well as three years of military service. Unfortunately, because of his one year with the Gothams (and despite intense lobbying from Tosheff), the NBA ruled that his military service and professional basketball career were not concurrent and denied his pension.

He's not bitter, but the lack of pension benefits did keep him driving a taxi in San Francisco until he was seventy-seven. Today, at eighty-one, he and his wife get by on twelve hundred dollars a month from Social Security and the help of family. "It's wrong, absolutely wrong," he says. "A pension would have helped me a great deal, but Tosh gave it a good fight. Unfortunately, those knuckleheads [the NBA] just won't comply."[18]

Isaacs says its cases like Ezersky's that fuel Tosheff's motivation to continue dogging the NBA on this issue. "Tosh has this genuine caring for his peers," says Isaacs. "He never forgot the experience of being around guys like John Ezersky, and it bothers him that they didn't get what they deserved."[19]

It's getting late now in that apartment living room that doubles as Tosheff's office. A clip from an interview with former Indiana coach Bob Knight comes on the TV, and Tosh immediately pops up to place a phone call to an old Indiana buddy to see if he is watching it, but ends up just leaving a boisterous message instead. "The man has more energy and gets by on less sleep than anyone I know," says Isaacs.

Every once in a while, early in the morning, Tosh still goes down to a park near the beach that has a couple of baskets and fires up a few two-handed set shots. "I used to go pretty regularly," he says. "I'd go down there about seven in the morning, and the homeless guys would hear me thumping the ball and say, 'Ah, geez, here he is again. How long you going to be out here?'"

"Well, I never, never quit until I hit a two-handed thirty-footer," says the seventy-nine-year-old. "Sometimes it might take me fifteen or twenty shots. Sometimes I'll make it on my first shot. But I always stay until I hit that last one."[20]

Bill Tosheff still never does anything halfway.

CHAPTER 7

He Could Have Been President

"Every man whom I have admired in history has willingly and courageously served in his country's armed forces in times of danger. It is not only a duty, but an honor, to follow their examples as best I know how. May God give me the courage and ability to so conduct myself in every situation that my country, my family, and my friends will be proud of me."

—Nile Kinnick

Walking into Red Frye's neat and orderly den, it instantly catches your attention. Among family photos of children who are now grown and an assortment of other life memories is a large color picture of a football team. Twenty-seven young men in black jerseys and gold pants, the straps from their leather helmets cinched tightly under their chins, their serious expressions failing to mask the natural brightness of youth shining from their faces. It's one of those unique images that prompt you to take a step forward—even if you don't really need to—and lean in for a better look. Underneath the photo is the inscription, "Iowa University Football Team, 1939."

Frye, now eighty-four and living in Albia, Iowa, where he attended high school some seventy years before, was a sophomore offensive lineman (No. 19)—the center—on that team. It's a team that is legendary in the annals of Iowa University football. Having won only two games the previous two seasons, they seemingly came out of nowhere to challenge Ohio State for the Big Ten title and lift the spirits of a state that had been knocked to its knees by the Depression. Because the team had only twenty-seven players on the roster, many of them never came out of games, playing both offense and defense. Their coach, Dr. Eddie Anderson, referred to them as the "Ironmen," and with each improbable victory they began to capture the interest of football fans across the country. "Iowa had lost all these games before, but all of a sudden the newspapers and radios started publicizing Iowa—not just the university, but *Iowa*—as having this great team," says Frye. "They'd put the hometowns of where the players were from in the newspapers, and people from across the state started really perking their ears up."[1]

Although their roster was small compared to other major college teams, the Ironmen had talent. Sophomore quarterback Al Couppee (No. 30), the primary signal caller and blocker in a formation in which the ball was centered directly to the running backs, would go on to play professional football with the Washington Redskins after his return from World War II. Senior left end Erwin Prasse (No. 37), who earned nine letters in three sports at Iowa, would play both professional basketball and baseball after serving in the war as an army platoon commander. Dick Evans (No. 35), the right end opposite Prasse, would play for the Green Bay Packers, as would left guard Chuck Tollefson (No. 27).

But when former players and longtime Iowa football fans discuss that team, invariably the conversation turns to number 24. The serious-looking, square-jawed young man seated in the second row, second from the left in the picture. His name was Nile Kinnick.

At 5'8" he was small for a running back and not particularly fast. "Hell, I was *a lot* faster than Nile," recalls Prasse, laughing.[2] But what Kinnick had in abundance were those qualities that coaches call the *intangibles*—toughness, an extraordinary feel for the game, and most important of all, a Michael Jordan–like ability to make the clutch play when his team needed it most. Time and time again during that magical fall of 1939, Kinnick would lead the Ironmen to one upset after another. His accomplishments, combined with the team's underdog appeal, catapulted him onto the national stage and in front of Depression-weary Americans hungry for something or *someone* to feel good about. They found exactly what they were looking for in Kinnick. President of his class, an honor student, and an eloquent speaker, to many he became the real-life version of fictional book and radio heroes Frank Merriwell and Jack Armstrong. As Bill Cunningham of the *Boston Herald* would write, "This country's OK as long as it produces Nile Kinnicks. The football part is incidental."[3]

Sixty-four years after he left Iowa for the navy in December of 1941, the legend of Nile Kinnick and the Ironmen continues to inspire those who are hearing the story for the first time. It's a story about a young man and a team who willed themselves to be the best they could be, and it's a story that in the end, like so many other stories from that generation, leaves you wondering what might have been.

Ironically, the Iowa football program's complete lack of success in the preceding decade was one reason the Ironmen were such a compelling story during the 1939 season. Although the Hawkeyes had won consistently throughout the 1920s, including back-to-back Big Ten championships in 1921 and 1922, the 1930s had seen the Hawkeyes fall to the cellar of the Big Ten and stay there. From 1930 to 1938 the team won a total of twenty-two games, and during five of those years they never beat a single Big Ten opponent. In 1929 a brand-new fifty-three-thousand-seat stadium was completed on the school's campus in Iowa City, but often during the late 1930s the number of fans in the stands seemed close to matching the number of players on the field. The school had sold bonds to finance the construction of the stadium, but poor attendance had reduced the athletic department's revenues to the point where they were no longer able to pay the interest on those bonds.

Kinnick arrived at the university in the fall of 1936. He had grown up on a farm in Adel, Iowa, but the Depression had forced his family to move to Omaha, Nebraska, before his senior year in high school, where his father took a job with the Federal Land Bank. The move didn't affect Kinnick's athletic career. Just like he'd done in Adel, he starred in three sports at Omaha's Benson High School, earning all-state honors in basketball and football. When it was time to pick a college, the University of Minnesota was his first choice. Minnesota had a reputation as one of the major football powerhouses in the Big Ten at the time, having won three national championships and going unbeaten for a stretch of twenty-eight games from 1933 to 1936. But Minnesota's coaches, concerned about Kinnick's size, did not express any real interest, so he headed to Iowa City.

Prasse, now eighty-five and living in Naperville, Illinois, remembers the first time he saw Kinnick at the start of freshman football practice. "I was looking around at some of the other guys and feeling a little intimidated. They were huge!" says Prasse. "Then another guy there leans over to me and says, 'Look, don't worry—if that little guy over there can play, so can we.' He was referring to Nile!"[4]

Kinnick was a standout on the Hawkeyes' freshman football, basketball, and baseball teams, but dropped baseball after that first year. He earned all–Big Ten honors as a running back in his sophomore year and played one more winter of basketball before deciding to focus his efforts solely on football and his studies. "The athlete learns to evaluate—to evaluate between athletics and studies, between playing for fun and playing as a business, between playing clean and playing dirty, between being conventional and being true to one's convictions," wrote Kinnick in his diary before the start of his junior year. "He is facing the identical conditions which will confront him after college—the same dimensions and circumstances. But how many football players realize this?"[5] It's the type of comment that is very much in line with how those who knew him describe Kinnick: serious, determined, and adept at seeing the greater meaning in the experiences and circumstances he—and others—found themselves in.

"I've never met anyone who had the self-discipline that 21-year-old had," Couppee once said about him. "There was just an aura about Nile. He didn't try to create it, it was just there. You really had the feeling you were in the presence of someone very special."[6]

"We obviously respected him and he was well-liked on the team, but Nile was not a great socialite," says Frye. "He was all business. That was the way he liked it and everyone knew it."[7]

After going 1–7 in 1937, Iowa had high hopes for a more successful season in 1938, but in their first game, against UCLA, Kinnick severely sprained his ankle in a 27–3 loss. It was an injury that would hamper him for the rest of the season. As a practicing Christian Scientist, he believed injuries and pain could be overcome through a combination of prayer and a "mind over matter" philosophy. He refused treatment on the ankle and tried to play through it, but he wasn't the same player. The team finished the season with a disappointing record of 1–6–1, scoring only three points in the final three games of the season. After amassing more than twelve hundred yards in total offense (running, passing, returning punts, and kickoffs) as a sophomore, Kinnick didn't reach even half of that as a junior.

Tired of being pummeled by the rest of the conference—and desperate to reverse their downward spiral in revenues—the athletic department fired coach Irl Tubbs and hired Dr. Eddie Anderson. Anderson had a resume that was tailor-made for the job. Having been raised in Mason City, Iowa, and later coaching at small Columbia College in Dubuque, he was a native Iowan who had a reputation for turning around ailing programs. After completing medical school at Rush Medical College in Chicago, Anderson had been hired by Holy Cross, where he'd taken a struggling program and in five years gone 47–7–2 with two undefeated teams in 1935 and 1937. Additionally, he was a Notre Dame man. Under Knute Rockne, the Fighting Irish had become the gold standard of college football, winning 105 games during Rockne's thirteen-year tenure and going unbeaten five times. Anderson was the captain of Rockne's 1921 team that went 10–1. To top it off, Anderson was also a certified urologist. When he wasn't tending to his football responsibilities, he worked in the Iowa University hospital.

Anderson arrived in Iowa City to an enthusiastic welcome on November 29, 1938, just ten days after the conclusion of the 1938 season, bringing with him two assistants who were also from Notre Dame: backfield coach Frank Carideo—a former all-American quarterback in 1929 and 1930—and line coach Jim Harris. They immediately let the state know that this was a new start for Iowa football. "Past performances don't mean a thing," Anderson told the *Des Moines Register*. "We want hard runners. And speed . . . You've got to have your offense ready when the season starts. I want the players to enjoy the game on Saturdays. They ought to get a kick out of confusing, out-hitting and outrunning the other team."

What that translated to for the players was an exhausting spring practice season. Obsessed with physical conditioning, Anderson's arduous practices were responsible for whittling his roster down from an initial eighty to less than thirty men by the time practice resumed in the fall. "He's the only physician I've ever known who thought the cure for everything from a hangnail to appendicitis was 'running it off,'" cracked Frye.

But Frye also says that by the time spring practice concluded, those who remained began to sense that they were going to surprise teams in the upcoming season. "We just started to get that feeling," he says. "We knew we had some good guys, and the new coaches just kind of put it all together. We started to build up some self-confidence, and that's kind of what happened."[8]

Perhaps because they saw so much of themselves in each other, Anderson and Kinnick hit it off immediately. Like Kinnick, Anderson prided himself on hard work and exhaustive preparation, and his tough practices, followed by lengthy strategy sessions that involved gathering the team together and going through plays and formations on a blackboard, were right up Kinnick's alley. As the 1939 season approached, Kinnick was like a well-trained thoroughbred eager to get out of the starting gate.

"For three years, nay for fifteen years, I have been preparing for this last year of football," Kinnick said in a letter home to his parents. "The season just past has removed much of the tension that might have attended this last effort . . . I anticipate becoming the roughest, toughest all-around back yet to his this conference."[9] It was an uncharacteristically bold statement from the usually humble and reserved Kinnick, but it spoke volumes about his determination going into his final season. As a runner, passer, punter, and kicker, he was without question one of the most versatile players in the country, but because of the team's poor record and his own injuries, not too many people outside the Midwest had ever seen or heard of Nile Kinnick. That was about to change.

The season started against South Dakota, the only team anyone gave the Hawkeyes a chance to beat in a schedule that included six Big Ten teams and Notre Dame. Because of that, an above-average opening-season crowd of eighteen thousand saw Iowa completely dominate South Dakota, with Kinnick putting on a dazzling all-around display. Kinnick's father, Nile Sr., had never seen his son win while at Iowa and had driven from Omaha to see the game, thinking, along with the rest of the crowd, that this would probably be the team's best and only chance for a victory. He was treated to quite a performance. In addition to gaining 110 yards on the ground in just eight carries—including a 65-yard run for a touchdown—the younger Kinnick had two touchdown passes and drop-kicked five extra points.

His kicking, which usually garnered less attention then his running and passing, was something Kinnick worked tirelessly on before and after practice with new backfield coach Carideo, himself an accomplished kicker during his years at Notre Dame. Frye remembers those practice sessions well, because he typically got roped in to centering the ball. "Nile would start at the twenty-yard line with the goalpost at a tough angle," remembers Frye. "I'd center the ball to him and he'd drop-kick it over the goalpost. Then he'd take a step or two this way and hit it from that angle, and he'd keep doing that until he got all the way across the field. I also remember him sending his receivers out and watching him kick perfect in-stride spirals to them."[10]

The team was feeling good after the win against South Dakota, but they also knew their first real test of the season was coming the following week against Indiana University—a team they had not beaten in eighteen years. Playing at home in Iowa City in ninety-degree-plus weather, they quickly fell behind the Hoosiers 10–0, but a furious second-half rally got them within a field goal—29–26—late in the fourth quarter. An interception by defensive back Bill Green (No. 43)—also the Ironmen's fullback—gave them the ball back one more time on Indiana's 31-yard line. Several Kinnick runs got the ball down to the 15, but the Indiana defense stiffened. A Kinnick drop-kick field goal would give Iowa a tie and a moral victory. "Forget the tie," Kinnick told his teammates. "We're going all the way."[11]

On fourth down Kinnick dropped back to pass and, with time running out, threw to Prasse, who made a fingertip catch in the end zone for the winning touchdown. Final score: Iowa 32—Indiana 29.

Kinnick had the type of all-around game that *he* knew he was capable of going into the season, but nonetheless it was startling to those watching him that warm autumn afternoon. He ran for 103 yards; threw touchdown passes of 25, 50, and 15 yards to Prasse; returned nine punts, for a total of 201 yards (a school record that still stands); and gained another 171 yards returning kick-offs. "A new gridiron star blazed across the Big Ten horizon here Saturday, a spectacular comet with brilliant touchdown tails which cleared away the shadows of despair which have hovered over Iowa's big stadium for the last six years," wrote Tait Cummins of the *Cedar Rapids Gazette*.[12] From then on, Kinnick had a new nickname—"The Cornbelt Comet."

But the following week, the Michigan Wolverines, led by running back Tom Harmon and quarterback Forest Evashevski, brought Iowa and Kinnick down to earth. Playing their first road game of the season, Iowa jumped out to an early 7–0 lead when Kinnick hit his backfield mate, right halfback Floyd "Buzz" Dean (No. 12), for a seventy-yard touchdown pass, but after that it was all Wolverines. Harmon, who would win the Heisman Trophy the following year, scored four touchdowns, one on a ninety-yard interception return of a Kinnick pass. The loss temporarily quashed the enthusiasm that had begun to percolate around the state after the Indiana win, but two weeks later the Ironmen got it going again when they came from behind to beat another Big Ten opponent, the Wisconsin Badgers.

Playing in Madison, Wisconsin—a place where they hadn't won in ten years—Iowa was behind 7–6 at the half and 13–12 in the fourth quarter, but they rallied behind the leadership and passing of Kinnick. After pushing to the Wisconsin 29-yard line midway in the fourth quarter, Iowa was stopped and forced to punt. Kinnick, though, worried that his team might not get close again to the Wisconsin goal line, faked the kick and threw to backfield mate Bill Green (No. 43) in the end zone for the go-ahead touchdown and a 19–13 lead. Interceptions by Max Hawkins (No. 64) and Dean snuffed out two final drives by Wisconsin, and Iowa had its third victory. Kinnick's passing was the key. He was seven for fourteen for 126 yards and three touchdowns. Of the twenty-six players who had made the trip to Madison, only eighteen saw action, and five—including Kinnick—played the entire sixty minutes. When a reporter brought up this point to Anderson after the game, he said he was coaching "Ironmen." The comment was picked up by papers around the Midwest, and the team's popularity took off.

The following week, the newly christened Ironmen traveled to Purdue for their third consecutive road game. The Boilermakers had been the preseason favorites to win the Big Ten. Only thirteen points had been scored against their defense all season, and Purdue thought if they could shut down Kinnick's passing game, their large offensive and defensive lines would eventually wear down the Ironmen. Their strategy partially worked. Kinnick was able to complete only one pass during the entire game, for twelve yards, but it was Iowa's defensive line that eventually made the difference in the game. Twice, tackle Mike Enich (No. 33) burst through the Purdue line to block two punts that led to safeties, and the Ironmen prevailed in a defensive war, 4–0. The game included a halftime outburst from Anderson that would prove pivotal in the team's next game against Notre Dame.

In the second quarter, the Hawkeyes had advanced to the Purdue eight-yard line, but four runs by Dean, Green, and Prasse had been unable to punch the ball across the goal line. When Anderson walked into the dressing room, he went directly to his sophomore quarterback, Al Couppee. "Couppee, when we get down on the goal line, there's just one guy on this football team who should get that football! Do you even know who he is?! Why don't you meet Nile Kinnick," yelled Anderson, telling the two to shake hands. "I was embarrassed as hell," Couppee later recalled.[13] The victory against heavily favored Purdue set off an impromptu celebration in Iowa City. When the team's train arrived, the coaches and players were put in cars and paraded around town behind the Hawkeye band. With a 3–1 record, the Ironmen had not only won more games than they had in the previous two years combined, but they were also tied for first place in the Big Ten. It was the perfect lead-in for their first home game in more than a month against the undefeated Notre Dame Fighting Irish.

Notre Dame's 1939 team was talented, deep, and unbeaten. In contrast to Anderson, Notre Dame coach Elmer Layden substituted liberally, knowing that the players he sent in from his bench were just as talented and athletic as those they were replacing on the field. Going into their November 11 game against Iowa, the Fighting Irish had won six straight games and were everyone's pick to win the national championship.

Friday night, ten thousand students and fans showed up for the campus pep rally—more than had attended many games in previous years—and the next day close to fifty thousand were packed into Iowa Stadium for the game. Similar to the previous week against Purdue, they witnessed a defensive battle played out primarily between the thirty-five-yard lines, with neither team able to move the ball. The difference was the punting of Nile Kinnick. Over and over again that cool, blustery afternoon, Kinnick's booming punts either pinned the Fighting Irish deep in their own territory or bailed out the Ironmen when their backs were against their own goal line. When they finally got a break, late in the second quarter, they made the most of it.

A fumble recovery by Buzz Dean gave Iowa the ball on the Notre Dame four-yard line. Two runs to the right side yielded nothing. Faced with third down, Al Couppee called a rare huddle and, remembering Anderson's half-time admonition the week before, told Kinnick (the left halfback) and Dean (the right halfback) to switch positions so that Kinnick would be in a better position to make a run at the goal line behind the left tackle. Several of the senior players immediately objected, afraid of making a change in such a critical situation, but the sophomore quarterback held his ground. "We're running that play the way I called it, let's go," he said.[14] The ball was snapped directly to Kinnick, who was met head-on at the goal line by a Notre Dame defender but still managed to bull his way into the end zone. His dropkick was good for the extra point, and the Ironmen had a 7–0 halftime lead.

The second half mirrored the first, with neither team able to generate much offense, but by the end of the third quarter, Notre Dame's superior depth began to wear Iowa down. On the second play of the fourth quarter, the Fighting Irish finally found the end zone, but they missed the extra point, allowing Iowa to maintain a 7–6 lead, but momentum had clearly swung in favor of Notre Dame.

With two minutes left in the game and the ball on their own thirty-four-yard line, Iowa was forced to punt the ball back to a Notre Dame offense that had begun to move the ball effectively against worn-out players who had yet to come out of the game—eight of the eleven, including Kinnick, had gone the distance. The ball was centered back to Kinnick, who launched a kick that sailed clear over the head of the return man, hit the ground, and bounced out of bounds at the Notre Dame six-yard line. "When I saw that ball sail over the safety's head, I knew we had beaten Notre Dame," Couppee would later say. "I have played in 147 football games, college, service and pro, but that was the single most exhilarating moment I ever experienced in sports."[15] Kinnick was carried off the field on the shoulders of his teammates. In addition to scoring the lone touchdown, he had punted sixteen times, for a total of 731 yards (both school records that still stand) and an average 45.6 yards per kick.

The Ironmen's shocking 7–6 victory set off a weekend-long celebration in Iowa City that also reverberated around the country. The score flashed continuously Saturday night at the Times building in downtown New York City at the corner of 42nd and Broadway, and movie theater newsreels nationwide included highlights of the big upset. On Monday, classes were canceled in honor of the football team's victory, and Anderson gave the team a rare day off to rest, but on Tuesday it was back to business. As Anderson quickly reminded them, the homecoming game was just five days away, and their opponent was perhaps even more daunting then Notre Dame. It was the Minnesota Golden Gophers, a team that had beat and embarrassed Iowa eight years in a row. Since 1934, Minnesota's margin of victory against Iowa had never been less than twenty-five points. Like Notre Dame, they were a team deep with talent, and they had an interior line that outweighed Iowa's line by an average of twenty-six pounds per man.

For the second straight week, nearly fifty thousand fans packed Iowa Stadium to see if Kinnick and the Ironmen could keep the magic going. For the first three quarters it didn't look good. Behind their big line, Minnesota ground out a 9–0 lead while stifling Iowa's own ground game. And as was usually the case against the Golden Gophers—"They just beat you up something terrible," Couppee would recall—the game took a physical toll on the smaller Hawkeyes. Nearly half the team was suffering from various sprains and bruises, including Kinnick, whose passing hand was swollen to nearly twice its normal size.[16]

Knowing that moving the ball through the air was their only chance, Kinnick began connecting with Dean and Prasse. After reaching midfield during their first offense possession of the fourth quarter, Prasse went long and the pair hooked up for a forty-five-yard touchdown strike. After Kinnick's dropkick, the Ironmen were down by only two points, 9–7. With just five minutes left, they got the ball back on their own twenty-one-yard line for what they suspected would be their last chance for a go-ahead score. They didn't need the whole five minutes. Kinnick quickly moved the team down the field, and with three minutes still remaining, hit Bill Green with a twenty-eight-yard touchdown pass that put the Hawkeyes ahead 13–9 and sent the homecoming crowd into complete delirium. When Kinnick sealed the victory a few minutes later by intercepting a Minnesota pass, the Iowa fans once again stormed the field, this time carrying the entire team off on their shoulders.

For Kinnick, beating Minnesota that day would be his "greatest thrill" in college football and the brightest highlight in a season of highlights. "I wish that I might be living at home so that you all might experience first hand the joys that I have had this fall," Kinnick wrote his parents.[17]

Not surprisingly, Kinnick's frequent letters to his family and friends were far from detailed rehashes of games or descriptions of his individual accomplishments. To the contrary, the letters reveal a young man whose interests and depth went far beyond what was taking place on the gridiron, and who thought deeply about life after football and Iowa. "Constantly, I am inquiring, wondering, speculating, philosophizing about what my future education, if any, should be: toward what I should really point as an occupation," wrote Kinnick in one letter home.

> For what line of endeavor am I best equipped? Is a happy, normal, honest upright life of the average man a sufficient goal toward which to strive, or is man duty bound if he is capable to try to serve his fellowman by serving his government and his country? Out of such musing and meditation I believe I have reached this definite conclusion. Man should be motivated in searching for employment and finding his place in society by the desire to benefit his fellowman . . . to leave his community and country a better place in which to live insofar as his effort, humble as it may be, will help produce that result.[18]

With just one game remaining in the 1939 season—against Northwestern—Kinnick knew that soon decisions would have to be made. He would have to decide what path he would take when he left the secure and comfortable surroundings of Iowa City.

The season finale against Northwestern would determine the Big Ten championship. An Iowa victory, combined with an Ohio State loss to Michigan, would give Iowa a share of the championship with Ohio State. But the back-to-back victories against much bigger Notre Dame and Minnesota had left the Ironmen emotionally drained and physically battered. "Everybody was beat up," recalled Couppee,[19] who would play most of the game with a brace on each shoulder. Sophomore George Frye started his first game at center and anchored a line that was far from 100 percent. Still, Iowa gave it all they had. With Northwestern up 7–0 and driving for a second score, Kinnick separated his shoulder tackling a Wildcat ball carrier. He stayed in the game, however, even trying to direct the Iowa offense, but when the pain became too great for him to throw the ball, Anderson forced him to come out. Up until then, Kinnick had played every minute of every game. Without their leader, the Ironmen still didn't quit, tying the game at 7–7 with less than two minutes left in the fourth quarter, with a patchwork lineup that had many players playing out of position.

When the Ironmen stopped one final Northwestern drive, sacking the quarterback at midfield, their magical season came to a close. Although Michigan had upset Ohio State, Iowa's tie was not enough. They were Big Ten runner-ups, but in the standings only. To the hundreds of fans who greeted the team on their return to Iowa City, as well as to the thousands more across the country who had been captivated by their story, the small, undermanned Hawkeyes were the true people's champions. They had also single-handedly returned the Iowa athletic department to prosperity. Where the football team was responsible for a ten-thousand-dollar loss the year before, the fall of 1939 saw the Ironmen generate eighty-five thousand dollars in revenue.

Nile Kinnick and teammates Erwin Prasse and Mike Enich were named to several all-American teams. Kinnick also won the Maxwell and Walter Camp Trophies as the most outstanding college football player for the 1939 season, and in a testimony to just how popular he and his teammates had become around the country, Kinnick was voted Outstanding Male Athlete of the Year by the Associated Press.[20] New York Yankee center fielder Joe DiMaggio and heavyweight champion Joe Louis finished second and third. On December 6, 1939, Nile Kinnick capped it all off by receiving the Heisman Trophy at the New York Downtown Athletic Club in New York City.

In a speech that has become legendary in Iowa football lore, Kinnick demonstrated the unselfishness and oratorical flare that had political party leaders eager to get him in front of voters. "A finer man and a better coach never hit these United States, and a finer bunch of boys and a more courageous bunch of boys never graced the gridirons of the Midwest than that Iowa team of 1939," Kinnick said about his coach and teammates. "I thank God I was born on the gridirons of the Midwest and not on the battlefields of Europe," he added. "I can speak confidently and positively that the players of this country would much more, much rather struggle and fight to win the Heisman Award than the Croix de Guerre."[21]

Kinnick returned to Iowa for his final semester, and with the rest of the Ironmen still basking in the warm glow of their magical season, he began contemplating his future. There were offers to go into business, play professional football (the Brooklyn Dodgers offered him a ten-thousand-dollar contract), and he was selected to receive a scholarship to Iowa's law school. Dr. Anderson also offered him an assistant coach's position for the upcoming season. "I'll be doggone if I can figure out what to do," he said in a letter to his parents in the spring of 1940. "If I were sure that law is my direction economic logic would say play a year of pro ball. I don't want to and I don't know how the shoulder would hold up."[22]

He decided to attend law school and accept Anderson's coaching offer, but not before putting on the pads one final time in the college football all-star game against the Green Bay Packers on August 29, 1940. The leading vote-getter, he left no doubt in anyone's mind that he would have been an excellent pro player, passing for two touchdowns and drop-kicking four extra points in a 45–28 loss, but by mid-September he was back in Iowa studying law. And as the grandson of a former Iowa governor, Kinnick also began dabbling in politics.

With his national celebrity, polished speaking ability, and all-American image, he was a people magnet wherever he went, and in the fall he spent a weekend introducing the Republican Party's presidential nominee, Wendell Wilkie, at several campaign stops in Iowa. He also addressed the Young Republicans state convention in Iowa Falls, and while "We Want Wilkie" was the cheer of the day, "We Want Kinnick" was seemingly the more popular chant. His appearances with Wilkie were noted in newspapers across the state, and when one gentleman wrote Kinnick cautioning him against getting involved in politics, Kinnick responded like a man who had found his calling. "I am addressing the Young Republican state convention not because I think that so doing will boost my prestige but because I am interested in government and have some ambition in that direction," he wrote back. "Politics are not very clean but they should be; politics need integrity and idealism . . . the feeling that politics and government is not the place for a gentleman has too long been accepted."[23]

Predictably, he did well in his first year of law school, standing third in his class, but by the summer of 1940, with war raging in Europe, Kinnick began leaning toward voluntarily joining the military. His correspondence to his family and the speeches he made around the community were increasingly filled with opinions and dissertations about America's involvement in the war. "Lincoln was a moral and upright man," he wrote in one letter to his family.

> He was a pacifist at heart. But when there was no other alternative he did not equivocate nor cravenly talk of peace when there was no peace. He grabbed the bull by the horns; realizing that the nation could not endure half slave and half free, he threw down the gauntlet and eradicated the evil. We are faced with the same thing and the longer we wait the worse it becomes. We are not people apart; there is no reason in the world why we shouldn't fight for the preservation of a chance to live freely; no reason why we shouldn't suffer to uphold that which we

want to endure.... And it is a matter of self-preservation right this very minute. Those are my sentiments—and they are RIGHT![24]

Rather than begin his second year of law school, Kinnick enlisted in the Naval Air Corps Reserve in September of 1941 and was called to active duty on December 4, 1941, three days before Pearl Harbor. "Every man whom I have admired in history has willingly and courageously served in his country's armed forces in times of danger," wrote Kinnick in announcing his decision to his family. "It is not only a duty, but an honor, to follow their examples as best I know how. May God give me the courage and ability to so conduct myself in every situation that my country, my family, and my friends will be proud of me."[25]

He did his initial training in Kansas City and New Orleans, enjoying the precision and exactness required to fly an airplane but grumbling a bit about some of the other aspects of military life. "It seems to me we spend more time on inspections, swabbing the decks and cleanup detail than we do on anything," he wrote shortly after arriving in Kansas City. "I have been here two weeks and the highest in the air I have been is a top bunk."[26]

Nevertheless, he progressed rapidly through the navy's aviation training pipeline. He soloed in February in New Orleans, received his advanced flight training in Pensacola, Florida, and by July 1942 was sent to Miami for fighter training, where he received his wings and his officer commission in September. "I guess I'm going to be a fighter pilot," he wrote to his parents. "When they asked me to indicate my choice I could no more refrain from saying fighters than I could refuse a second dipper of ice cream."[27]

Throughout his travels and his now-intense training schedule, Kinnick continued to maintain his vigorous appetite for reading and writing ... and for learning. His steady correspondence with family and friends and his daily diary entries were peppered with the titles of books that he was reading as well as a running commentary on world events and politics. He particularly admired the speeches of Winston Churchill. "Some of the passages in those speeches are just beyond any description that can be given," he told his family after reading *Blood, Sweat, and Tears,* a compilation of Churchill speeches. "It makes my spine tingle just to read those lines over to myself. I'd rather write a speech like any one of those than do anything else I can think."

And the more time went on, the more apparent it became that once the war was finished, he intended to run for a political office in Iowa. "Gus [referring to his father], I wish you would cagily and unobtrusively sound the political opinion of the men and women in different areas with whom you come in contact," he wrote to his father. "[Ask them] what are their convictions and hopes for the post war world . . . what they think of the different political candidates . . . store up your observations for the day when once again we can sit down and discuss them face to face. Would suggest you give no indications of your son's possible intentions."[28]

After finishing his fighter training in Miami, Kinnick had two weeks before being required to report to Norfolk, Virginia, for operational training in the Grumman F-4F Wildcat, so he raced home for one last visit to Iowa, expecting it would be his last opportunity before being assigned to an aircraft carrier in the fall. He spent a week with his family in Omaha and then made the rounds in Iowa, visiting friends in Adel and Cedar Rapids before making a final stop in Iowa City to watch his old team play a nonconference game against Washington University of St. Louis. It was a nostalgic trip for the former all-American and Heisman Trophy winner. "[It was] just like old times—eager appetite, good food, lusty, happy companionship, the prospect of a game the next day; I enjoyed every minute of it," he commented to his parents about his attendance at the Hawkeyes' Friday evening meal.

The next day, after doing a radio interview in the Iowa press box, a chant began to pick up steam around the stadium: "We want Kinnick! We want Kinnick!" Although it had been three years since the Ironmen's magic of 1939, Iowa's fans had not forgotten the "Cornbelt Comet." It was the last time they would ever see him.

In Norfolk he spent several months mastering the F-4F Wildcat and learning to land and take off from aircraft carriers before heading to Quonset Point Naval Air Station in Massachusetts to join a squadron, VF-16, and wait for the aircraft carrier USS *Lexington* to be commissioned. On May 11, 1943, the *Lexington*, with Kinnick and his squadron aboard, set sail for a month-long training cruise that would take them south to the safer waters off South America. In a sense, after nearly eighteen months of training and preparation, the cruise marked Kinnick's official entry into the war, and as he said in a final letter to his parents before he shipped out, he was ready. "This task which lies ahead is adventure as well as duty, and I am anxious to get at it," he wrote. "I feel better in mind and body than I have for ten years, and am quite certain that I can meet the foe confident and unafraid."[29]

On June 2, 1943, Kinnick took off from the *Lexington* early in the morning in his F-4F Wildcat on a routine practice flight. An hour into his flight his plane developed a serious oil leak. "Can you give us ten minutes?" the *Lexington* asked him. With their flight deck full of planes waiting to take off, an emergency landing would have put too many other lives at risk. "I'm not sure, but I'll try," was Ensign Kinnick's reported response.[30]

But shortly after, with the engine in his aircraft completely empty of oil, he was forced to land in the water about four miles from the *Lexington*. It was a clear day with calm seas, and those who were aboard the ship, as well as those in planes circling overhead, saw him make a textbook water landing. Rescue boats were immediately launched from the *Lexington*. One of his squadron mates circling overhead to mark the exact spot where the plane entered the water said he saw Kinnick get clear of the aircraft, but when the rescue boats arrived on the scene less than eight minutes later, he had disappeared without a trace.

"Knowing Nile to be a very good swimmer, an excellent athlete and in wonderful physical condition, it is inconceivable that he could have failed to remain afloat for the short period of time required for the crash boat to arrive unless he had been seriously hurt in the landing itself," Lt. Cdr. Paul Buie wrote in a letter to Kinnick's parents. Buie's best guess was that Kinnick's safety belt broke on the landing, causing him to strike his head and "injuring him to the extent that he could not remain afloat."

"Nile was an outstanding man in every respect," said Buie. "His calm and determined manner, his quick grin, his sound common sense, and his outstanding all around abilities made him a wonderful asset to the squadron and a man we were all proud to call our friend. His loss was a terrible blow to all of us and a serious loss to the country he so ably served."[31]

At the age of twenty-four, five weeks shy of his twenty-fifth birthday, Nile Kinnick was gone. The news of his death was greeted with shock and disbelief throughout Iowa and the Midwest. How could someone whose light shone so brightly, who seemed so indestructible and destined for further greatness, suddenly be gone? "Offhand, it is hard to think of any good quality which Nile Kinnick did not possess in abundance," wrote Eric Wilson in the *Daily Iowan* after Kinnick's death.[32] "And now he is gone forever and his dreams with him," added Whitney Martin of the Associated Press.[33]

In the sixty-one years following his death, Kinnick's teammates and his university never forgot him. Every few years, the Ironmen would gather for a reunion and dust off the memories of their magical 1939 season. They'd swap tales, catch up on one another's lives, and every now and then talk about their friend Nile. What would he have accomplished if he'd survived the war? Al Couppee loved to lead that discussion. "I tell you where Nile Kinnick would be right now," he used to say. "He'd be in the White House, and with him there we wouldn't have any of the junk that's going on now. Nile would've been so far ahead of these people."[34]

Today, before every football game in the Big Ten Conference, the captains from each team meet the officials in the center of the field for the coin toss. The face on the coin is that of Nile Kinnick. And the same stadium that he and his teammates filled in 1939 is now known as Nile Kinnick Stadium. "He just epitomizes that ideal of a student athlete," says George Wine, Iowa University's sports information director from 1968 to 1993. "In terms of scholastic achievement, being a campus leader and accomplishing what he did in athletics . . . Nile Kinnick had the whole package."[35]

There are just a few Ironmen left now: Erwin Prasse in Naperville, Illinois; Dick Evans in Chicago; and Red Frye in Albia, Iowa. Every month or so Frye will pick up the phone and call his old teammates to "check up on them." The conversation is always warm and friendly. He misses Al Couppee, who passed away a few years ago. "He'd come back here and stay for a week at a time from San Diego," says Frye. "He said he always needed to come back to Iowa to recharge his batteries."

While looking at the color picture of the 1939 team on his den wall, Frye is asked where that season ranks on his list of life experiences. He lets out a gentle laugh that seems to say, "Hey, let's remember it was still just football." This, after all, is a man—a former Marine—who was one of the first pilots to land on Pelileu Island after the Marines' landing there and who returned after the war to eventually run hospitals for the Veteran's Administration. "Well, it was one of those notches in your life that you never forget and that you got a lot of gratification from," he says politely. "But then we all moved on to the war and did some things that were noteworthy and got on with the rest of our lives once we came home."[36]

And it's that comment that brings you back to the tragedy of number 24, Nile Kinnick, and the thousands and thousands of other young men just like him who paid the ultimate sacrifice in World War II and left their families, their friends, and their classmates forever wondering what might have been. The difference in Nile's case is that there really has never been much wondering among those who knew him well. As far as they are concerned, he could have been president.

Tom Landry, head coach of the Dallas Cowboys, is carried from the field of the Superdome after his team beat the Denver Broncos, 27 to 10, for the NFL crown at Super Bowl XII in New Orleans, Louisiana, Sunday, January 16, 1978.   *Courtesy of AP (APA9449975)*

Capt. Ted Williams orders a "care package" from Desa Cucuk, director of the
CARE program for Northern California.   *Courtesy of the United States Marine
Corps History Division*

Robert Chappuis, all-American halfback for University of Michigan
football, photographed in 1947.   *Courtesy of the Bentley Historical Library,
University of Michigan (BL001324)*

Lt. Col. Jerry Coleman was trained to fly the Douglas SBD Dauntless dive bomber. He flew a total of 120 combat missions in World War II and the Korean War.   *Courtesy of Jerry Coleman*

CS Robert William ("Bob") Feller poses alongside a 40-mm quadruple antiaircraft gun mount, probably on board USS *Alabama* (BB-60) in late 1942 or early 1943. The original caption (released March 5, 1943) read: "GUN CAPTAIN FELLER—Bob Feller, one of the finest baseball pitchers of the era, is all set to do a different kind of pitching these days. As a Chief Specialist, he is the captain of a 40-mm gun crew aboard one of Uncle Sam's new battleships. The former American Leaguer joined the U.S. Navy as a physical education instructor and later applied for Gunnery School. Subsequently he was assigned to sea duty and here he is—grin and all—beside his guns on a cold winter day." *Courtesy of the Navy Historical Center (NH 102847)*

1st Lt. Jack Lummus, USMC, was awarded the Medal of Honor posthumously in 1945.
Courtesy of the United States Marine Corps History Division

Monte Irvin was one of the best all-around players in the Negro Leagues when he was drafted into the U.S. Army. If not for the army, many believe it would have been Irvin, not Jackie Robinson, who would have been the first to crack the major leagues' color barrier.   *Courtesy of the National Baseball Hall of Fame Library, Cooperstown, New York*

Teammates of Bert Shepard, relief hurler on the Washington staff and former U.S. Army combat pilot, admire the distinguished Flying Cross awarded to Shepard in a colorful home-plate ceremony between games of the New York–Washington twilight doubleheader on August 31, 1945, in Washington. Undersecretary of War Robert P. Patterson presented the award. Left to right are: Joe Judge, Roger Wolff, Mario Pieretti, and Bert Shepard.   *Courtesy of AP*

Mario "Motts" Tonelli was a star fullback for Notre Dame and went on to play professional football for the Chicago Cardinals before joining the U.S. Army. He survived the Bataan Death March and forty-two months in a Japanese prison camp. *Courtesy of the Notre Dame Archives*

Washington Senator shortstop Cecil Travis was one of the American League's best hitters and a perennial all-star. After serving four years in the U.S. Army, he returned to the Senators. He never regained his prewar form, but he never questioned for a minute his obligation to serve his country. *Courtesy of the National Baseball Hall of Fame Library, Cooperstown, New York*

Lou Brissie nearly lost a leg fighting in Italy, but he came back to pitch for the Cleveland Indians.   *Courtesy of the National Baseball Hall of Fame Library, Cooperstown, New York*

Specialist Pat Tillman, U.S. Army—a former Arizona Cardinal—participates in graduation ceremonies on October 25, 2002, at Fort Benning, Georgia. Tillman was killed in action in Afghanistan on April 22, 2004.
Copyright KRT

CHAPTER 8

A Legend and a Patriot

"You'll never hear me cry about those lost four years. I've always felt that one big win—World War II—and being a part of that was a heck of a lot more important than me winning another 100 ball games."

—Bob Feller

When the 1941 season came to a close, there was no question that the three best players in baseball were the New York Yankees' Joe DiMaggio, the Boston Red Sox's Ted Williams, and the Cleveland Indians' Bob Feller. DiMaggio was coming off a season in which he hit in a record-setting fifty-six straight games on his way to batting .357 with thirty home runs and 125 RBIs (runs batted in). Williams hit .406 and became only the ninth player in major league history to bat over .400. And for the third consecutive season Feller led the American League in wins (25), strikeouts (260), and innings pitched (343).

By 1943 all three men would be serving in the military—DiMaggio in the army and Williams and Feller in the navy—but only one of these future Hall of Famers would hear the news of Pearl Harbor and decide to immediately enlist: Bob Feller.

Like most people of his generation, Feller remembers exactly where he was on that seventh day of December in 1941. He had spent the first few months of the off-season at his family's farm in Van Meter, Iowa, but had agreed to meet Roger Peckinbaugh, the Indians' general manager, in Chicago to negotiate his contract for the 1942 season. "I'd just crossed the Mississippi River and entered Illinois when the news came over my car radio that the Japanese had bombed Pearl Harbor," says Feller.[1]

He had registered for the draft in the fall of 1940, but the Cleveland draft board had granted him a deferment because his father was terminally ill with cancer and he'd become the sole support for his family. That hadn't changed, but he'd always told himself if war broke out, draft deferment or not, he was going to enlist.[2] When he heard the news of the Japanese attack, he knew that time had come. "Like a lot of people, I really thought we were in serious trouble," says Feller. "The British were getting beaten up, and the war effort just seemed more important than anything else."[3]

Feller's contract in 1941 had paid him more than forty thousand dollars, but after his third straight season with more than twenty wins, the Indians were planning to reward their superstar with a substantial raise. But he never got it. On December 9, he walked into a navy recruiting office in Chicago and signed enlistment papers that would pay him eighty dollars a month—less than one thousand dollars a year—to serve in the U.S. Navy.

It was a life-changing decision for the then twenty-two-year-old Feller. During the next three and a half years he would serve in both the North Atlantic and South Pacific and see extensive combat as a gun mount captain on the battleship *Alabama*. By the time he was discharged in August of 1945, he had missed the better part of four baseball seasons and the prime years of his career. But to Bob Feller that never mattered. Like the tens of thousands of other young men his age, he believed it was his duty to serve.

Numbers alone can't articulate just how good—how dominant—Bob Feller was when he put baseball aside to enter the navy in 1941, but they paint a fairly clear picture. In the three years leading up to the war, he'd won twenty-four, twenty-seven, and twenty-five games; averaged 250 strikeouts a season; and had an earned run average (ERA) of 2.87, the best in the major leagues. He'd pitched the first-ever opening day no-hitter against the Chicago White Sox in 1940 and set the American League's single game strikeout record, fanning seventeen Cleveland Browns as a seventeen-year-old rookie in 1936. "Feller is the best pitcher living," Joe DiMaggio said during the 1941 season. "I don't think anyone is ever going to throw a ball faster than he does. And his curve ball isn't human."[4]

Because of his national prominence, Feller could have easily spent his military service coaching and playing baseball. Just about every base or command had a team, and both the army and navy frequently fielded traveling all-star teams comprised of former major leaguers to raise money and attract new recruits. Cdr. Gene Tunney, the boxing heavyweight champion from 1926 to 1928, had been commissioned by the navy to run its physical fitness program and had actively recruited Feller and other professional athletes to serve as physical training drill instructors. The navy thought it would be good for morale and great publicity to have well-known athletes whipping new recruits into shape. In return, the athletes were given the rank of chief petty officer upon their completion of basic training.

Feller joined Tunney's program and after six weeks of boot camp was assigned to the Norfolk Training Station in Norfolk, Virginia, as a physical training supervisor, where his job was to give recruits physical fitness tests. When spring rolled around he played baseball for the base team, joining Detroit Tigers pitcher Fred Hutchinson, Philadelphia Athletics outfielder Sam Chapman, and several other former major leaguers assigned to the base. But by the end of spring the nature of his service began to bother him. "I just wanted to do more than jump up and down and do deep knee bends and do the jumping jacks," he says.[5]

He had learned to fly in 1940, but when he applied for military pilot training he was rejected for poor hearing. He decided instead to enter gunnery school and spent the summer of 1942 learning about the various guns aboard navy ships. When he graduated he requested assignment to his home state's namesake, the battleship *Iowa,* but no billets were available, so the navy sent him to the battleship *Alabama.* He was assigned to the gunnery department and took charge of one of the ship's 40-millimeter, quadruple antiaircraft gun mounts.

John Brown was a twenty-year-old seaman working in one of the *Alabama*'s sixteen-inch gun turrets and remembers when Feller came aboard in September 1942. He says that despite his notoriety, Feller was able to blend in with the rest of the crew. "We certainly all knew he was on board and who he was," says Brown, now eighty-two. "But like all of us, he had a job to do and he did it. He was well respected."[6]

Feller says although he missed the freedoms of civilian life, his experience being involved with team sports helped him adjust to the navy. "I was accustomed to getting along with groups of men, so I didn't find the transition as difficult as some men did," he says.[7]

Commissioned in August 1942, the *Alabama* took to sea shortly after Feller's arrival, and for the next two and a half years was under way a lot more than it was in port. It spent the remainder of 1942 training off the East Coast and was then deployed to the rough waters of the North Atlantic to escort convoys with the British Fleet. *Alabama* never encountered the German U-boats or ships that still lurked in the area, but Feller's days were full with constant gunnery practice and standing regular watches. He also got to know his shipmates.

"We had eighty-two chief petty officers, and I got to know all of them real well," says Feller. "We had our own mess and our own cooks. I also knew lots of guys in different departments, particularly the guys in the radio shack. I was always going up there and getting the ball scores. I certainly won't say everybody loved me, but I did my job and treated everyone the best I could."[8]

With the focus of the war shifting to the Pacific, the *Alabama* was detached from the North Atlantic in August 1943 and returned to Norfolk, but its stay back in the United States was a brief one. After just ten days in port the ship was ordered to proceed through the Panama Canal and head to the Pacific to join the island-hopping campaign that would bring the allies closer to the Japanese mainland. It would be eighteen months before Feller and the *Alabama* crew set foot again in the United States.

In the South Pacific, the *Alabama*'s sixteen-inch guns were put to work bombarding shorelines in support of marine invasions at places such as Saipan, Guam, Leyte, and the Philippines. And as the Japanese became more desperate, Feller and his antiaircraft gun crew saw more and more action shielding their ship from kamikazes. "The Japanese suicide pilots were like blind, maddened bulls," says Feller. "A number of their bombs dropped too close for comfort, and we were forced to outmaneuver a few torpedoes, but we came through unscathed."[9]

In one instance in March 1944, six Japanese aircraft staged an attack on the aircraft carrier *Yorktown,* but a barrage of antiaircraft fire from the *Alabama* and other ships in the battle group shot two of them down and drove off the other four. It was good preparation for a battle that took place several months later, which Feller would later describe as the most exciting thirteen hours of his life.[10]

In June 1944 the Japanese launched an all-out attack from their remaining carriers and air bases, sending wave after wave of aircraft against the American naval forces in the Philippine Sea. It was a last-gasp effort to try to stem the allies' steady advance toward their mainland. Of the estimated 430 Japanese aircraft that were launched, only 35 survived. For those involved, the battle of the Philippine Sea came to be known as the "Marianas Turkey Shoot," and Feller and the *Alabama* were right in the middle of it.

Asked how many planes his gun mount crew shot down, Feller volunteers only that they "bagged a couple of them. You never really knew who shot down what, because there were other ships around shooting at the same aircraft," he says, "but it was certainly the most exciting 13 hours of my life. After that, the dangers of Yankee Stadium seemed trivial."[11]

Following the battle of the Philippine Sea, the *Alabama* spent six more months in the South Pacific, supporting the liberation of the Philippines and escorting the carrier *Enterprise* during the battle of Leyte Gulf, before finally heading home in December 1944 for repairs and crew rotation. During its eighteen months in the South Pacific, the ship earned eight battle stars as well as the distinction of never allowing a carrier under its escort to be damaged from enemy attack. For Feller, the *Alabama*'s return home in January of 1945 marked the end of his time at sea. He was ordered to the Great Lakes Training Center in Great Lakes, Illinois, to relieve former Detroit Tigers catcher and manager Mickey Cochrane as head baseball coach. In his 1947 autobiography, *Strikeout Story,* Feller says when he left the ship it wasn't without some sadness and regret. "It had been a safe home in the most grueling battle between men and machinery the world had ever known," he wrote. "*Alabama* produced its share of gallant men, and men who merely did their duty uncomplainingly."[12]

When Feller had enlisted in the navy, back in 1941, there had been real concern and doubt among Americans about the direction and final outcome of the war. By the time he arrived at Great Lakes, early in the spring of 1945, the outcome was no longer in question. The only unanswered question was how long the Japanese would hold out before surrendering. No one thought it would be long, but until then Feller used the time to get ready to return to the major leagues. As the manager of the team, he had the luxury of setting his own pitching schedule, and he began diligently getting himself back in shape. It took a while. "Once the action became hot in the Pacific, I played little baseball," said Feller. "I was able to work out occasionally by playing catch on the deck, but it wasn't nearly enough. Frequently the call to battle stations interrupted our workouts."[13]

However, once he started to pitch again at Great Lakes, he felt he really hadn't lost anything in terms of his physical ability to throw the baseball. In fact, looking back, Feller says he thought he was better. "In my opinion, I had lost nothing," he says. "I felt I still threw as hard, probably had a better curveball, a better slider, and a better changeup to left-handed hitters."[14]

By the time the Japanese surrendered on August 14, 1945, Feller had been pitching throughout the summer against former major leaguers on other base teams. He was in top shape and ready to return to the Cleveland Indians, who were more than ready to welcome him back. On August 21, 1945—forty-four months after he had turned down a new contract with the Indians to enlist in the navy—Chief Petty Officer Feller was honorably discharged at Navy Pier in downtown Chicago. Three days later he was on the mound in Cleveland's

League Park, pitching against the Detroit Tigers in front of 46,770 cheering fans who had turned out to thank him and welcome him home. "They gave me a great reception, and I appreciate it to this day," says Feller.[15]

Before the game, community leaders held a luncheon in his honor, and after several speakers praised his patriotism, Feller spoke. "I told them I was happy to be back, but I asked them not to forget about the men we had left in the islands who were never coming back. I intend to remember them," he said.[16]

By the time the game finally started that evening, Feller says, he was already exhausted, but his performance didn't show it. He struck out the first hitter he faced and eleven others on his way to a 4–2 win. He would go on to win four more games during the remaining six weeks of the season, including a one-hitter in another win against the Tigers. The feelings and confidence he had voiced in his pitching at Great Lakes prior to leaving the navy had been correct—he *hadn't* lost a thing. Bob Feller was still the best pitcher in baseball.

The next several seasons would be an affirmation of that fact. In 1946, his first full year back, he had the best season of his career, winning a league-best twenty-six games while striking out a record 348 batters. He followed that up with another twenty-win season in 1947, and then averaged eighteen wins a year during the next four seasons.

"I've always thought that Feller and Sandy Koufax were physically the two best pitchers I've seen," says Eddie Bockman, a teammate of Feller's in 1947 and a major league scout for forty-five years with the Philadelphia Phillies. "He could throw harder than anybody, and what people forget is that he had a helluva curveball. As the players like to say today, it was 'nasty.'"[17]

Bockman remembers one game in particular that Feller pitched against the Phillies: "He struck out twelve of the first fifteen hitters he faced, all of them on fastballs. Then it started raining. We had a thirty- to forty-minute rain delay. Bob came back in and only pitched another inning before they took him out. I've always wished I could have seen him pitch that whole game. His stuff that night was just mind-boggling. I never saw him quicker."

Feller retired from baseball in 1956 and in 1962 became the first pitcher since Walter Johnson to be elected to the Baseball Hall of Fame in his first year of eligibility. In eighteen years with the Cleveland Indians he compiled a record of 266–162, with 2,581 strikeouts and an ERA of 3.60. He pitched three no-hitters and an astounding twelve one-hitters, a major league record he still shares with Nolan Ryan. Considering he was in his prime when he left for the service in 1941, it's generally believed that Feller's nearly four years in the navy easily cost him another one hundred wins and one thousand strikeouts.[18] But that has never bothered Feller. "You'll never hear me cry about those lost four years," he says. "I've always felt that one big win—World War II—and being a part of that was a heck of a lot more important than me winning another one hundred ball games."[19]

Today, Feller and his wife, Anne, live in a quiet neighborhood in Gates Mill, Ohio. Their home backs up to about a mile of woods, and Feller enjoys the birds, wild turkey, and deer that frequently come into view. Listening to him, you get the sense that in many ways, even with all the fame and public adulation that has followed him throughout his life, the lessons he learned from his parents back on that farm in Van Meter, Iowa, always stayed with him—lessons of hard work, honesty, loyalty, and love for country. "Oh, yeah, every kid should grow up on a farm," he says when asked about Iowa. "I'd come home from school, change clothes, and get to work. You never had to ask what needed to be done, you knew."[20]

He says the war and his service in the navy changed him, made him more mature, more willing to voice his opinion on things he believed in. During his postwar career he became a key figure in labor relations, pushing baseball's owners to adopt a pension plan and to give players a greater say in the way the game was run. And while his image was tarnished by a public rift with Jackie Robinson,[21] Feller was a strong advocate for integrating baseball, openly including black players in his barnstorming tours around the country and later vocally supporting their inclusion in the Baseball Hall of Fame. "Bob Feller did as much for the integration of baseball as Happy Chandler, Jackie Robinson and Branch Rickey by playing so many exhibition games with African American players immediately after World War II," said Monte Irvin, a former New York Giant teammate of Willie Mays and a member of the all-African-American team that toured with "Bob Feller's All-Stars."[22]

Feller remained active in retirement. He was the first baseball player to incorporate himself, establishing Ro-Fel, Inc., to take advantage of endorsements and other business opportunities, and he was a frequent spokesman for his generation of baseball, unhesitant about commenting on the current health of the game. Now eighty-six, he still receives frequent requests for interviews and appearances at baseball card shows, but he says he's become more selective and reserved. "There are certain [controversial] things I just don't want to talk about or comment on anymore," says Feller. "I'm done doing those types of interviews, but for example when Larry Doby [the first black player in the American League and Feller's teammate] died, I was asked to say some things about him, and I was happy to do it."[23]

That doesn't necessarily mean he's mellowed. After the war Feller gained a reputation for his straightforward, matter-of-fact manner, and his friends say that hasn't changed. "You got 'im," says former teammate Ray Boone when given a description of Feller as someone who calls them like he sees them. "I've always enjoyed being around Bob," says Boone. "He tells it like it is and has always been that way."[24]

But although Feller has become a bit more reluctant to wade into the controversial topics surrounding today's game or even his own career, the same is not true when it comes to sharing his feelings about his country or the military. He says he thinks most American youth would benefit a great deal from two-year tours in the military to help them learn to be on time, to take and give orders, and to learn to "have an agenda and accomplish something."

He is very proud of his own service and over the years has remained active in the USS *Alabama* Crew Members Association and the Navy League, a civilian-run organization dedicated to supporting the sea services. And perhaps because of the experiences of his generation, he is more mindful than most of the cliché that freedom isn't free. "Our ancestors—those that wrote and signed the constitution—gave up everything to live in this country. They gave up their lives, their homes, and their property," says Feller. "We get so distracted sometimes that it's easy for us [Americans] to forget that."[25]

But Bob Feller has not. When he came back from the war, everyone—his own teammates, reporters, and fans—was quick to label him a hero. Feller has always been swift to deny that label. "I'm not a hero," he said. "The heroes were the ones who didn't come home."

CHAPTER 9

The Quiet Revolutionary

"My father came to San Francisco from Italy just after the 1906 earthquake. He was a very quiet man, and he worked in restaurants from six in the morning until ten at night. He was grateful for the opportunities this country gave him. When I was growing up he told me, 'This country's been good to us. If you get a chance, do something in return.'"

—Angelo "Hank" Luisetti

E very generation has them. Those unique people who, for whatever reason, suddenly veer off the well-trodden path of tradition and decide to approach a problem, a task, in a completely new way. Invariably, they endure initial criticism, but in the end they find their creativity embraced, emulated, and built upon by the generations that follow. Sports has always been ripe with such trailblazers. Athletes who, once on the scene, changed the way their respective games would be played forever. In 1934 an eighteen-year-old son of an Italian immigrant began playing basketball for Stanford University. His name was Angelo "Hank" Luisetti, and by the time he graduated, the game of basketball would never be the same.

Born in a neighborhood just above North Beach in San Francisco, Luisetti grew up playing basketball on the playgrounds near his home. Back then, the game was slow and focused around the basket. If an occasional shot was taken outside twelve feet, it was done with two hands, with the player's feet never leaving the ground—a set shot.

"It's easy to guard a man that does that," Luisetti once said, "because he has to put his feet together. I learned that when I was a little kid. I was small, playing against high school kids. I was only in grammar school. The only way I could shoot was to throw the ball up with one hand. I couldn't shoot with two hands. They'd block it."[1] He also learned that if he shot on the move, it made him more difficult to guard. "I didn't jump and shoot at the height of my jump, the way they do now," he said. "I'd let the ball go right near my face and shoot off my fingertips."[2]

He perfected the shot, but that wasn't the only thing that made Luisetti stand out on the basketball court. As he moved through San Francisco's Galileo High School—earning all-city honors three times—it became increasingly apparent that he played differently than everyone else. A lean 6'3", Luisetti covered the court with a speed and athleticism that people had never seen before. He shot from all angles and distances, dribbled and passed behind his back, and played every position on the court. Stanford gave him a scholarship, and soon word began to get out about this "do everything" player who eschewed basketball tradition and shot with one hand.

In December of 1936 Stanford traveled to basketball's biggest stage, the old Madison Square Garden in New York City, to play against Long Island University—the top-ranked team in the country and holders of a forty-three-game winning streak. In front of an audience of 17,623 people, the majority of whom had never seen a player shoot with one hand, Luisetti scored fifteen points; played center, forward, and guard; and demonstrated a dizzying array of basketball skills. When he left the game late in the fourth quarter with Stanford comfortably ahead, the capacity crowd gave him a standing ovation.

"The coast sensation surpassed everything that had been said about him," the New York Times reported the next day. "It seemed that Luisetti could do no wrong. Some of his shots would have been deemed foolhardy if attempted by any other player, but with Luisetti doing the heaving, these were accepted by the crowd as a matter of course."[3]

Basketball traditionalists were less convinced. "That's not basketball," said Nat Holman, the coach of New York's City College, when asked to comment on Luisetti's style of play. "If my boys ever shot one-handed, I'd quit coaching."[4] But it was too late—the revolution had begun.

By the time Luisetti left Stanford in 1939, he had been selected twice as college basketball's player of the year (in 1938 and 1939), was the game's all-time leading scorer, and held the single-game collegiate scoring record, putting in fifty points against Duquesne. He was the best basketball player in the world, and the one-handed shot he had made popular was showing up on basketball courts everywhere. With the NBA still seven years from being born, and the other professional basketball leagues disorganized and centered largely in the Midwest, Luisetti continued playing competitively at the AAU (Amateur

Athletic Union) level, leading the San Francisco Olympic Club to the finals of the 1941 National AAU tournament. He had just accepted an offer to work and play for the Phillips Petroleum Company when the war started. Newly married and with a young daughter, Luisetti could have received a draft deferment but remembered something his father had once told him. "My father came to San Francisco from Italy just after the 1906 earthquake. He was a very quiet man, and he worked in restaurants from six in the morning until 10 at night. He was grateful for the opportunities this country gave him. When I was growing up he told me, 'This country's been good to us. If you get the chance, do something in return.'"[5]

He enlisted in the navy and was first stationed close to home at St. Mary's College in nearby Moraga. His job as a physical training officer for the navy's preflight program allowed him to continue playing basketball, and in 1943–1944 he led St. Mary's preflight team to an undefeated season. He was also in charge of one of the enlisted barracks. Ironically, it would be this assignment—not combat—that would eventually end Luisetti's basketball career.

One day, a recruit in his barracks became violently ill with what appeared to be a bad case of the flu. He was hospitalized, so Luisetti collected the recruit's personal belongings to take to him. Shortly thereafter, Luisetti was ordered to the *Bon Homme Richard* in Norfolk, Virginia, an aircraft carrier preparing to deploy to the Pacific. One evening, Luisetti was out with some other officers when he suddenly became dizzy and nauseous. Thinking the feeling would pass, he got into a cab to go to the movies, but when he began drifting in and out of consciousness, the other officers rushed him to the hospital. He was diagnosed with spinal meningitis. It was the same illness the recruit in his barracks unknowingly had several months earlier.

"I remember somebody saying, 'He's got spots all over his body.' And that's the last thing I remember," Luisetti said later. "I woke up 10 days later. They had strapped me down because I'd been thrashing around so violently."[6]

It was November 1944. The *Bon Homme Richard* sailed without him, and Luisetti spent the next four months in the hospital. His weight dropped 45 pounds to a rail-thin 140, and his doctors firmly told him that his basketball-playing days were over. "The world had not seen many survivors of spinal meningitis and advice on how much activity an athlete could endure was uncertain. Doctors told him the new sulfa drugs that had cured him had weakened his heart. They warned him against the painful aftereffects of swelling scar tissue lining his brain, and at the very least predicted the onset of horrific headaches should he undergo prolonged activity on the baseball court."[7]

He was assigned to the U.S. Naval Academy to serve as the assistant basketball coach, and gradually his strength returned. The navy discharged him at the end of the war, and a pro team tried to lure him back with a ten-thousand-dollar contract—more than three times what most professional basketball players were being paid—but Luisetti turned it down. His body just couldn't do it anymore.

He dabbled briefly in coaching, than dropped out of basketball for good to begin a long, successful career in the travel business. His friends say he never had any regrets about not being able to play after the war. There was no bitterness. "That just wasn't his way," says Jack Laird, a former Stanford teammate who kept in touch with Luisetti over the years. "He never relished the attention that he received during his playing days. He was always very modest about that."[8]

"My mother once said, 'If you're good enough, Angelo, people will know,'" said Luisetti when asked why he didn't like talking about himself.[9] And his mother was right. In 1950 Luisetti finished second to George Mikan as the best basketball player in the first half of the century, and in 1959 he was selected to be a member of the Basketball Hall of Fame's charter class. "He was closer to dominating the game than anyone other than Michael Jordan," legendary coach Pete Newell once said. "Hank Luisetti did things as sensational as what Michael did. Him scoring 50 points in a game would be the equivalent of damn close to 100 now. I mean it. You just didn't do that. It was astounding."[10]

Luisetti died on December 21, 2002, at the age of eighty-six. A bronze statue of him shooting his trademark one-hander sits outside Maples Pavilion on the campus of Stanford University.

CHAPTER 10
A Texas Hero

"Dearest Sis, It's been a long time since you heard from your long legged brother. . . . I needn't explain why I haven't written. . . . Our outfit is aboard ship and going into combat—just where I can't say . . . don't get excited if there is a delay because I'll write the first chance I get when we are ashore. There will be lots of work to be done before we have everything secured and little time for writing. . . . Take good care of yourself and say an extra prayer for your bud."

—1st Lt. Jack Lummus, February 9, 1945

Around six-thirty in the morning on February 19, 1945, fifty thousand U.S. Marines began boarding landing craft for the five-mile ride that would take them to the shores of a small, porkchop-shaped South Pacific Island called Iwo Jima. They were a diverse group of men. Some were teenagers just a few years removed from high school. Others were recent college graduates. Some were grown men with teenage sons of their own back home. They had been together for the better part of a year, training for exactly the type of mission they had now been asked to do—invade and capture an island that would move the American military one step closer to mainland Japan.

As the first waves of the landing force moved forward under the umbrella of the U.S. Navy's withering preinvasion bombardment, no one—not the military planners at Pacific Fleet Headquarters nor the Marines themselves—expected the type of battle that actually awaited them. They knew the Japanese would put up a stiff fight, but with the overwhelming size and firepower of the American invasion force, those who planned the operation had anticipated it would take less then a week to secure the eight-square-mile island and seize control of its three airfields. They were wrong.

For the next thirty-six days U.S. Marines would engage in one of the fiercest and bloodiest battles in their storied history, fighting the Japanese literally hand-to-hand to uproot them from the island. By the time the battle was over, one in every three Marines who fought on Iwo Jima would be either wounded or killed. In the end, victory was won for one reason—the courage, determination, and individual heroism of the American Marine.

"Uncommon valor was a common virtue," Adm. Chester Nimitz, commander in chief of the U.S. Pacific Fleet, would say when asked to describe what took place on Iwo Jima. One of the Marines he was referring to was 1st Lt. Jack Lummus.

Four years before he set foot on Iwo Jima, Jack Lummus was finishing up his senior year at Baylor University in Waco, Texas. It had been a year of uncertainty and indecision for Baylor's class of 1941. With news of the German army's advances through Europe, most figured it was only a matter of time before America entered the war. Congress had passed the Selective Service Act the year before, requiring unmarried men between the ages of twenty-one and thirty-six to register for military service, and the question facing Baylor men was, "Do I wait to be drafted or go ahead and enlist now?"

"We were kind of an uncertain group of guys," recalls Franklin Golden, a 1941 Baylor graduate and baseball letterman. "We all saw the war coming, but at the time we left school in May no one was quite sure what was going to happen or what to do."[1]

Jack Lummus was no exception. Quiet and mild-mannered, he'd grown up playing sports in the small, northeast Texas cotton-farming town of Ennis. He had arrived at Baylor in 1937 on an athletic scholarship and become a three-time all-Southwest Conference center fielder and an all-American football end. "We used to call him 'the blanket,'" said Golden, "because of the amount of territory he could cover in center field. There were numerous times when I was pitching that he got to balls I thought were just unreachable when they were hit."

At 6'3" and 195 pounds, Lummus's size and speed also had made him one of the most talented ends in the country and had caught the eye of a scout from the NFL's New York Giants. As his last year at Baylor came to a close, Lummus found himself in the enviable quandary of having offers to play both professional baseball and football, but like his classmates he felt the tug of military service. When an Army Air Corps recruiter came to Baylor's campus that spring, Lummus thought flying would suit him and signed up. He managed to get in twenty-six games in the minor leagues, playing center field and hitting a respectable .257 with the Witchita Falls Spudders, before reporting to Hicks Field in Fort Worth, Texas, for flight training.

Flying, though, didn't come as naturally to him as he had hoped. He made it through preflight training, but when a wing on his P-19 Fairchild clipped a fence after a solo flight, he washed out. He was honorably discharged and put back into the draft pool, but this time, with America still not in the war, Lummus decided to accept the Giants' invitation for a tryout. Their preseason camp had already started several weeks earlier, but Lummus quickly demonstrated to Giants coach Steve Owen that he had the talent to play in the NFL. When the Giants broke camp and headed to New York City, Lummus was on the roster, earning $125 a game as a backup end to Giant veteran Jim Poole, at that time considered one of the best ends in the NFL. "Jack was very, very good, but there were some veterans in front of him who were also very good," recalls George Franck, himself a rookie running back from Minnesota. "But he had that quiet confidence and was sure of himself. I'll tell you something else—you couldn't find a more likeable guy then Jack Lummus."[2]

It was the era of professional football when players wore leather helmets with no face masks and played both offense and defense. Broken noses, cuts, and an assortment of other injuries were common parts of the game. "It seemed liked the routine was 'play a few games, go get patched up at the hospital, play a few more games, go back to the hospital,'" Franck recalls, laughing. Although Lummus was a backup, the rules didn't allow the wholesale substitutions seen in the NFL today. Once a player entered the game, he had to play the remainder of that quarter unless injured, so Lummus saw quite a bit of playing time, usually entering games in the second or third quarter as a defensive end.

"He was shy until he got on the field," recalls Ward Cuff, a running back with the Giants at that time. "Then he became one of the boys."[3]

Having grown up in the Depression without ever experiencing life outside the Southwest, living in New York City and traveling to cities such as Pittsburgh, Washington, D.C., and Philadelphia was an eye-opening experience for the young Texan.

But the Giants' game on December 7, 1941, against the Brooklyn Dodgers at the polo grounds, jerked Lummus—and the rest of America—back to reality. Midway through the first half, the Associated Press ticker in the press box began spitting out the news that the Japanese had bombed Pearl Harbor. Fans in the stands who had been listening to the game on their radios also heard the news and spread the word. "I was carrying the ball, and they made the announcement that the Japanese just bombed Pearl Harbor," recalls Cuff. "It just took the wind out of everybody."[4] The game was completed, with the Dodgers beating the Giants 21–7, but football suddenly seemed very unimportant—to both the fans and the players.

Lummus played his final professional football game two weeks later at Wrigley Field against Coach George Halas's Chicago Bears for the NFL championship. After a close first half, the Bears pulled away in the second half and won easily, 37–9. Lummus pocketed the $288.70 paid to each player on the losing team, returned to New York City just long enough to check out of his hotel, and drove back to Ennis. Several days later he went to Dallas and enlisted in the Marine Corps. "Once the war came on, he lost all interest in playing sports," says his nephew Pete Wright, whose mother, Thelma, was Lummus's sister. "He wanted to fight."[5]

"He just felt like it was his duty to serve . . . we all did," says Jack Willis, a close friend and former Baylor teammate, who was with Lummus when he enlisted. "It wasn't really whether you wanted to or not. It was your duty."[6]

Lummus completed boot camp at the Recruit Training Depot in San Diego and was on the security force at Mare Island Navy Yard near San Francisco, as well as on the baseball team. He probably could have remained at Mare Island for the duration of the war, but he was not content. "My dad followed Jack into the Marines, and he told me he had tried to convince Jack to stay with baseball because he thought it would keep him out of heavy combat situations, but my dad said Jack wouldn't listen," said Wright. "He was determined to get into the war."[7]

Shortly thereafter, the course of Lummus's life suddenly veered toward Iwo Jima. At the time, 400,000 men in the 1st, 2nd, 3rd, and 4th Marine Divisions were engaged in combat in the Pacific, but military leaders feared those numbers would not be enough for the ongoing march toward the Japanese mainland. They decided to create the 5th Marine Division, but needed more officers to fill the dozens of battalion, company, and platoon officer positions in the 22,500-man division. They turned toward their enlisted ranks, looking through records for Marines with the educational background and leadership potential to serve as officers. Lummus was an easy choice.[8]

He was sent to Quantico, Virginia, where he completed Officer Candidate School in the spring of 1943. He spent several months as an advanced combat training instructor at Camp Elliot in San Diego and then joined the 5th Marine Division thirty miles north at Camp Pendleton in January 1944, as a company commander in the 2nd Battalion, 27th Marines.

Lummus was a natural leader, quickly earning the respect and admiration of his men and his superiors. If his company had an inspection, his appearance would resemble a Marine in a recruiting poster. If he ordered the company on a long hike, he was out front leading the way. If weapons training was on the schedule, he was right in the middle of it, offering encouragement and instruction. "The men who served under him loved him," said Dr. Tom Brown, the surgeon assigned to Lummus's battalion. "They'd go anywhere with him and they said so."[9]

"He was always considerate of others and more than anxious to help everybody and anybody," said his commanding officer, Maj. John Antonelli. "No matter what his orders were he carried them out with cheerfulness, thoroughness and rapidity. He did this not once or twice or in order to impress people, but always. He was sincere."[10]

In August 1944 the 5th Marines boarded ships and left Camp Pendleton for the big island of Hawaii to move one step closer to the war in the South Pacific, and fine-tune their training in amphibious landings. Their home was barren Camp Tarawa, located twelve miles inland. "We arrived there in Hilo, Hawaii, and I remember Jack looking around and saying he thought the Marines had gone soft on us putting us in this paradise," recalls Bill McCann, a good friend and fellow officer of Lummus's in the 2nd Battalion. "Then they put us in these trucks and drove us up the hillside and put us right between these two volcanoes. I guess we should have known then we were headed for something like Iwo Jima."[11]

In October the 5th Marines' commanding general, Maj. Gen. Keller Rockney, and a handful of his key staff members were called to Pearl Harbor and told by Admiral Nimitz that they would lead the next major offensive in the Pacific. The target was Iwo Jima. If the Americans could capture Iwo Jima, it would eliminate the island as an "early warning" radar site for the Japanese, while at the same time providing an ideal pit stop for American bombers returning after attacking the Japanese mainland. It would also give the United States a place to base fighter aircraft to protect bombers on their way into Japan from the Mariana Islands, something that previously had been impossible.

As the days inched closer to Christmas and they continued to fine-tune their training, Lummus sensed that real combat was right around the corner for the 5th Marine Division. "Just came back from a very interesting amphibious landing operation at our beach," he wrote to his sister Thelma. "It kind of looks like we might be getting ready for something big pretty soon."[12]

After another series of amphibious landing exercises on the island of Maui, the 5th Division boarded navy ships on January 27, 1945, and began the three-week, five-thousand-mile transit to Iwo Jima, stopping in Saipan for one last rehearsal. It was there Lummus wrote the letter to Thelma asking her to say an "extra prayer for her bud."

Finally on February 19, after three days of bombarding Japanese defenses on the island from the air and the sea, the fifty thousand Marines of the 4th and 5th Marine Divisions boarded their landing craft and headed toward the long-awaited battle. Lummus, now 2nd Battalion's liaison officer, would go ashore in the invasion's first wave. His job would be to keep Antonelli informed at all times of the other battalion actions and movements.

Despite near-daily photo reconnaissance flights in the weeks leading up to the invasion, what these Marines didn't know was the depths—literally—that the Japanese army had gone to in order to turn Iwo Jima into an underground fortress. Approximately twenty-one thousand Japanese soldiers lived in rooms twenty to thirty feet below the ground. Sixteen miles of tunnels connected these rooms, along with command posts and storage areas, and led to concrete bunkers that poked out above the ground just enough to allow the Japanese to fire their weapons. Tanks and long-range artillery were also buried and difficult to detect from the air.

Precisely at 9:00 AM, with navy ships continuing to lambaste Japanese positions along the island's eastern coast, Lummus and seven battalions from the 4th and 5th Marines landed on Iwo Jima. At first, because the Japanese were still rebounding from the preinvasion bombardment, they were greeted by only moderate fire. What did slow them—and all the Marines who went ashore—was the island's volcanic sand. "When we landed, nobody could run, because it was so soft," said John Scarfo, then a seventeen-year-old corporal in the 2nd Battalion. "Some people sunk up to their knees. I remember sinking up to my ankles."[13]

Second Battalion's orders were to quickly get across to the west coast of the island and begin heading north toward the airfields with the 4th Division, while other elements of the 5th Marines attacked the Japanese on Mount Sarabachi at the southern end of the island. They made it by early evening on the nineteenth, but when they turned north the next day they were met with stiff resistance. Their daily progress could be measured only in yards, and with Mount Sarabachi behind them still under the control of the Japanese, they were being shot at from the back and the front. "We'd trained for combat but not when people were shelling us and shooting at us," said Brown. "But we adapted in a hurry."[14]

On the fourth day of fighting, 2nd Battalion got a lift. "All at once someone said, 'Look at the flag!'" remembers Brown. The American flag was flying atop Mount Sarabachi, plainly visible in the bright morning sunshine to Marines all over the island. "It was inspirational and also made us feel somewhat protected, because that meant the gunfire from behind us had been shut off," said Keith Neilson, another member of the 2nd Battalion. "We thought we'd go ahead and take the island," added McCann. "Little did I know that was just the start."[15]

The Japanese still occupied key high ground in several other locations in the northern part of the island— specifically, two hills the Marines had designated 382 and 362A. While they were not as large as Sarabachi, they were equally dangerous. The Japanese had hollowed them out, turning them into concrete blockhouses that contained not only dozens of soldiers but anti-tank guns and concealed artillery as well. From these locations, the Japanese inflicted heavy casualties on the slowly advancing Marines, so much so that the 3rd Marine Division, which had been held in reserve aboard ships off the coast, was brought in to assist the 4th and 5th Divisions, bringing the total number of Marines who would set foot on the island to seventy thousand.

Because of mounting casualties, units were forced to reorganize to continue the push toward Iwo Jima's northern coast. Major Antonelli, in need of platoon commanders, pulled Lummus from his job as battalion liaison officer and assigned him to lead the 3rd platoon in 2nd Battalion's E Company. Shortly thereafter the order was given for Marines to take the remainder of the island in their zones and advance to Iwo Jima's northern coast.[16]

For 2nd Battalion that meant the difficult task of advancing along a rugged, heavily defended ridgeline on the island's west coast, the Nishi Ridge. But after two days of bitter fighting, the battalion had made little progress. On the evening of March 7, Antonelli called in his company and platoon commanders and told them they needed to break through the Japanese resistance the next day. One platoon was selected to lead the attack—the 3rd Platoon, under the new leadership of First Lieutenant Lummus. "It wasn't an easy decision for him to make," says Brown. "He and Jack were good friends, but I really believe he felt Jack was the only one who could do it. We had been at a standstill for almost three days, and he was just confident Jack could lead the charge that would break through."[17]

They would need tanks to do it, however, and after the Japanese repelled their first attempt that next day, Lummus requested tanks to give his platoon additional firepower. Ignoring enemy fire, he personally guided the tanks over difficult terrain to get to their position, running between them and using the butt of his rifle to bang on them to get their attention and direct fire. When they arrived, Lummus again ordered his platoon forward.

When the platoon was stopped by a heavy concentration of enemy fire coming from several concealed concrete pillboxes, Lummus charged ahead of his men and attacked one pillbox, sticking his rifle through a hole in the concrete and destroying it with several fragmentation grenades. As he did this he came under fire from a second pillbox and was knocked to the ground by an enemy grenade, suffering shrapnel wounds to his shoulder. Undeterred, he got up and attacked, destroying the pillbox and then returning to his platoon to rally his men forward. "He was not a pushing force, he was a leader," recalls Neilson. "He was out in front of us, and we all had a very high respect for his bravery."[18]

When a third enemy pillbox erupted, stopping the platoon's advance, Lummus again rushed forward, charging it and destroying the enemy inside. "He ran without concern for his own safety, shouting orders and throwing rocks at anyone he thought was shirking, always moving forward," said Brown.[19]

Inspired by their leader, 3rd Platoon broke through the enemy line and was rushing toward Kitano Point on Iwo Jima's northern coast when they heard an explosion. Lummus had stepped on an antipersonnel mine. As he lay there, his legs and the lower half of his body torn apart by the mine, he immediately raised himself on an elbow and shouted to his men, "Don't stop now! Keep going!" Several Marines, though, immediately came back to assist him.

"I went up and laid down beside him. I had this satchel with little bottles of apricot brandy," said Neilson. "I gave him one bottle, and he asked me if we took the ridge. I told him yes, we were clear out to the edge of the ridge. We blasted them and went through the gorge. We went clear out to the ridge and looked down and could see the water. And he said, 'Well, I won't play anymore football, will I?' I told him 'No, Lieutenant, you won't.'"[20]

Three Marines and a corpsman from E Company gently placed Lummus's broken body on a stretcher, started a plasma bottle, and carried him past the battalion's command post on their way back to the aid station. Noticing it was their good friend, Antonelli and several of his staff members followed close behind. Dr. Brown was waiting and immediately began administering emergency aid. As he started a second unit of plasma, Lummus slowly opened his eyes, grinned at

Brown and Antonelli, and in a frail voice with his characteristic Texas drawl said, "Well, Doc, the New York Giants lost a mighty good end today."[21]

After fifteen or twenty minutes he was evacuated to a field hospital close to the same beach the Marines had landed on seventeen days before. He died on the operating table shortly thereafter. He was twenty-nine. The next day, his friends and fellow Marines buried him in the 5th Marine Division cemetery near the base of Mount Sarabachi.

The fighting would continue on Iwo Jima for another eighteen days. "That same shelling and shooting, horrible killing and destruction of man . . . it began to slow down because there were fewer troops on either side," recalls Brown.[22]

By the time the island was finally declared secured, on March 26, 1945, a total of 6,821 U.S. Marines had been killed and another 19,217 wounded. Twenty-seven Marines would be awarded the Congressional Medal of Honor, the highest number from a single battle in U.S. military history. One of those men was Jack Lummus. In an evening Memorial Day ceremony in Ennis, Texas, on May 30, 1946, Mrs. Laura Francis Lummus received the Medal of Honor awarded to her son.

Today, the memory of Jack Lummus still elicits admiration and smiles in those former teammates, friends, and fellow Marines who knew him so well when they were young. "I like to remember him as a great football player and a great guy," said Cuff. "I never heard him say a bad word about anybody. I'm sure if he'd have stayed with the Giants he would have been a real star."[23] "There just aren't that many who resemble Jack," adds McCann. "He was kind of one all by himself, I thought."

There is a park in Ennis named in Lummus's honor, and Baylor has an encased Jack Lummus display, containing the original copy of his Medal of Honor citation signed by President Harry Truman. But for his family in Texas, perhaps the most meaningful and long-lasting remembrance came on February 22, 1986, when the navy christened their then-newest maritime prepositioning ship, the MV (motor vessel) *1st LT Jack Lummus*. Appropriately enough, its primary mission is to carry equipment and supplies for a marine division.

"His memory has never diminished in my mind and heart," said Lummus's sister Thelma at the ship's commissioning. "I have immense pride in the belief that his memory lives today in your minds and hearts. Growing up, America responded to Jack with freedom and opportunity. Jack responded to America with pride, honor, and heroism."[24]

CHAPTER 11

Determination and Grace

"In 1942 . . . I felt that I was really coming into my own. But then I had to go into the Army and that wiped out everything that I had accomplished. There's no question that World War II made some radical changes in my life."

—Monte Irvin

I n October of 1941, executives from the Negro Leagues met in Chicago with the NAACP. The purpose of the meeting was to develop a strategy for pressuring major league baseball to give blacks the opportunity to play in the majors. A part of that discussion focused on choosing the right player to be the first to break the color barrier. Various players were discussed—Josh Gibson, Satchel Paige, Buck Leonard, Ray Dandridge. All were well-known stars in the Negro Leagues, but the group instead decided on a young, college-educated, twenty-two-year-old outfielder with the Newark Eagles named Monte Irvin.

Irvin had been playing with the Eagles since he was eighteen and had become one of the league's brightest stars, hitting .405 in 1940 and .395 for the 1941 season. He was, in baseball parlance, a "five-tool" player. He could hit, field, run, throw, and hit for power. Additionally, he had the even disposition and good nature that Negro League executives thought would be essential to handle the criticism and racial abuse that would undoubtedly come his way. Everyone agreed. Monte Irvin was the right choice.[1]

But before their movement could gain momentum, America—and Irvin—was thrust into World War II. He was assigned to an all-black engineering unit in the army, and for the next three years found himself in Europe, trailing the front lines, building and repairing bridges. By the time he returned home in September of 1945, the skills and athleticism that had made him the Negro League's best all-around player were buried under three years of rust. Jackie

Robinson had become the chosen one, signing a contract with the Brooklyn Dodgers in the fall of 1945 and entering the major leagues in 1947.

It is the type of twist of fate that would have sent many spiraling into a lifetime of "what ifs" and "what should have beens." Not Monte Irvin. Like his fellow veterans, he returned home after the war and promptly went to work, determined to make up for lost time, determined to prove what he had been sure of when he had left for the war in 1943—that he was good enough to play major league baseball.

Born on February 25, 1919, Irvin was one of thirteen children. His early childhood years were spent on a farm in Haleburg, Alabama, where his father was a sharecropper, who grew cotton and gave a portion of it to the owner of the land, who was white. During cotton-picking season, Irvin remembers spending all day out in the fields as the designated water boy. "My father, brothers, and sisters all worked in the field," says Irvin. "They would put pads on their knees and they'd get down and straddle a row and pick both sides as they went along. Now *that* was hard work."[2]

Separate but equal was the law of the land, but in the south, although segregation was strictly enforced, equality between blacks and whites was not. Irvin says the owner of the farm where his family lived frequently cheated his father, taking more than his share of cotton profits and regularly bumping up the rent on the land. When Irvin's father finally objected, they were run off. "At that time a black man had no recourse whatsoever in such a matter," said Irvin. "If a white man said something was true, then that's the way it was."[3]

In the 1930s countless black families were fleeing the racism "and poverty that existed throughout the south, moving to large urban centers in the North and Northeast."[4] The Irvin family became one of them, making their way up to New Jersey and eventually settling in an integrated neighborhood in Orange. It was the Great Depression. His father's salary was eighteen dollars a week, and Irvin remembers his parents growing a garden and canning vegetables and fruits to help put food on the table. Their life centered on church and the local YMCA.

It was at the Y that Irvin learned he excelled in sports. "We were always there doing something . . . basketball, Ping-Pong, swimming . . . something . . . and it became noted that [my brothers] and I were the best at almost anything we were playing," said Irvin.[5]

That continued at Orange High School. Playing football, basketball, and baseball as well as participating in track events, he earned sixteen varsity letters and all-state recognition in each sport. During the spring he often found himself playing baseball, then running over to the track to throw the javelin, shot, or discus in a meet.

The University of Michigan took notice and offered him a football scholarship, but when Irvin couldn't come up with the expense money to get himself set up at Ann Arbor, he accepted a scholarship to Lincoln University, a small all-black college in Pennsylvania. He was a multisport star once again, playing football, basketball, and baseball, but after a year and a half, feeling like a big fish in a small pond and tired of being broke, he left Lincoln to dedicate himself full-time to playing professional baseball. "At the time, if you thought about playing professionally, you thought about playing baseball," says Irvin. "I'm talking about black or white. Baseball was *the* game. Even though you didn't make much money, you made more money playing professional baseball than any other game."[6]

He had played with the Negro National League's Newark Eagles during each of the past two summers, playing only in away games and under the assumed name of "Jimmy Nelson" to maintain his college eligibility. After leaving Lincoln in February 1939, he re-signed with the Eagles. At the age of twenty, "Jimmy Nelson's" professional baseball career was over, but Monte Irvin's was officially about to begin.

The Negro Leagues of the late 1930s and early 1940s were a barnstorming league of ten to twelve teams, traveling "from city to city, playing whoever would play them."[7] Playing conditions were difficult and the travel was worse, but what the league lacked in facilities and organization it more than made up for in talent. There was Satchel Paige of the Kansas City Monarchs, Josh Gibson and Buck Leonard of the Homestead Grays, and James "Cool Papa" Bell of the Pittsburgh Crawfords, all players who would have been stars if allowed to play in the major leagues. The Newark Eagles team Irvin joined in 1939 included pitcher Leon Day, third baseman Ray Dandridge, and shortstop Willie Wells, all of whom would eventually be inducted in the Baseball Hall of Fame.

"There was so much raw talent available and it showed up in many different ways," said Irvin. "Bunting, base-stealing, sensational pitching, flashy plays in both the infield and outfield and daring plays of all kinds occurred daily. We played for the love of the game and I think that was reflected in our style of play."[8]

Devoting himself full-time to baseball, Irvin improved rapidly and by the end of the 1941 season was widely recognized as one of the league's best young players. "There wasn't anything Monte couldn't do and there wasn't any position he couldn't play," said Roy Campenella, the Brooklyn Dodgers Hall of

Fame catcher who initially got his start in the Negro Leagues playing for the Baltimore Elite Giants. "He was one of the fastest men for his size I ever saw, and what most people don't know is what a tremendous arm he had. Oh, what an arm."[9]

Talk of blacks entering the major leagues had increased, and it was widely accepted around the Negro Leagues that Irvin should be the one to break the color barrier. But then came December 7, 1941. Irvin was playing winter baseball in Puerto Rico when he heard the news of the Japanese attack on Pearl Harbor. "I had just doubled and was standing on second base when the announcement came over the loudspeaker," he recalls. "When it was over, the people really began to cheer and I remember saying to myself, 'Don't they realize what this means? Don't they realize what a hardship it's going to create on this island? And don't they know that many of the soldiers stationed at the bases here in the Caribbean will go to war?'"[10]

While Irvin sensed the impact of America's entry into the war, with a wife and a five-month old daughter, he says he didn't think he would be immediately called to serve, and he was correct. With talk of integrating major league baseball on hold, he played the 1942 season in the Mexican League, accepting an offer from an owner in Mexico City to play for $500 a month, a $350 raise over his salary with Newark. Hitting .398, he led the Mexican League in batting average and home runs and planned to return to Mexico for the 1943 season, but a February visit to his draft board changed those plans.

"I asked permission to go down to spring training. They said, 'Sure you can go if you don't pass your physical, but you have to take your physical exam first.'" Because of a knee injury he'd suffered playing football at Lincoln, Irvin didn't think he'd pass. "Along with the fact that I was married with a child and I had a job, I thought that I would have no problem. I didn't have any idea that I was going into the armed services. But I took the physical and they passed me."[11]

It was March 9, 1943, and Monte Irvin, the best all-around player in the Negro Leagues, the player who had been pegged to be the first black to play in the majors, was headed into the army. Like the rest of America, the army was segregated, with blacks placed in all-black units. Irvin was assigned to an engineering unit and after several months of stateside training was sent to England in the winter of 1944. He vividly remembers his trip across the Atlantic.

"We sailed 19 days in the North Atlantic," said Irvin.

On the second day out, we connected with a convoy of about five hundred other ships. The ship I was on was called the *Brittania*. It was a huge English luxury liner but, naturally, all the luxuries had been taken away. I think at that time the capacity was about three thousand people, but there must have been ten thousand troops aboard ship. Since it was an English ship, they served a lot of mutton and just to smell mutton would make you sick. So I spent a lot of time up on deck in the fresh air, trying to keep from getting sick.

After arriving in Liverpool, Irvin's unit took a train to the southern part of England, where they experienced their first close call. They had been guarding a supply depot near Plymouth when they received their orders shipping them out to France. "We moved out of the area on a Saturday morning and that evening the area was plastered by the German air force," said Irvin. "If we hadn't moved, all of us might have been killed. We went back later and saw where they had bombed, and they had really blasted the place."[12]

It was August of 1944, two months after D-day, when Irvin's unit, the 1313 General Service Engineers, landed on the coast of France. "By that time, when we landed at Omaha Beach, the beach had been cleared and a path had been made so that we could land safely," said Irvin.

Hundreds of German prisoners were coming through France at the time, and one of his first jobs was guarding them before they were processed and sent somewhere else. "They were just happy to be safe behind our lines because for them the war was over," said Irvin. "Some were very young and some were very old, but they were all completely defeated and glad to be out of the war."[13]

Irvin's unit was constantly on the move, "building bridges and tearing down others that had been mined."[14] They were in Reims, France, in December 1944 when the Battle of the Bulge brought them to combat's doorstep. The Germans, in a last-gasp effort to reverse the tide of the war, had mounted an offensive that pushed to the outskirts of Bastogne in Belgium. If they broke through at Bastogne, the next city in their path was Reims.

"So we were put on the lines, mainly guarding a big French gasoline depot," said Irvin. "It was cold as could be and must have gotten down to four below zero. We were told to look out for Germans who were dressed in American uniforms. We were told to ask them, 'Who was Joe DiMaggio?' Or 'Who was Ted Williams?' and any baseball questions or other technical questions that only a true American would know. But it never got to that. Our troops stopped them at Bastogne, so we never did actually start any fighting."[15] Irvin remembers the unit being disappointed they didn't see combat until paratroopers from the 101st Airborne passed through their position.

"We wanted to fight and we didn't feel like we were really making any contributions," he says. "Then some of the 101st Airborne paratroopers came back and said, 'Fellows, you don't know how lucky you are. You don't want to be up there at the front. . . . Know when you're well off. Just go ahead and do your thing right here because you're lucky to be here.' After that, I didn't hear too much complaining anymore."[16]

Shortly after the Germans' surrender, in May 1945, Irvin developed an inner-ear problem and was sent back to the States. A month after the Japanese surrender in August he was discharged from the army. His thoughts immediately returned to baseball. He spent the last few weeks of the 1945 season in Newark playing with the Eagles, but it was a discouraging experience. He learned he wasn't the same player he'd been when he entered the service. "Right away, I realized that I had lost something," said Irvin. "I'd lost my timing . . . I was older."[17] "Just too much Army."[18]

The word was out that Jackie Robinson, a three-sport athlete during his years at UCLA, had signed a contract with the Brooklyn Dodgers to play the 1946 season with their top minor league team in Montreal. Robinson, not Irvin, would be the first to break the color barrier. "I was very happy for him," said Irvin. "I wasn't jealous of Jackie's success, but I was envious. I thought, 'Gee whiz, why couldn't that have been me.'" Irvin had actually been contacted by the Dodgers several months after his return from the army and had met with Branch Rickey, the Dodgers' owner, who had expressed interest in signing him, but Irvin had told him his skills weren't "up to par yet." Rickey had responded, "Fine, when you get ready just let us know."[19]

With renewed determination, Irvin headed to Puerto Rico for the winter to see if he could regain his old form. "I always knew I could make it," says Irvin, "and so I decided to go all out and give it everything I had."[20]

Gradually, the game that had seemed so easy to him before the war started to come back. "I had a pretty good year in Puerto Rico and started to hit the ball again. I was also fielding and throwing the way I had before the war, but I still was not quite ready yet."[21]

He returned to the Negro Leagues for the 1946 season and played for a Newark Eagles team that now included second baseman Larry Doby, who would later become the first black player in the American League. Irvin continued to regain his form, hitting .398 and leading the Eagles to the Negro League World Series Championship, all while keeping an eye—as every player in the Negro Leagues was—on Jackie Robinson's progress in Montreal. "He tore up the International League," says Irvin. "He hit, ran and played good all-around baseball. And he just constantly improved. I knew if he succeeded there would be new opportunities for the young Negro ball players coming along after Jackie."[22]

And those opportunities came. In quick succession the Cleveland Indians signed Irvin's teammate Larry Doby, and the Brooklyn Dodgers picked up the Baltimore Elite's catcher Roy Campenella and pitcher Don Newcombe. But Irvin, now twenty-eight, was not called. Playing-wise, he felt he had returned to where he was before he had left for the army, but many teams now considered him too old. He responded the same way he always had when confronted with adversity. "I just kept going," said Irvin, "and waited for my chance."[23]

In 1949, twelve years after making his first appearance in the Negro Leagues, that chance finally came when the National League's New York Giants picked up Irvin's contract from the Newark Eagles for five thousand dollars. Along with Hank Thompson, another outfielder from the Negro Leagues, he spent several months playing for the Giants' minor league team in Jersey City before they were both called up to the majors in July. It had been four years since Irvin's return from the war—four years of backbreaking travel on buses, and winters in Puerto Rico and Cuba trying to rediscover his game—but Monte Irvin had made it.

"When Hank and I reported to the Polo Grounds, our uniforms were laid out for us," recalls Irvin. "I went over to the locker to get dressed, and when I put on the New York Giants uniform for the first time, that had to be one of the greatest thrills of my life. It was like a dream coming true, and something that I never expected to ever happen. I thought about the long road that I had traveled to get there, and the fact that it was finally happening was a feeling that is indescribable."[24]

Having heard the stories of what Jackie Robinson had gone through in Brooklyn, Irvin was nervous and unsure how he and Thompson—the Giants' first black players—would be received by their white teammates. Leo Durocher, the Giants' manager, quickly answered that question. He walked over to Irvin and Thompson and welcomed them, then brought the team together for a quick meeting. "About race, I'm going to say this," said Durocher. "If you're green or purple or whatever color, you can play for me if I think you can help this ballclub. That's all I'm going to say about race."[25]

"After that, we felt great," said Irvin. "Each player came over and wished us good luck."[26]

"When Monte joined the team, he was obviously such a gentleman and a high-class person that there was no way you couldn't like him," said pitcher Whitey Lockman.[27]

Seeing only limited action, Irvin hit .224 the remainder of the year and started the next season back in the minor leagues in Jersey City. But after hitting more than .500 with ten home runs in his first fifty at-bats the Giants brought him back up, and he never went back.

A year later, in 1951, the Giants brought up a young black nineteen-year-old center fielder to team with Irvin and Thompson in the major league's first all-black outfield. His name was Willie Mays. "Take care of the kid," Durocher told Irvin. In Mays, Irvin saw the type of player he had once been. In Irvin, Mays found the mentor and example he needed to maximize his tremendous natural talent and get his career started on the right foot. The two quickly developed a closeness and friendship that would last a lifetime.

"Monte roomed with Willie and had a lot of influence on him," said Giants outfielder Dusty Rhodes. "Monte was like an old professor. When he talked, you listened. He helped Willie get straightened out."[28]

"Monte was like my father," Mays would later say. "By 9 or 10 o'clock I was in bed, no girls, no lights on in my room. I can thank him for the fact that I am here today."[29]

With Irvin and Mays, the Giants advanced to the World Series in 1951 and 1954, losing to the New Yankees in 1951 but defeating the Cleveland Indians in 1954. In the 1951 World Series, Irvin hit .458 and stole home in the opening game, something he looks back on as his "greatest thrill in baseball." After five seasons with the Giants, Irvin was released by the club in 1955. The Chicago Cubs picked him up, and Irvin had a solid 1956 season, hitting .271 with fifteen home runs, but at the age of thirty-seven it was his final season in the major leagues. He played a handful of games the following year for the Los Angeles Angels in the Pacific Coast League, but when his back began to give him problems, he drove back to Newark and, at the place where his career had started twenty years earlier as an eighteen-year-old with the Newark Eagles, officially retired from baseball.

Sixteen years later, on August 6, 1973, Monte Irvin was inducted into the Baseball Hall of Fame in Cooperstown, New York. His selection was recognition of his major league career, but even more so, it was acknowledgement of his tremendous accomplishments and success during his years in the Negro Leagues. "Goodness knows what he might have achieved in the major leagues had be been able to come and spend those ten or twelve earlier years with us," said baseball commissioner Bowie Kuhn during his introduction of Irvin.[30]

Irvin's acceptance speech that day was typical of the man Kuhn had described as one of the most decent, kind, and beloved men in baseball. There was no anger, no resentment from being unfairly denied an opportunity. He thanked his family for their support and mentioned his father, the man Irvin always said was the "real hero" in his life. "When I was growing up, he was always there to give me a word of encouragement and say the right thing to keep me going," said Irvin.

Then, always mindful of where he came from, he remembered his friends in the Negro Leagues. "I hope my induction will help ease the pain of all those players who never got a chance to play in the majors," he said.[31]

Irvin is now eighty-six years old. He and his wife, Dee, live in Homosassa, Florida. Irvin admits that every so often he'll catch himself wistfully wondering what kind of numbers he might have been able to put up had he been able to play in the big leagues during his prime, how his life might have been different if he had been the first to break the color barrier, but they aren't things he dwells on for very long. "My only regret was that I didn't get a chance sooner," said Irvin. "But I hold no bitterness. I'm just happy that I finally did get a chance."

"We didn't have an easy time," he added, making reference to all who played in the Negro Leagues. "We knew it was tough, but it made us better men."[32]

CHAPTER 12

A Lesson in Perseverance

*"I was happy to be in the service. I wouldn't have stayed home for anything.
The war just had all priority."*

—Bert Shepard

The call finally came on August 4, 1945. In the top of the fourth inning, with the Red Sox pounding the Washington Senators in the second game of a doubleheader, Senators manager Ossie Bluege summoned a twenty-four-year-old rookie left-hander named Bert Shepard from the bullpen. A smattering of applause rippled through Washington's Griffith Stadium as the crowd of thirteen thousand recognized the new pitcher who was walking in from right field. Some had seen him on the newsreels shown in movie theaters downtown. Others had read about him in newspapers earlier that spring. They had been humbled by his courage, inspired by his determination.

Now, as Shepard neared the pitcher's mound to face Red Sox center fielder George "Catfish" Metkovich, they were about to see for themselves whether this young man, just fifteen months removed from a German POW camp, really could pitch in the major leagues with an artificial leg.

You would think that after having been cut by four minor league teams before the war and within an eyelash of losing his life during it, the moment would have been incredibly emotional for Shepard. Not really, says the now eighty-four-year-old Shepard. "More than anything, I was just excited and happy as heck to be getting in a ball game," he says. "I'd been pitching batting practice for a while, and all I remember thinking was that I really wanted to do well so I could get in more games!"[1]

It's the completely unassuming and unpretentious type of response America has come to appreciate from this generation of men. But the truth is, the story of how Robert "Bert" Shepard found himself on the Griffith Stadium pitcher's mound that warm August afternoon is far from ordinary. It's a story of how a young man from a small Indiana town chased his dream of playing professional baseball and ended up inspiring millions of Americans along the way.

Bert Shepard was born on June 20, 1920, in Dana, Indiana. One of six boys, "Bertie," as his family called him, grew up hunting, fishing, and playing sports with his brothers. "The thing about Bertie was that he was just naturally good at everything he did," says younger brother John. "He was a good swimmer, a good football player, and he played basketball well. He made things look easy."[2]

In 1930, with the country entering into the Depression, the Shepards moved to Clinton, Indiana, where Bert's father, who had lost his delivery business, took work as a farmhand. It was in Clinton, located about twenty miles from Terre Haute, that Bert developed a passion for baseball. "They didn't have a school team, so we'd all meet down at the park in the morning and choose up sides. If we had a couple of balls we'd play for quite a while," recalls Shepard. "The semi-pro team would then come out and practice at five. I'd stay and practice with them until dark. I'd shag flies, do whatever I could just to be around them."[3]

Having heard on the sand lots that Southern California was the place to go if someone really wanted to become a baseball player, Shepard left Clinton after his junior year in high school and headed west—on top of a freight train boxcar. "I got as far as Amarillo, Texas, before a sheriff there caught me and put me in jail for ten days for illegally riding a train," says Shepard.[4]

He hitchhiked the rest of the way, working odd jobs along the way to pay for his meals. Eventually he made it to California, found work in a tire retread plant, and resumed chasing his baseball dreams on Sunday, his one day off. "I'd go out to the parks and watch everyone play, and they all looked pretty darn good to me," recalls Shepard. "I remember saying to myself, 'I've got a lot to learn.'"[5]

He returned to Indiana in the spring of 1939 and began playing with the same semi-pro team he had once shagged flies for, catching the eye of a White Sox scout, who signed Shepard to a contract for sixty dollars a month and sent him to the team's minor league training facility in Longview, Texas. Shepard spent almost as much time on the ball field in Longview as he had the previous summer in the Amarillo jail.

"I got there and they asked me if I wanted to pitch," says Shepard. "I said, 'Sure.' The next day, they asked me again, and I said, 'Sure.' Well, I ended up pitching three days in a row and got a sore arm. They released me shortly after that."[6]

During the next two summers, he hooked up with any minor league team that would give him a chance, playing for the Wisconsin Rapids in the Wisconsin State League, for the Philadelphia A's minor league team in Anaheim, California, and then landing in the Arizona-Texas league. At each stop, the story was the same: Shepard's lively left arm would get him a chance, but his wildness eventually prompted each team to send him searching for another opportunity.

When baseball season rolled around in the spring of 1942, Shepard found himself in a different uniform. Like thousands of other young men his age, he had been drafted into the U.S. military. Showing the same spirit of adventure that had sent him to California on top of a boxcar, Shepard decided he wanted to fly.

"I actually flew the first plane I ever saw," he says. "During primary flight training in Santa Ana, California, the instructor asked me if I'd ever flown before, and I told him that this was the closest I'd ever even *been* to an airplane! But the more I flew, the more I liked it, and realized I could really fly an airplane."[7]

After completing his flight training, he joined the U.S. 8th Air Force's 55th Fighter Group in Scotland and began flying combat missions over Germany in a P-38 Lightning. On May 21, 1944, he flew in the first daytime bombing raid over Berlin. "We were getting ready for the invasion [of Europe] and were going in to strafe an aerodrome. I'd shot up a fuel tower that supplied oil to trains and heard on the radio there was some aircraft on the field up ahead. When I leveled off, I could see this column of smoke. I thought I could stay low, avoid the flak, and make one pass and keep on going. I was about two or three miles away from the airfield, down real low, and darn if they didn't go and shoot my right foot off. I called back to my colonel at the base and told him I'd had a leg shot off and would call him back to tell him what I was going to do."[8]

He never got a chance. Another bullet ripped through his cockpit, hitting Shepard in the chin and knocking him unconscious. His plane crashed into a farmer's field in Ludwigslust, Germany, a small town between Hamburg and Berlin. Despite the threats of local farmers who had run to the burning plane wielding sticks and pitchforks, a German doctor pulled Shepard from the cockpit and brought him to a nearby hospital. He woke up several days later, finding that his right leg had been amputated eleven inches below his knee and learning that the frontal sinus bone around his right eye had been fractured from his head hitting the cockpit gun sight.

After recovering from his injuries Shepard was immediately sent to a German POW camp. Back in Clinton, his family didn't know if he was alive or dead. "We had gotten a letter saying he was missing," recalls John, now seventy-one and still living in Clinton. "Bert's wingman had also come by and told us that he had been flying with him when he was shot down and didn't see anyone get out. But he also said that if anyone can survive a crash like that it was Bert."[9]

Three months later, the family received a letter from him. "I remember my Mom screaming and crying that Bert had lost a leg, but I also specifically remember him saying in the letter not to worry, that he was okay."[10]

A Canadian medic and fellow POW, using whatever odds and ends they could find, made him a makeshift artificial leg, and Shepard soon discovered he was a lot better off than he had initially thought. Using a cricket ball, he began playing catch with the other prisoners and learning just what he could still do on a baseball field. As far as he was concerned, the answer was, "Everything!"

"He had this indomitable will," columnist Wright Bryan once wrote about Shepard. Bryan had been a POW with him at Stalag IX-C, one of several camps Shepard was sent to. "He told me he would be playing ball again, and I would say, 'Sure you will,' and then feel sick inside myself for the disappointment I thought Shep was going to face."[11]

Bryan was wrong. After eight months as a POW, Shepard was returned to the United States in the winter of 1945 in a trade of POWs between the Germans and allies. While being fitted for another artificial leg in Washington, D.C.'s Walter Reed Hospital, he was called to the secretary of war's office, along with three other former POWs. At the end of the conversation, the secretary, Robert P. Patterson, asked them what they wanted to do now that they were home.

"Play professional baseball," said Shepard.

"Well, you can't really do that now, can you?" said Patterson, motioning toward Shepard's amputated leg.

"Why not?" said Shepard. "I did it before."

Impressed by his determination, Patterson called his good friend Clark Griffith, the legendary owner of the Senators, who promptly invited Shepard to Griffith Stadium to work out with the team. Senator players and manager Ossie Bluege were amazed by his versatility and how hard he threw the ball.[12] "He certainly didn't just toss it over," says Buddy Lewis, the Senators' right fielder and a pilot himself throughout World War II. "He had a good curve ball and he ran well. You couldn't tell he had a leg off."[13]

Griffith was also impressed. Figuring Shepard would be a symbol of courage for the team and the city, as well as a good batting practice pitcher, he signed him to a contract. Shepard's teammates quickly accepted him. "He was great to have around," says Lewis, Shepard's roommate on road trips. "He was the most open-minded person in dealing with this adversity in his life that I've ever known. If he had any bad days I sure never heard about it."[14]

In July, when Shepard pitched four strong innings against the Brooklyn Dodgers during a midseason exhibition game, Bluege moved him to the active roster, opening up the possibility that he would pitch in a regular major league game that season. Several weeks later, Shepard found himself facing Boston Red Sox center fielder George "Catfish" Metkovich with the bases loaded on August 4, 1945, at Griffith Stadium.

Although he quickly threw two balls to Metkovich, Shepard insists it wasn't because he was nervous. "You know, when Warren Spahn first came back after having fought in the Battle of the Bulge, someone asked him if he was nervous, and he said, 'No! There was no one in the stands pointing a gun at me.' And I guess that's exactly how I felt."[15]

With the count to Metkovich full, he reached back and threw a waist-high inside fastball. Metkovich took a full swing and missed. Four years after having been cut by his fourth minor league team and less than a year removed from a German prison camp, Shepard had struck out the first official big league hitter he ever faced.

Shepard pitched five more innings that afternoon, giving up three hits, striking out three, and allowing just one run. "I thought I might get into more games after that, but it just never materialized," he said later.[16]

The Senators went on to lose the pennant to the Tigers on the final game of the season when Hank Greenberg, another recently returned army veteran, hit a dramatic home run on the final day of the season.

For the 1946 season the Senators invited Shepard back as a coach, but after a short while, he asked to be sent down to the team's minor league AAA team in Chattanooga, Tennessee. "I just wanted to go where I could play," says Shepard.[17] For the next nine years, that's exactly what he did, once again bouncing around from team to team—some in the minors, some semi-pro—going wherever he could to play the game he loved.

He remembers scoring from second on a single to center field while in Chattanooga, stealing five bases and hitting five home runs during a stint as player-manager in Waterbury, Connecticut, and his arm finally dying out on him in 1955 playing and managing a semi-pro team in Williston, North Dakota.

"Wherever he played, Bert would always make it a point to visit veterans hospitals and other amputees," says his brother John. "He was a tremendously positive example for those people. I can remember being with him on one of those visits. A man came up to me and said, 'God sent me an angel today. His name is Bert Shepard.' Bert showed those people that just because you were an amputee, it didn't mean you couldn't have a good life."[18]

After throwing his last professional pitch in 1955, Shepard hung up the cleats for good, going to work first as an IBM typewriter salesman and then as a safety engineer for several companies. "He'd come back home after he left baseball, and I remember our mom saying, 'Bertie, you ever find out who saved your life over there in Germany?'" recalls John. "He would say, 'You know, Mom, I never did. One minute I was flying, the next I was in a German hospital.'"[19]

That changed one Sunday in 1993, when out of the blue Bert received a call from England. "Are you the same Bert Shepard that woke up in a hospital in Ludwigslust, Germany, in 1944?" the voice asked. When Shepard said yes, a man explained that a friend of his living in Austria, Dr. Ladislaus Loidl, had told him about an American pilot whose leg had been shot off, whom he'd pulled from a burning airplane during the war. As luck would have it, the Englishman had read about Shepard in a newspaper article and thought there was a good possibility that pilot would be him.

Shepard eventually traveled to Germany and met the man who, forty-nine years earlier, had pulled him out of his burning aircraft and took him to the hospital. "I had always wondered about it," says Shepard. "Always wondered who it was that saved my life. In a way, when I met Dr. Loidl, I felt a sense of closure. I felt I could say I really had a full life."[20] Which—as is typical of the humble Shepard—is an understatement of significant proportion.

"He's actually had enough experiences for about six lives," says Bill Gilbert, a writer who got to know Shepard when he served as the Senators' batboy in 1945. "He's just an incredible man, who loves life. He's taken whatever life has thrown his way and made the best of it. He has this positive attitude that really is incomparable."[21]

Today, Shepard and his wife of forty-eight years, Betty, live in Hesperia, California. They have four children and eight grandchildren. Earning the title of National Amputee Golf Champion in 1968 and again in 1971, Shepard continued to play golf regularly—always walking—until a stroke sidelined him. "He used to get insulted if you ask him to ride in a cart," says Gilbert.

Asked if all his experiences and nearly sixty years as an amputee had created a "life philosophy" he felt compelled to share, Shepard says only that he puts a lot of stock in perseverance. "And I think you have to be willing to try new things without worrying about failing. Everyone fails sometimes, and everyone gets embarrassed. You've just gotta overcome that."[22] Bert Shepard's life has been a living testimony to that.

CHAPTER 13

Just a Kid from the Neighborhood

"I went in as a PFC. And I came out as a PFC. . . . I was twenty years old and remember before I got on the train to come home I tried to get a beer in a tavern in San Diego, and the guy wouldn't serve me because I wasn't old enough. I'll never forget that. I'd nearly got my ass blown off in the South Pacific . . . but I was too young to drink in a California bar."

—Art Donovan

Art Donovan knows how to tell a story. In fact, he's great at it. Its one reason he's been a guest on just about every late-night talk show in the country, including three appearances with David Letterman. And it's why, although nearly forty years have passed since he last anchored the defensive line for the great Baltimore Colts teams of the 1950s, he's still a favorite of writers and sports talk-show hosts whenever the subject is old-school NFL football. Ask Donovan a question and you can guarantee his answer will contain three things: humor, colorful language, and most of all, honesty. As he likes to say in his still-thick New York accent, "If you ask me somethin', I'm gonna tell you what I think. Now it might not be right, but it's how I feel." In a day and age where most professional athletes are masters of the cliché and ten-second sound bite, Art Donovan is a veritable quote machine.

So it's no surprise that when you ask him to talk about his time as a Marine in World War II, what comes forth is a story with all the trademark Donovan elements. It's the story of an eighteen-year-old boy from the Bronx who, like the rest of his buddies from the neighborhood, left home to serve to his country and ended up on the other side of the world, fighting the Japanese in the South Pacific.

It was April 1943 when Donovan, as he puts it, got his "green slip" from Uncle Sam. He'd entered the University of Notre Dame early so he could take part in spring football practice, but he knew his days as a student were numbered. The Donovan family had a long history of military service. His grandfather had joined the Union Army at fourteen and fought for Generals Grant and Sherman in the Civil War, and his father had been in both the Mexican Wars and World War I. He says there was kind of a matter-of-fact expectation, not just in his house, but throughout his neighborhood, that it was his generation's turn. So when he returned from Notre Dame in early April, he and a group of his friends decided to go down to the Grand Central annex next to the train station to enlist.

"No matter which of the five boroughs you were from, everyone had to go to the annex," says Donovan. "So we walk in there, and there were lines set up for all the different services with guys coming up trying to recruit you for their service. Well, this sergeant comes up and says, 'If you guys join up right now, we'll give you a good deal. We'll get you set up in a good job in the army.' We were all a bunch of wise guys, so we immediately asked him 'Doing what?' And he told us they'd send us to cooks and baker school. I said, 'Get the hell out of here! I'm not going to be a cook for the rest of the war.' So we went across the aisle and joined the Marines."[1]

His father, Mike—a famous fight referee who had been in the ring for most of Joe Louis's championship fights, including the two against German Max Schmeling—was not happy with his choice.

> I got home and my Dad says, "So Arthur, you're going into the Army huh?" And when I told him no, I had joined the Marines, Jesus Christ, he began hollering at my mother, "Kiss him goodbye, Mary, he's going to get killed! He's going to get that fat ass shot right out from under him!" I tried to explain to him that I had to join something and that the Marines seemed to promise the most action. But he wouldn't hear any of it. Through all his years in the service, the Marines were always the ones my father had seen die first.[2]

A few weeks later, Donovan received a call from his recruiter telling him he needed to report to boot camp at Parris Island. And it was then that Donovan says things began to sink in.

I remember the night before I left, I sat next to my mother on her bed and said, "Mom, I don't want to go," and she said, "Well, Arthur, I don't want you to go either, but if you don't go I'd be ashamed of you," and that was it. The next day a group of us went around the corner, got on the subway, and went down to the annex again. From there we took a barge across the Hudson River to Jersey City, got on the B&O railroad going to Washington, D.C., then the Atlantic Coast line to South Carolina. We're thinking, where the hell are we going! We were just a bunch of kids, we didn't know what was happening.[3]

Once he got to Parris Island, though, Donovan discovered he felt comfortable in the disciplined environment of the Marine Corps. Having just completed spring practice at Notre Dame, he was already in great shape, and he liked the regimentation of the Corps. "It was a hell of an experience. They worked my ass off, but it was great training and I really loved it."

He learned to fire 20- and 40-millimeter machine guns and after boot camp was assigned to a Marine Corps gunnery detachment on the USS *San Jacinto*, an aircraft carrier headed through the Panama Canal for the South Pacific. It was while patrolling the Mariana Trench southwest of Guam that Donovan, an ammunition loader on one of the ship's 40-millimeter twin gun mounts, experienced a steady diet of increasingly desperate attacks by Japanese dive bombers and kamikazes.

"Well, I'll tell you what, and everyone tells it differently, but there was many a morning and night that I almost pissed in my pants. Those [Japanese] bombers kicked the living shit out of our navy in '44. I remember one night at dusk, these Japanese planes got between two of our ships and while we were shooting at the planes, we were actually hitting each other. We almost destroyed one of our own ships; it was really terrible. Often, there were so many kamikazes coming down we didn't know which ones to shoot at."[4]

But by the summer of 1945, with the tide of the war having turned in the South Pacific, the Corps began moving Marines off ships to secure islands that had been recently liberated. Donovan volunteered and was sent to Okinawa on a navy tanker, where he joined an eight-man .50-caliber machine gun crew. Their job was to combat lingering Japanese snipers who had retreated into the jungles after the Marine Corps' defeat of the Japanese main defense forces two months earlier. "They were still all over the place and you'd never really see them. You'd just hear their bullets whistling past your ear when you'd get into a fire fight. But it still beat the hell out of facing the kamikazes."[5]

After two months on Okinawa he was sent to Guam, where the 3rd Marine Division was doing the same mission while also preparing for the invasion of Japan.

> It was just like Okinawa. It was supposed to be secured, but there were Japanese all over the place. You could hide on Guam for years, for Christ's sake. One night they came down out of the hills and stole the tent over our commode, and we had to go out looking for them at night. We couldn't find them, and I think everyone was kind of happy. Nobody wanted to get killed over a tent from the latrine. They stole the tent. What the hell did we care? Let them steal the tent. Those guys never gave up. They always went down fighting. And Guam was a big island.[6]

It was on Guam that he also got into what he likes to refer to as "his most memorable experience" in the South Pacific. It didn't involve fighting, however. It involved food—Spam, to be specific. He had been assigned to help empty the cargo ships arriving with supplies for the invasion of the Japanese mainland. While off-loading a troop transport ship, Donovan and some buddies found a case of Spam that they decided to take as a self-declared reward for their hard work and stash it underneath the floor of their tent for future consumption. Unfortunately, a torrential rain storm washed away the dirt covering the Spam, leaving it exposed when their tent was inspected the next day by a young lieutenant—a "real greenhorn," says Donovan—just in from the United States.

"He said to us, 'What's that?' Nobody said nothing, so he ordered us to pull it out. Finally he asked, 'This is government property. Where did you guys steal it from?' Still nobody said nothing. He asked again, 'Who does it belong to?' After a long pause I told him it was mine. He asked me where I got it, and I lied to him. I told him I found it on the side of the road."[7]

Later that day a messenger showed up at Donovan's tent with instructions for him to report immediately to the regimental adjutant's office. Donovan still remembers his name. "It was Major Joe McFadden. He was from New Jersey and had been the quarterback of Georgetown's football team." Donovan first attempted the "found on the side of the road" excuse, but McFadden would hear none of that.

"Damnit, Donovan, don't lie to me," he said. So Donovan admitted he had taken it while cleaning out a troop transport ship.

"And then he said to me, 'What were you going to do with it? Sell it to the gooks?' And I said, 'No sir, I'm going to eat it!' He said, 'I told you not to lie to me. Nobody eats that crap!' I told him, 'I do. I like it.'

McFadden then asked Donovan where he was from and if he was related to Mike Donovan, the famous fight referee. "I told him the ref was my father. Now, I figured a McFadden from New Jersey who played football at Georgetown is not going to throw a Donovan from New York who played football at Notre Dame into the brig over a case of Spam. Sure enough, Major McFadden told me he was going to give me a week to eat the whole case, or as he put it, 'your ass belongs to me.' I ate the whole case in six days. Thirty pounds of Spam. I was the company hero. The cooks used to come over to our tent and put the Spam in batter and cook it up for me. Twenty-four hours a day I'd be eating Spam. And loving it. They let me off the hook, and I still have a soft spot in my heart for Spam."[8]

Donovan says the main topic of discussion on Guam was always the pending invasion of Japan. "We all talked as if it was certain. What we didn't talk about, but what we knew, was that not a lot of us were going to be coming back from that hornet's nest."[9]

But in early August, Donovan remembers watching comedian Charley Ruggles during a visiting USO show when suddenly the regimental commander appeared on stage and announced the atomic bomb had been dropped on Japan. "We didn't know what the hell he was talking about," recalls Donovan. "Then he said that he felt that the Japanese would sue for peace. Now we figured he was drunk, because everyone knew they were digging in on the beaches of Japan. In fact, I had a captain named Mike Heinz sitting next to me, and when the general made this announcement, I turned to him and asked him if this meant we were going home. And he laughed and said, "I'll tell you where the hell it means we're going. It means we're going to Tokyo."[10]

Three months later, though, Donovan was on a troop transport ship headed for California. It was October 1945. "I went in as a PFC. And I came out as a PFC. I suppose they just didn't recognize my leadership abilities," he jokes. "I was twenty years old and remember before I got on the train to Bainbridge [Maryland], I tried to get a beer in a tavern in San Diego, and the guy wouldn't serve me because I wasn't old enough. I'll never forget that. I'd nearly got my ass blown off in the South Pacific for twenty-four months but I was too young to drink in a California bar."

The Marines officially discharged him on December 10, 1945, and Donovan promptly hopped on a train and headed back to the Bronx. "I got off the train at Penn Station and went over to Thirty-fourth Street to catch the subway home," he says, laughing at the memory. "I'm in my uniform. I've got my seabag, and I'm really feeling like one of the returning heroes, you know. Well, there's a kid from my neighborhood on the train, Tommy Ianetti, and I'll never forget it. I saw him and said, 'Hey, Tommy, how ya doin'?' And he says, 'Artie! Where ya' been?' He didn't even know I was gone!"[11]

A few of his cousins met him when he came out of the subway. When he walked in the door, his mother was in the kitchen cooking a ham. It was all such a familiar scene, he says, it was if he'd never left. "I looked at her and said, 'Here I am, Ma. I just won the war.'" The tears she was trying to hide told him how glad she was he had made it back.

"You see, in my neighborhood everybody hung out in front of the candy store," says Donovan.

> Whether you were a few years older or a few years younger, that's what we did. But when the war started, one-by-one, we all left. I remember some guys who went in right away, saying, "I'll be back in a year," and then not coming back until five years later! And some guys who left never made it back at all. But when we did come back, we'd go back to the wall in front of that store. The thing was, nobody ever talked about their experiences in the service. I guess we looked at it like it was something that happened in our lives, but now that we were home, it was time to get on with it.[12]

For Donovan, that meant college and football. Still passionate about the game, he turned down an invitation to return to Notre Dame and accepted a scholarship to Boston College, because he felt he'd have a greater opportunity to play at Boston. By the end of his junior year, he was one of the country's best defensive linemen and had attracted the attention of teams from the NFL and the All-American Football Conference (AAFC). The competition between the two leagues had created a bidding war for players, and in 1948 the AAFC's Buffalo Bisons offered him a guaranteed $25,000 contract that included a $5,000 signing bonus and a new car if he'd forgo his senior season and play for them. After some strong arm-twisting from his mother—"She wanted me to finish my education"—Donovan turned it down and graduated the following spring, but by then the professional football landscape had changed. The

AAFC had folded and the NFL was king. The Baltimore Colts selected him in the fourth round and offered him a nonguaranteed contract for $4,500. "The bidding war was a thing of the past," says Donovan. "If you wanted to play professional football, it was take it or leave it."

It was 1950. He was twenty-five and figured if there was a chance he might be able to get paid for playing a sport he still loved, then why not give it a try? So he returned to the Bronx, packed up the car his mom had bought him with the money he'd sent home while he was in the Marines, and, with forty-five dollars in his pocket, headed to Baltimore. "And that was it," says Donovan with a shrug, too humble to get into the particulars of the tremendous career he would go on to have with the Colts, a career that would span twelve years and would include five straight Pro Bowl appearances, two NFL championships, and a place in the Pro Football Hall of Fame.

Donovan is eighty-one now. He and his wife, Dottie, live in Towson, Maryland, ten miles outside of Baltimore. During his years as a Colt, Donovan and his teammates were beloved in Baltimore. They were part of the fabric of the community in a way that is difficult to find today in professional sports. "We had a good group of guys and would get invited to roasts, crab feasts, schools . . . all kinds of functions," says Jim Mutscheller, the Colts' wide receiver from 1954 to 1961. "We did that kind of stuff year-round and really got to know people in town, and they got to know us. So during the season, you had this feeling like the people in the seats were your personal friends, and I think that's also the way they looked at us. We weren't these million-dollar athletes that they only saw on Sunday. We were just like them."[13]

"The thing about those guys was that they all lived in the same communities as we did," says Maureen Kilkullin, who grew up in Towson and remembers attending Sunday mass and always seeing Donovan, Gino Marchetti, and Johnny Unitas. "We'd sit next to them in church, go to school with their kids . . . as loved as they were, you just felt like they were regular guys."[14]

And no one typified that more, says Kilkullin, than Art Donovan. "He was a blue-collar guy in a blue-collar town and just always gave off this feeling that he was accessible," she says. "Even after he retired and became well-known around the country from his appearances on Letterman and other shows, he never changed. You always felt like he was just a regular guy that you could go up to and have a conversation with if you saw him out in town."[15]

"Art has about as broad an appeal as you'll ever find," says Ordell Brasse, who played alongside Donovan on the Colts' defensive line for four years. "And I think a lot of that has to do with where he grew up. In his neighborhood he was exposed to lots of different types of people . . . Italians, Irish, you name it. It was a real melting pot, and he just became very perceptive about things. He's one of kind."[16]

And it's in listening to those who have known him best that you understand the real reason behind the popularity of Art Donovan. It's not because he was a great professional football player, or because he makes people laugh with funny stories. It's because, despite all the notoriety and fame that has followed him throughout his life—even as a young boy with a famous father—Art Donovan has never thought he was anything more than just a big Irish kid from the Bronx who was fortunate enough to be able to play football.

"Somebody once came up to me and told me that my dad was like Forrest Gump," says Debbie Donovan, his oldest daughter. "And the more I thought about it, the more I realized they were right. He's had this amazing life and done and seen so many things, but he's always stayed the same."[17]

She says she can't ever remember her father telling anyone that he played professional football or is in the Hall of Fame. "He underplays everything he's ever done," she says. "He's just a very humble man." But she does say that as he's grown older, she's become more aware of how much his experience in the Marines meant to him. In 2004 the commandant of the U.S. Marine Corps, Gen. Richard Hagee, officially inducted him into the Marine Corps Sports Hall of Fame at a formal dinner in Quantico, Virginia. "He would never tell anyone that, but I know how honored both he and my mom felt being there."[18]

And Debbie is right. When it's mentioned to him, he deflects any talk about himself, and instead tells a short story about what meant the most to him that evening. But unlike others, this is a story that cuts to the core of who Art Donovan has always been.

"Seeing all these young Marines was what meant the most to me," says Donovan. "You know, these are people who are willing to sacrifice their lives for something they believe in, for all of us. I was introduced to this young Marine who had just come back from Afghanistan, and you know what I told him? I told him, 'Young fella, you know all these baseball, football, and basketball players everyone's always talking about? They're not heroes. *You're* a hero. Thank you for what you're doing for all of us."[19] That's vintage Art Donovan.

A Will to Live

"All we had was life and our fellow man. In the end, that is enough to fight for. We have to be willing to help each other and never take freedom for granted. That's the kind of spirit we should have in America today."

—Mario "Motts" Tonelli

Three months. That was all Sgt. Mario "Motts" Tonelli had left on his army enlistment when the Japanese attacked Pearl Harbor in December 1941. He had voluntarily enlisted the previous March for a one-year hitch, leaving behind a new bride and a budding professional football career, because it had "seemed like the right thing to do." Many of his teammates and buddies from his old neighborhood in Chicago's north side had enlisted—in fact, some were already back home—and Tonelli just felt like it was his turn. "Don't worry," his friends had told him. "The time will fly by." And for the most part, they had been right.

After completing his initial training at Camp Wallace and Fort Bliss in Texas, he was assigned to the 200th Coast Artillery, an antiaircraft unit formed from the New Mexico National Guard. In October they were shipped out to the Philippines and stationed at Clark Field outside of Manila. By then, talk of war was rumbling throughout the Pacific, as it was back in the States, but for Tonelli and his unit the routine wasn't much different then it had been back in Texas. There were drills, marches, and cleaning—and then more drills, marches, and cleaning. They thought about home and talked about the grand plans they all had once they "got out." And they did their best to adjust to the tropical heat and clouds of mosquitoes that were such a part of life in the Philippines.

Tonelli often found himself daydreaming of his wife and of football. He had hated leaving Mary. They'd met at a party at Northwestern University and after a brief courtship had married in Las Cruces, New Mexico, just five days before he'd shipped out. He was eager to get back and lead a normal life with her. And though the jungles of the Philippines were a far cry from the crisp autumns of Illinois, the calendar still said it was football season, and Tonelli wondered how his Chicago Cardinal teammates were doing without him. "One year, and I'm out, boys," he had told them before leaving. "I'll be back knocking you in the head before you can kick the mud off your cleats."[1]

With December's arrival, he thought he was just a few months from heading home to make good on that promise. But December 7 changed everything. At 5:00 AM, he was awakened by the sound of sirens calling everyone to their battle stations. The Japanese had bombed Pearl Harbor, they were told, and the army's leadership at the base was certain the Philippines would be next. They were right. The next day, at approximately 12:30 PM, Tonelli was emerging from the base mess hall after standing down for lunch when he noticed a swarm of planes approaching on the horizon. "We initially thought they were American planes," said Tonelli. "But then they started bombing the air fields."[2]

Unable to get back to his unit, he picked up an abandoned Springfield rifle, hit the ground, and began firing at the planes as they passed overhead. For two straight hours they bombed and strafed Clark Field and other island defense positions. But unlike Pearl Harbor, the air attacks didn't stop after just one day. They continued, and were soon accompanied by Japanese ground forces that landed on the island.

It was the beginning of a four-year battle for survival for Mario Tonelli. He had been so close to going home, but he would spend the next four months valiantly fighting to keep the Japanese from overrunning the island, then the next forty-two as a prisoner of war, enduring horrific torture and abuse that would eventually take the lives of nearly two of every three men captured in the Philippines. But even though the Japanese would ravage Tonelli's body, reducing the once bruising 205-pound fullback to a 92-pound skeleton, they never broke his will to live.

The story of how Motts Tonelli survived that four-year hell really begins back at his alma mater, the University of Notre Dame. A multisport star at Chicago's DePaul High School and the son of Italian immigrant parents, he had planned to attend the University of Southern California until Elmer Layden, Notre Dame's legendary coach and one of the famed "Four Horsemen," visited his parents, accompanied by a priest. As the story goes, Layden extolled the virtues of Notre Dame football on Motts and his father while the priest quietly went into the kitchen and in perfect Italian spoke with Mott's mother, Celi, about where a good young Catholic boy should really be going to school. A few minutes later, Mrs. Tonelli, who knew nothing of football, or any other American sport for that matter, emerged from the kitchen and told Motts he could forget about California.

"You're going to Notre Dame," she said. "It's a Catholic school, and you won't be far from home."

"And that was it," said Tonelli.[3]

Success came slow to him in South Bend. Homesick and relegated to the practice squad his freshmen year, he questioned whether the school was the right place for him and wondered if he'd ever get a chance to play. But after some encouragement from a young priest named John O'Hara (who later become president of the university and a cardinal in the Catholic Church), he decided to stick it out, and gradually things improved. By his junior year he was a regular in the Notre Dame backfield, and in the team's final game of that 1937 season against USC, it was Tonelli who made the big play, taking a handoff on a fullback reverse and rumbling seventy yards down to the USC thirteen-yard line. Two plays later, he dragged a tackler into the end zone to score the go-ahead touchdown for the Irish and give them a share of the national championship. It was a game that four years later would save his life.

When the Japanese invaded the Philippines on December 8, 1941, they encountered a combined Philippine-American force of more than one hundred thousand soldiers, who were inexperienced but determined to defend the island. From his headquarters on Corregidor in Manila Bay, Gen. Douglas MacArthur immediately ordered the force into the jungles of the Bataan Peninsula with the hope they could make a stand until reinforcements arrived.

For three months, despite dwindling supplies of food, ammunition, and medicine, that's exactly what Tonelli and his fellow soldiers did. In mid-January they went to half-rations. By the end of February those rations were reduced again to one thousand calories a day—some rice, a little fish, and whatever meat they could find.[4] But the promised reinforcements didn't come. With the Pacific Fleet still reeling from Pearl Harbor and the country adopting a "Hitler First" approach to the war, the "battling bastards of Bataan," as they were now calling themselves, were on their own. "There are times when men have to die," Secretary of War Henry Stimson had privately conceded back in Washington when confronted with the worsening situation on Bataan.[5]

On April 9, 1942, with his remaining forces starving, out of ammunition, and suffering from disease, Maj. Gen. Edward King ordered his soldiers to surrender. They had fought bravely. "No Army did so much with so little," MacArthur later said.[6] But now Tonelli, roughly ten thousand Americans, and sixty-five thousand Philippine soldiers were prisoners of war. *At least there will be some food and water,* they thought. *It can't be much worse than what we've just gone through.* The next day Tonelli began to realize just how wrong that was.

They had spent the night in several large fields outside the town of Mariveles in the southern tip of the Bataan Peninsula, forming what amounted to large refugee camps. But the Japanese, eager to continue pressing forward to attack MacArthur and the remaining U.S. forces on Corregidor, weren't prepared to handle such large numbers of POWs, particularly ones in such poor physical condition. Their solution was to march them sixty miles north to the town of San Fernando, then pack them like sardines in railroad boxcars and move them to Camp O'Donnell, an abandoned Philippine military training base that the Japanese had converted into a POW camp. On the morning of April 10, Tonelli, grouped with several hundred soldiers, began the hike north. Shortly after they started walking, a Japanese soldier approached on horseback carrying a dark object atop a long bamboo pole. As he got closer, Tonelli realized what he was looking at. It was the head of an American soldier, its eyes and mouth open, completely engulfed by flies.

"The things I saw on that march can't be described by words," remembers Tonelli. "Words don't do justice to that kind of horror. It happened so quickly. One day we had our freedom, the next day we were being treated like animals."[7]

They were not given food or water, and many soldiers, already starving and dehydrated before the march, immediately began to falter. Those who fell to the side were shot, bayoneted, or decapitated by Japanese soldiers. The same fate befell Philippine civilians who tried to pass them water or food from the side of the road.

The Japanese moved up and down their ranks, taunting them and taking anything of value that they were carrying. If an American or Philippine soldier was found to have Japanese money, he was shot on the spot. One of the soldiers spotted Tonelli's gold graduation ring and, jabbing his bayonet toward Tonelli's hand, motioned for him to hand it over. Tonelli refused.

"Motts," a friend whispered, "Give it to him or he'll kill you."

Reluctantly, Tonelli handed it over, watching with a combination of disgust and despair as the Japanese soldier smiled and walked away.

But a few moments later, a Japanese officer approached Tonelli and in perfect English asked him if one of his soldiers had taken something from him.

"Yes, my graduation ring from Notre Dame," responded Tonelli. Reaching into his pocket, the Japanese officer pulled out the ring.

"Is this it?" he asked. Tonelli said it was.

"You know," the officer said. "I was educated in America at the University of Southern California. I know a little about the famous Notre Dame football team. In fact, I watched you beat USC in 1937. I know how much this ring means to you, so I wanted to get it back to you."

As the officer walked away, he turned around to the stunned Tonelli. "I'd advise you to put that away," he said. "Or someone is going to take it from you."[8]

Later known as the Bataan Death March, the grueling walk lasted seven days. Each night Tonelli removed his shirt and put it on the grass to catch the morning dew. It was the only water he drank the entire week. By the time they arrived in San Fernando, an estimated seven hundred Americans and ten thousand Philippine soldiers had died. And those numbers would continue to grow. In San Fernando, they were packed one hundred to a boxcar for the twenty-five-mile, four-hour train ride to Capas. They couldn't move, let alone sit down, and hundreds died from dehydration and heat exhaustion in boxcars that turned into saunas under the midday tropical sun. When they finally arrived in Capas, they were forced to march another eight miles to Camp O'Donnell.

At O'Donnell, soldiers finally received water, waiting in line for as long as ten hours to fill their canteens from one of two water spigots. Disease ran rampant within the overcrowded barracks, and Tonelli, assigned to grave-digging detail, found himself burying thirty to forty of his fellow soldiers a day. He came down with scurvy, beriberi, and malaria, diseases that made his joints throb and left him in a constant state of either cold chills or fever. "The nights were terrible," he recalls. "You'd hear grown men crying, 'Lord, why did you do this to me?' The next day they would be dead on the floor."[9]

Their torturous treatment by the Japanese didn't improve. By surrendering, the Japanese told them, they had disgraced their country. "The commander of the prison camp told us the Japanese were very good people and that when the war was over we would be welcome there since we no longer would be welcome in the United States," said Tonelli. "We didn't believe him."[10]

After seven weeks—and the deaths of sixteen hundred more Americans— the Japanese evacuated O'Donnell and moved the prisoners northeast to a camp near the town of Cabanatuan, where they spent the next year doing slave labor. A diphtheria epidemic swept through camp and contributed to the deaths of another twenty-five hundred men. Their meals were bowls of rice or rice soup, both infested with worms. But Tonelli refused to give in to the despair that was all around him. Each night he removed his gold Notre Dame ring from its hiding place, a silver soap container, and remembered happier days—Chicago, football, Mary. The ring renewed his hope that someday he would return to them.

In the fall of 1942 Tonelli and one thousand other men left Cabanatuan and were shipped south to a prison farm on the large island of Mindanao to grow food for the Japanese army. For a while, things improved. The Japanese commander, understanding that starving workers would be of little use to him, gave them fish, bananas, papayas, and rice, but when several prisoners escaped, conditions became more harsh. Tonelli's days were spent in the rice fields, and he contracted an intestinal parasite that often made him double over with stomach pain. But he continued to work. If he didn't, his meager rations would be even further reduced.

By the summer of 1944 the tide of the war in the Pacific had turned. U.S. forces were pushing north with their island-hopping campaign, and the Japanese, aware of MacArthur's pledge to return and retake the Philippines, decided to move the POWs to Japan and put them to work in their factories and mines. By the thousands they loaded the prisoners into the dark bowels of unmarked merchant ships and kept them there for weeks—in some cases months—while the ships dodged American air and submarine attacks en route to Japan. Several of these ships were sunk, killing thousands of American POWs. For example, on September 7, 1944, the Japanese vessel *Shinyo Maru* was sunk with 750 POWs. Only 82 would be rescued by Filipino guerillas. On October 24, 1944, the *Arisan Maru* was sunk on the first day of the battle of Leyte Gulf with 1,790 POWs on board. Only five survived. And on December 13, the *Oryoku Maru* went down with 1,619 POWs. They had been at sea for forty-nine days. This time, 1,300 survived.[11]

For Tonelli, his journey aboard what POWs and historians later referred to as "hell ships" began on July 1, 1944. He and one thousand prisoners were crammed into the dark forward hold of a captured merchant ship named the *Canadian Inventor* (*Mati Mati Maru*). They were never allowed on deck. There were no lights, no water, and no toilets. Their bathroom was a five-gallon bucket the Japanese lowered down on a rope. They used the same buckets to pass the Americans their daily ration of three baseball-sized balls of rice. "They washed out the buckets, put the rice in them, and sent them down to us. Then the buckets were washed out again and filled with water and sent down so we could fill our canteens," Tonelli recalled.[12]

Because there wasn't enough room for them to all lie down at once, they slept in shifts. Every now and then the ship would stop and they would drift to avoid attack from American submarines. For sixty-two days they remained sequestered at sea like the slaves they had become. Tonelli says that in his nearly four years of captivity it was the closest he ever came to giving up all hope. "It made us think the guys on Bataan who didn't make it were the lucky ones."[13]

When they finally arrived on the Japanese mainland, they spent ten months at a work camp in Yokkaichi before being moved to a scrap metal plant in Toyama in June 1945. Something told him it would be his final stop. He knew his once two-hundred-pound frame, now down to less than one hundred pounds, would not be able to hold up much longer. "I felt that I was going to either die or be liberated," said Tonelli.[14]

At each new camp they were assigned a number. When Tonelli arrived in Toyama, he was handed a cap with his assigned number scrawled on it. He did a double take when he saw it—number 58. It was the same number he had worn at DePaul Academy, Notre Dame, and his year with the Chicago Cardinals. "I'm going to make it," he said quietly to himself.

Throughout that summer Tonelli and his fellow prisoners saw American planes flying overhead. Each week they seemed to come in lower, and they prayed the end was near. On August 1, Toyama was firebombed and the plant where they worked nearly destroyed. They continued working for the next several weeks, but on the fifteenth they unexpectedly were given the day off. The next day several B-17s flew directly over their camp, flying so low that the prisoners could see soldiers in the planes' bomb-bay doors, kicking out fifty-five-gallon drums attached to parachutes. The drums were full of the food the prisoners had been dreaming of for years—canned beef and bacon, powdered milk, coffee, canned fruits and vegetables, cheese, candy. On a carton of cigarettes was this message: "Hostilities have ceased. We'll see you soon."

"We built our own little fires in the compound and did our own cooking," said Tonelli. "We ate so much, we got sick. Our stomachs weren't used to it."[15]

During the next several days, U.S. Army trucks arrived and retrieved their fellow countrymen. After 1,236 days in captivity, Mario Tonelli was once again a free man. Within the month, he was on a steamship headed for San Francisco, still battling the lingering effects of malaria, but savoring the feeling of the sea air on his face. He read magazines and newspapers, caught up on the news, and slept a lot, treasuring the sensation of clean sheets and a soft pillow. When he arrived in San Francisco, he immediately hopped a train for

Chicago and the reunion with his parents and Mary—a reunion that he had never given up on.

When his train arrived at the station in Chicago on that mid-September day in 1945, there was no band, no crowd of appreciative, flag-waving admirers to welcome him home. After all, men were returning home daily from the war now. Men who, in their own minds, had simply done their duty . . . done what they had been asked, because, as Tonelli himself had said four years earlier, "it seemed like the right thing to do." Their reward, their recognition, was simply in making it home, and that's how they felt about it. They knew many who had not made it home. So when he stepped down on to the station platform, wearing his uniform, with his green duffel bag slung over his shoulder, he didn't feel special. He knew he was one of the lucky ones. He had got word to his parents and Mary about his arrival, and he spotted them standing together at the end of the platform, but it wasn't until he removed his hat that they recognized the rail-thin soldier who was walking toward them. Mary's hands immediately went to cover her mouth. He made it to them, then collapsed in their arms. His incredible journey of survival was truly over.

In retrospect, Tonelli's survival and return from the Bataan Death March marked the completion of one journey and the beginning of another. As he had promised his Chicago Cardinal teammates when he left them in March 1941, he *did* play with them again. Two months after returning home, Cardinals owner Charlie Bidwell renewed Tonelli's contract, and on October 28, 1945, less than three months after being liberated from the prison camp in Toyama, he carried the ball twice for no gain against the Green Bay Packers. It was a noble gesture by Bidwell to ensure that Tonelli qualified for an NFL pension, and Tonelli never forgot it. "I wasn't forgotten about by the organization," he said. "The Cardinals did the honorable thing and let me fulfill my contract."[16]

It was the last NFL game he would play in. In 1946, at the age of thirty, Tonelli entered politics and became the youngest man—and only Republican—ever to win election as a Cook County commissioner. It was the beginning of forty-two years of public service within Cook County.

For years, the lingering effects of the diseases he'd contracted as a POW put him in and out of hospitals, but he gradually healed, and despite the horrific things he endured and witnessed, he was never bitter. "As I got older and started to read about Bataan, I wondered how he *couldn't* be bitter," says his daughter Nancy. "But back then everybody just wanted to start over."[17]

He never forgot, though, and as he got older it became increasingly important to him for younger generations to understand the sacrifices made for them at Bataan and other places during the war. He spoke at schools and talked about his experiences, but often the students (and some of the teachers) had never heard of Bataan and seemed disinterested. It frustrated him, but he kept at it, determined to do what he could to remember those who hadn't made it home.

A few months before he passed away, on January 7, 2003, Tonelli was inducted into the Italian American Sports Hall of Fame. It was a long evening, with numerous former athletes recounting stories from their glorious athletic pasts. By the time Tonelli was introduced, the ceremony was into its fourth hour. "At nearly midnight, Mr. Tonelli shuffled up to the microphones," wrote Bryan Smith in Tonelli's obituary. "He squinted at the bright lights, his voice soft and raspy in the microphone. He merely asked the audience to pray for America's soldiers and expressed his love for his country. The moment brought the crowd to its feet, in tears. Mr. Tonelli shuffled off the stage and back to his table."[18]

At the age of eighty-six, at a ceremony honoring him and all that he accomplished in his life, Motts Tonelli chose to remember his country and all those who continue to serve it.

That's really who he was, Nancy would recall. "He had this uncanny ability to make everyone feel like they were a good friend," she would say after he passed away. "It was one of the things I loved most about him. I could [not] have cared less about the football stuff. Who he was and his ability to inspire had everything to do with his character."[19]

CHAPTER 15
Forever Changed

"One thing I believe is, if you come back from war and the only thing you bring back is bitterness from the hardships you endured, then you didn't learn anything. I was blessed to have made it back."

—Lou Brissie

No sport in America was affected more by the war than professional baseball. At the zenith of its popularity in 1941, both the major and minor leagues struggled to survive in the four years that followed as thousands of players joined the military. By war's end, some 340 major leaguers and nearly 3,000 minor leaguers had been in uniform. Like the 16 million soldiers, sailors, airmen, and Marines they served with, their experiences in the service of their country would have a lasting impact on their lives and on their careers. For some, it was a significant detour in a career that was successfully resumed at war's end. But for others, World War II derailed dreams and careers that before December 7 seemed destined for greatness. This is the story of three of those players.

From his very first game in the big leagues, Cecil Travis could hit. On May 16, 1933, the nineteen-year-old Georgian was called up to the majors to fill in for the Washington Senators' injured third baseman, Ossie Bluege. Travis went five for seven that day and never put on a minor league uniform again. During the next eight seasons, primarily playing shortstop, he hit for an average of .327 and was well on his way to the Baseball Hall of Fame. In 1941 Travis hit a career-best .359. Only Ted Williams hit better. "Cecil Travis, a guy most people have never heard of, had a hell of a year," Williams would write in his biography, "and never had another one like it."[1]

Williams was right. In January 1942, at the age of twenty-eight and at the pinnacle of his baseball career, Travis was drafted into the army. After spending eighteen months stateside, his 76th Infantry Division was sent to Europe in the summer of 1944 and then into Belgium that winter, right on the heels of the Battle of the Bulge. "We were more of a supply and support unit," recalls Travis, "following right behind the front line guys. We were moving so fast taking all these towns that we just slept anywhere we could. And there were booby traps everywhere."[2]

He remembers Gen. George S. Patton coming through his division, waving and shaking hands, but most of all he remembers the cold his division endured. "We'd just shiver all night long. It was mighty cold, and I ended up getting a couple of frozen toes," he says.[3]

When his limp was so bad he could no longer keep up with his division, he was sent to a hospital in France to recuperate. "It was three weeks before I was able to rejoin my unit. By this time, I'd been in the service about as long as anybody. I'd been overseas for about nine months, and I knew my wife at home was pregnant and that maybe she'd already had the baby [indeed she had—the second of their three sons], so I was anxious to get home, at least for a little while."[4] He'd heard that if you volunteered for duty in the Pacific, they allowed you a brief pit stop at home before shipping you out again. His request was approved. In August he was home on leave, "waiting to go overseas, when they dropped that thing on Japan, and the war was over."[5]

He was discharged from the army and wasted no time in returning to his former team. He arrived in Washington for the final fifteen games of the 1945 season, hitting .241—very respectable for someone who just months before had been on the battlefield. But in 1946, his first full season in five years, he struggled. "Every once in a while I'd get it back, but my timing was just off," says Travis. "Pitches that I used to wham out, I was missing."[6]

He hit just .252, and the next year, 1947, playing just as a utility player, he hit only .217. Travis always had been popular with fans and the media, and reporters attributed the drastic drop-off of the Senators' onetime star shortstop to the frostbite he suffered during the war. Travis says that wasn't true. "I just didn't have it anymore," he says. "My toes had nothing to do with it."[7]

When he realized he no longer could play like he used to, he retired to his farm just south of Atlanta, the same one on which both he and his father had grown up on. Today, at ninety-two, Travis is still there, tending to some cattle he keeps on his sixty-five acres, "just to give me some exercise."

He says there was never a doubt in his mind as to whether or not he should have been called to serve. "Good gracious, no," he says in his southern drawl. "Everyone who was able was supposed to go in. Whether you were a baseball player ... shouldn't—and didn't—have anything to do with it at all."[8]

Late in the afternoon of December 7, 1944, Cpl. Lou Brissie lay in a creek bed in the mountains of northern Italy, his left leg shattered from a German artillery shell that had fallen upon his company in the 351st Infantry, 88th Division earlier that morning. Eight of his company mates died instantly. Brissie was in such bad shape that several corpsmen, seeing his condition, passed right by him, figuring he, too, was dead.

When someone finally noticed he was still alive, Brissie was rushed to a field hospital, where doctors took one look at his leg and said they would have to amputate it if he was going to survive. Through the fog of painkillers Brissie heard this and sat up. "You can't take the leg off," he said. "I'm a ballplayer."

And a very good one. After high school, Brissie had been offered a twenty-five-thousand-dollar bonus to sign with the Brooklyn Dodgers. Instead, he accepted an invitation by Philadelphia Athletics owner Connie Mack to hone his skills at Presbyterian College before joining the Athletics for spring training at the end of his sophomore year. His entry into the army in 1942 at eighteen put that plan on hold. The injury to his leg made it look like it might never happen.

After nine months and twenty-three operations to remove bone and shrapnel, Brissie's leg was saved, but doctors said his baseball days were over. Again, Brissie disagreed. "If God lets me walk again, I'll play. That's my ambition," he said.

He got a leg brace and in 1946 began his comeback, pitching for a semipro team near his hometown in Ware Shoals, South Carolina. In his first game, he threw just ten pitches, giving up two home runs and seven hits. But Brissie battled on, and by the end of the year he had shown enough progress that the Athletics assigned him to their Class A minor league team in Savannah, Georgia, for the 1947 season.

Although an infection in his leg sidelined him for six weeks, Brissie caught fire halfway through the season, winning twelve games in a row and drawing huge crowds whenever he pitched. On opening day in 1948, less than four years after his near death in the mountains of Italy, his comeback was complete. He was the starting pitcher against Ted Williams and the Boston Red Sox.

He won that game, and thirteen more that season, finishing fourth in the voting for Rookie of the Year. That season, a writer from the Associated Press called him "one of the most courageous and determined players of all-time."

month. Lefty thought he was worth a lot more, and in a brash move for a player who had never pitched an inning in the big leagues, sent the contract back. The Senators sent him another one, but that contract was never signed either.

In the winter of 1941, Lefty was drafted into the army and became a paratrooper, primarily because it paid an extra fifty dollars a month. Although Lefty knew his dream to play in the majors had been delayed, Bill says his older brother took an immediate liking to military service. "Life in the service was a better life than where we came from," he says. "You received standard-issue clothes and three meals a day. But Lefty in particular took to the military. He looked like he was made to wear the uniform."[12]

Throughout the war, just about every military unit had its own baseball team. In Brewer's case, he not only jumped out of planes, but he also pitched for the 508th Parachute Infantry Regiment "Red Devils." "When the war is over," he wrote to his mother, "I'm really going to town. My arm is in better shape than it's ever been."[13]

In March 1944 the Red Devils were sent overseas to Nottingham, England, in preparation for the D-day invasion. On the evening of June 5, Brewer and the rest of the 508th parachuted into France along with twenty-four thousand other allied paratroopers to start the invasion of Europe. "The paratroopers got scattered everywhere," says Bill. "Lefty's group captured a road, and he fought for about eleven hours."[14]

About noon, they were overrun by Germans and made a dash for the Merderet River. "I was aware someone was running just behind me," recalls Bill Dean, another paratrooper from the 508th. "In my panic I took a quick look and saw Lefty, at port arms, running like he was going to stretch a double into a triple."[15]

A German machine gun opened fire a split second later, and Lefty Brewer was killed instantly. After being buried at an American cemetery in France, Brewer's body was returned to Jacksonville in 1947. Today, Bill, who is eighty-two and served in the navy and merchant marines during the war, keeps Lefty's medals encased next to his own.

He pitched another five years in the big leagues for the Athletics and Cleveland Indians, winning forty-four games. But fans and his teamm never fully understood the pain he endured. His frail leg was inflicted w osteomyelitis, a bone infection that continued to flare up, often sending hi to bed or the hospital for treatment between starts.

Following the 1953 season, Brissie retired at age twenty-nine, accepting an offer from the American Legion to become their director of youth base- ball. Hollywood asked permission to make a movie of his life, but he politely declined. "I'm not a hero, and I just didn't feel comfortable with that," says Brissie, now eighty-two and living in North Augusta, South Carolina.[9]

He says the fact he was able to make it back from that creek bed in northern Italy left a lasting impression that he's carried throughout his life. "Whenever I'd start to get bothered by something, I'd think about that inci- dent and remember how lucky I was," says Brissie. "One thing I believe is, if you come back from war and the only thing you bring back is bitterness from the hardships you endured, then you didn't learn anything. I was blessed to have made it back."[10]

"**G**rowing up, Lefty was just good at everything." That's what Bill Brewer says when asked about his older brother, Forrest "Lefty" Brewer. "Volleyball, football, baseball, hunting, whatever, he was just naturally good at all of them."[11]

It was one of the things that helped the Brewer boys—Frank, Lefty, and Bill—fit in as their family bounced from place to place in northern Florida during the Depression years, finally settling down in Jacksonville. And it was there that Lefty zeroed in on the one talent in which he was particularly gifted: throwing a baseball.

In the spring of 1938 Brewer dropped out of his senior year in high school at nineteen to pitch for the St. Augustine Saints in the Florida State League—at Class D, the lowest possible rung on the minor league ladder. He pitched like a man among boys, winning twenty-five games for the Saints, striking out more than 230 hitters, and pitching a no-hitter on June 6. His performance was so dominant that the Washington Senators, who had a working agreement with the Saints, bought Brewer's contract and brought him to Washington so they could watch him while he practiced with their team.

They liked what they saw, and during the next two years Lefty moved through the Senators' minor league farm system, first in Orlando, Florida, and then in Charlotte, North Carolina. After the 1940 season the Senators offered him a major league contract for the 1941 season at two hundred dollars a

The Throwback

"My great-grandfather was at Pearl Harbor and a lot of my family has gone and fought in wars, and I really haven't done a damn thing as far as laying myself on the line like that. And so I have a great deal of respect for those that have and what the flag stands for."

—Pat Tillman

"There is in Pat Tillman's example, in his unexpected choice of duty to his country over the riches and other comforts of celebrity, and in his humility, such an inspiration to all of us to reclaim the essential public-spiritedness of Americans that many of us, in low moments, had worried was no longer our common distinguishing trait."

—Senator John McCain

On September 11, 2001, Pat Tillman was a defensive back for the Arizona Cardinals. Beginning his fourth season in the NFL, he was making more than a million dollars a year playing a game he loved and stood to make a lot more once his current three-year contract expired. Seven months later, moved by the images of 9/11 and an inner voice reminding him of his family's own tradition of military service, he and his brother Kevin, a minor league baseball player in the Cleveland Indians organization, quietly enlisted in the army, adamantly insisting that there be no publicity about their decision, because they felt it would be disrespectful to those already serving. They wanted to be Rangers.

"For someone to walk away from several million dollars and a life of relative ease to put his neck on the line literally for $18,000 to $20,000 with no guarantee for tomorrow, you had to be surprised by that," said Pete Kendall, his Cardinals teammate at the time. "Pat is the only one I know in our modern day of athletics who did it. This was sort of out of the blue and totally unexpected nationally. But the more you knew Pat, the more you understood why."[1]

When he arrived at Arizona State University in 1994, he was a lightly recruited eighteen-year-old from San Jose, California, who, with his long hair, flip-flops, and penchant for calling everyone "dude," looked more like a surfer than a football player. At 5'11" and 195 pounds, he was small for a Pac-10 linebacker, and his coaches considered redshirting him, figuring the extra year would give him a chance to get stronger and adjust to college. But there was something in Tillman's response when they approached him with the idea—a sense of urgency and intensity—that made them change their minds. "I've got things to do with my life," the freshman had told them. "You can do whatever you want with me, but in four years I'm gone."[2]

By his senior year, he was the Pac-10 defensive player of the year on a team that went to the Rose Bowl, and a star in the classroom, graduating in three and a half years with a 3.84 grade point average and a degree in marketing. The NFL was interested, but the general feeling was that Tillman's size and average speed would restrict him to special teams and an occasional role as an extra defensive back. Like Arizona State, the pros underestimated his determination. The Arizona Cardinals decided to take a chance and selected Tillman in the last round of the 1998 draft—the 226th player chosen out of 241 total picks. Two years later, now a fixture at safety in the Cardinals' defense, he set a franchise record with 224 tackles in a season and was suddenly a sought-after commodity.

The St. Louis Rams, winners of the 1999 Super Bowl, offered him a five-year, nine-million-dollar contract, but Tillman, adhering to his own code of loyalty, turned them down. "It wouldn't be fair to [the Cardinals] to leave," he explained to his agent when told about the offer.[3]

On September 11, 2001, he was at the Cardinals' training facility when terrorists flew commercial planes into the World Trade Center and the Pentagon. The next day he gave his last on-camera interview as a professional athlete, his words and tone of voice reminiscent of those athletes who had responded to similar questions almost sixty years before following the attack on Pearl Harbor. "My great-grandfather was at Pearl Harbor and a lot of my family has gone and fought in wars, and I really haven't done a damn thing as far as laying myself on the line like that," he said. "And so I have a great deal of respect for those that have and what the flag stands for."[4]

He and his brother enlisted, made the Rangers, and did a three-and-a-half-month combat tour in Baghdad. When he returned home he called his friend and agent, Frank Bauer, to say hello. "I told him a lot of clubs were calling about him," said Bauer. "He said he knew he could probably put his papers in to get out because he'd been in combat, but he said, 'I made a commitment for three years and I'll fulfill it.'"[5]

On April 22, 2004, while on a combat patrol in Afghanistan with his Ranger platoon, Tillman was killed by friendly fire after his unit was ambushed by al-Qaeda and Taliban fighters in mountains along the Pakistan border. His tragic death was front-page news across the country. Magazines, newspapers, and television stations recounted his decision to forgo professional football for the military, and people from former teammates and coaches, to senators, and even the president of the United States, lauded his selflessness and patriotism.

Although it was exactly the type of public adulation Tillman abhorred and had diligently avoided, his story reminded Americans about service. It reminded them of the time in our country's history when professional and college athletes were *expected* to put their athletic careers on hold to serve. And even more importantly, it reminded them that there are still young people in America who place serving their country above all else—thousands of young men and women who are not famous, who are not professional athletes, but who are out there, deployed all around the world, putting their lives on the line on behalf of us all. They are the ones who truly deserve our admiration and respect. They are the ones who matter most.

NOTES

Introduction

1. David Halberstam's introduction in Michael MacCambridge, ed., *ESPN Sports Century* (New York: Hyperion, 1999), 1.
2. Bob Feller, interview with Rob Newell, July 2003.
3. Gary Bloomfield, *Duty, Honor, Victory: America's Athletes in WWII* (Guilford, CT: Lyons Press, 2003), 30.
4. Geoffrey C. Ward and Ken Burns, *Baseball—An Illustrated History* (New York: Knopf, 1994), 276. An image of Roosevelt's original letter can be seen at http://www.baseball -almanac.com/prz_lfr2.shtml.
5. Bloomfield, *Duty, Honor, Victory,* 73.
6. Ibid., 30.
7. Ward and Burns, *Baseball,* 279.
8. William Marshall, *Baseball's Pivotal Era, 1945–1951* (Lexington: University Press of Kentucky, 1999), 16.
9. Bloomfield, *Duty, Honor, Victory,* 96.
10. Pat Zacharias, "The Wolverines' Legendary Tom Harmon," *Detroit News,* n.d., n.p. Available at http://info.detnews.com/history/story/index.cfm?id=60&category =people.
11. Paul Baender, *A Hero Perished: The Diary and Selected Letters of Nile Kinnick* (Iowa City: University of Iowa Press, 1991), 58.
12. David S. Neft, Richard M. Cohen, and Richard Korch, *The Complete History of Profes- sional Football from 1892 to the Present,* 2nd ed. (New York: St. Martin's, 1994), 112–13.
13. Bloomfield, *Duty, Honor, Victory,* 249.
14. Jacklummus.com, http://www.jacklummus.com.
15. Peter C. Bjarkman, *The Biographical History of Basketball: More than 500 Portraits of the Most Significant On- and Off-Court Personalities of the Game's Past and Present* (Lincolnwood, IL: Masters Press, 2000), 15–16.
16. Bloomfield, *Duty, Honor, Victory,* 104.
17. Fimrite, "A Half Century Removed, World War II Seems but a Distant Thunder," *Sports Illustrated,* October 16, 1991, 98.
18. John Wooden with Jack Tobin, *They Call Me Coach,* (1972; Chicago: Contemporary Books, 1988), 69.
19. Bloomfield, *Duty, Honor, Victory,* 77.

20. Ibid., 133.

21. Cecil Travis, telephone interview with Rob Newell, September 2000.

Chapter One—The Man in the Hat (Tom Landry)

1. D. D. Lewis, telephone interview with Rob Newell, June 2004.

2. Tom Landry, *Landry* (Grand Rapids, MI: Zondervan Books, 1990), 44.

3. Ibid., 40.

4. Ibid., 47.

5. Bob St. John, *Landry: The Legend and the Legacy* (Nashville, TN: Word Publishing, 2000), 128.

6. Landry, *Landry,* 51.

7. St. John, *Landry: The Legend and the Legacy,* 128.

8. Ibid., 135.

9. Landry, *Landry,* 65.

10. Ibid., 68.

11. Ibid., 69.

12. Ibid., 71.

13. Ibid.

14. Ibid., 72.

15. Ibid.

16. St. John, *Landry: The Legend and the Legacy,* 159.

17. Landry, *Landry,* 73.

18. St. John, *Landry: The Legend and the Legacy,* 172.

19. Ibid., 173.

20. Ibid.

21. Bill Minutaglio, "Thrown for a Loss," *Sporting News,* February 21, 2000, 33.

22. Larry Cole, telephone interview with Rob Newell, July 2004.

23. Charlie Waters, telephone interview with Rob Newell, July 2004.

24. Cole, telephone interview.

25. Waters, telephone interview.

26. Lewis, telephone interview.

27. Tom Landry Jr., telephone interview with Rob Newell, July 2004.

28. St. John, *Landry: The Legend and the Legacy,* 18.

Chapter Two—The Perfectionist (Ted Williams)

1. Michael Seidel, *Ted Williams: A Baseball Life* (Chicago: Contemporary Books, 1991), 113.

2. Ted Williams, *Ted Williams: My Turn at Bat,* (1969; New York: Simon & Schuster, 1988), 97–98.

3. Seidel, *Ted Williams,* 112.

4. Associated Press, "Williams Decides to Play One Season: Red Sox Batting Star Says He Will Enlist after Coming Baseball Campaign," *New York Times,* March 6, 1942, 26.

5. Bobby Doerr, telephone interview with Rob Newell, June 2003.

6. Ward and Burns, *Baseball*, 276.

7. Ibid.

8. Seidel, *Ted Williams*, 122.

9. Ibid., 125.

10. Associated Press, "Red Sox Ace to Get Training as Flier: Williams Asks No Deferment but May Not Be Called by Navy until Season's End—Passes His Tests Highly Rated as Seaman 2d Class—Says Finances Remove 3-A Reclassification Cause," *New York Times*, May 23, 1942, 17.

11. Associated Press, "Ted Williams, Near Solo State, Eager for Naval Flying Career: Red Sox Star Proves a Hard-Working Cadet in Civilian Pilot School at Amherst—Wins Praise of His Instructors," *New York Times*, December 2, 1942, 36.

12. Williams, *My Turn at Bat*, 100.

13. Jim Prime and Bill Nowlin, *Ted Williams: The Pursuit of Perfection* (Champaign, IL: Sports Publishing, LLC, 2002), 81.

14. Williams, *My Turn at Bat*, 104.

15. Ibid., 103.

16. Seidel, *Ted Williams*, 139.

17. Dom DiMaggio, telephone interview with Rob Newell, June 2003.

18. Williams, *My Turn at Bat*, 173.

19. Ibid., 175.

20. Prime and Nowlin, *Ted Williams*, 81.

21. Williams, *My Turn at Bat*, 176.

22. Prime and Nowlin, *Ted Williams*, 82.

23. Williams, *My Turn at Bat*, 179.

24. Prime and Nowlin, *Ted Williams*, 85.

25. Williams, *My Turn at Bat*, 181.

26. Prime and Nowlin, *Ted Williams*, 85.

27. Doerr, telephone interview.

28. Prime and Nowlin, *Ted Williams*, 81.

29. Joe Burris, "Glenn Pays Respects to Proud Fighter Pilot," *Boston Globe*, July 23, 2002, F-5.

Chapter Three—Dr. Jack (Jack Ramsay)

1. John Papanek, "A Man Who Never Lets Down," *Sports Illustrated*, November 1, 1982, 80.

2. Vicki Michaelis, "Ramsay Takes Lessons to Heat," *Palm Beach Post*, October 13, 1994, 1C.

3. Dr. Jack Ramsay, telephone interview with Rob Newell, September 2004.

4. Ibid.

5. Ibid.

6. Ibid.

7. Ibid.

8. Bob Sweet, telephone interview with Rob Newell, September 2004.

9. Bob McKay, telephone interview with Rob Newell, September 2004.

10. Ibid.

11. Jack Ramsay, *Dr. Jack's Leadership Lessons Learned from a Lifetime in Basketball* (Hoboken, NJ: Wiley, 2004), 8.
12. Ramsay, telephone interview.
13. Ramsay, *Dr. Jack's Leadership Lessons,* 9.
14. Ibid.
15. Ibid., 10.
16. Ibid., 8–10.
17. Ramsay, telephone interview.
18. Ramsay, *Dr. Jack's Leadership Lessons,* 11.
19. Papanek, "Man Who Never Lets Down."
20. Ramsay, *Dr. Jack's Leadership Lessons,* 13.
21. McKay, telephone interview.
22. Sam McManis, "Jack Ramsay: In Addition to Being the Coach of the Portland Trail Blazers, He Has a Doctorate in Education and Likes to Compete in Triathlons," *Los Angeles Times,* May 5, 1985, Sports section, 3.
23. Frank Davies, *Miami Herald,* May 26, 1996, Tropic section, 6.
24. Ramsay, *Dr. Jack's Leadership Lessons,* 137.
25. Ramsay, telephone interview.

Chapter Four—Thanks to the Kindness of Strangers (Bob Chappuis)

1. Bob Chappuis, interview with Rob Newell, June 2003.
2. Don Lund, interview with Rob Newell, October 2003.
3. George Ceithmal, interview with Rob Newell, October 2003.
4. Chappuis interview, June 2003.
5. Ibid.
6. Ibid.
7. Ibid.
8. Ibid.
9. "The Specialist," *Time* 50, no. 18, November 3, 1947, 76.
10. Ron Fimrite, "A Half Century Removed, World War II Seems but a Distant Thunder," *Sports Illustrated,* October 16, 1991, 98.
11. Ibid.
12. Chappuis interview, June 2003.
13. Fimrite, "Half Century Removed."
14. Bob Chappuis, interview with Rob Newell, November 2003.
15. Chappuis interview, June 2003.
16. Ibid.
17. Chalmers Elliot, interview with Rob Newell, October 2003.
18. Ceithmal interview.
19. Chappuis interview, June 2003.
20. Ceithmal interview.
21. Don Lund, telephone interview with Rob Newell, October 2003.
22. Chappuis interview, June 2003.

23. Quoted in Chappuis interview, October 2003.
24. Chappuis interview, June 2003.

Chapter Five—Still Serving Others (Jerry Coleman)

1. Jerry Coleman, interview with Rob Newell, May 2003.
2. Coleman interview.
3. Irv Noren, telephone interview with Rob Newell, June 2003.
4. Chuck Greenwood, "Around the Horn," *Sports Collectors Digest*, April 17, 1998, 50.
5. Noren, telephone interview.
6. Bob Aguilina, telephone interview with Rob Newell, June 2003.
7. Coleman interview.
8. Joe Williams, "Ted Williams and Coleman Get Raw Deal," *New York Times*, March 26, 1952.
9. John Drebinger, "Coleman to Open with Yanks," *New York Times*, April 14, 1951.
10. Aguilina, telephone interview.
11. Coleman interview.
12. United Press International (wire), "Coleman Batting 1,000: Yankee Infielder on Successful Air Mission," February 4, 1952.
13. Coleman interview.
14. Ibid.
15. Jim Lucas, *World Telegram and Sun Saturday Magazine*, July 11, 1953, 4.
16. Tom Cushman, "Coleman Never Flinched When War's Shadow Loomed," *San Diego Union Tribune*, March 9, 2003, C4.
17. "Coleman Humble Hero," *New York Times*, September 14, 1953.
18. Greenwood, "Around the Horn."
19. Ted Lightner, interview with Rob Newell, May 2003.
20. Dave Marcus, interview with Rob Newell, May 2003.
21. Bruce Bochy, interview with Rob Newell, May 2003.

Chapter Six—The Pioneer's Champion (Bill Tosheff)

1. Bud Palmer, telephone interview with Rob Newell, February 2003.
2. Alex Tosheff, telephone interview with Rob Newell, February 2003.
3. Bill Tosheff, interview with Rob Newell, January 2003.
4. Dale Vieau, telephone interview with Rob Newell, February 2003.
5. Bill Tosheff interview.
6. Alex Tosheff, telephone interview.
7. Bill Tosheff interview.
8. Ibid.
9. Ibid.
10. Dr. Vince Ruscelli, telephone interview with Rob Newell, February 2003.
11. Palmer, telephone interview.
12. Bill Tosheff interview.
13. Ibid.

14. Ibid.
15. "Pension Fairness for NBA Pioneers," NBA statement during the hearing before the subcommittee on employer-employee relations, U.S. House of Representatives, July 15, 1998.
16. Neil Isaacs, interview with Rob Newell, February 2003.
17. John Ezersky, interview with Rob Newell, February 2003.
18. Ibid.
19. Isaacs interview.
20. Bill Tosheff interview.

Chapter Seven—He Could Have Been President (Nile Kinnick)

1. George "Red" Frye, interview with Rob Newell, July 2003.
2. Erwin Prasse, interview with Rob Newell, July 2003.
3. Ron Fimrite, "With the Wartime Death of the '39 Heisman Winner, America Lost a Leader," *Sports Illustrated*, August 31, 1987, 112. Available at http://iowa.scout.com/2/247034.html.
4. Prasse interview.
5. Fimrite, "With the Wartime Death."
6. Ibid.
7. Frye interview.
8. Ibid.
9. Paul Baender, *A Hero Perished: The Diary and Selected Letters of Nile Kinnick* (Iowa City: University of Iowa Press, 1991), 58.
10. Frye interview.
11. Scott M. Fisher, *The Ironmen* (Philadelphia: Xlibris, 2003), 69.
12. Fimrite, "With the Wartime Death."
13. Fisher, *Ironmen,* 95.
14. Ibid., 103.
15. Fimrite, "With the Wartime Death."
16. Baender, *A Hero Perished,* 106.
17. Fisher, *Ironmen,* 111.
18. Baender, *A Hero Perished,* 29.
19. Fisher, *Ironmen,* 111.
20. Ron Flatter, "Everybody's All-American," September 11, 2003, espn.com, http://espn.go.com/classic/kinnick_nile.html.
21. Fisher, *Ironmen,* 132.
22. Fimrite, "With the Wartime Death."
23. Baender, *A Hero Perished,* 45.
24. Ibid., 58.
25. Ibid.
26. Ibid.
27. Ibid., 89.
28. Ibid., 128.

29. Ibid., 134.
30. Fisher, *Ironmen,* 136.
31. Baender, *A Hero Perished,* 137.
32. Fimrite, "With the Wartime Death."
33. Ibid.
34. Ibid.
35. George Wine, interview with Rob Newell, June 2003.
36. Frye interview.

Chapter Eight—A Legend and a Patriot (Bob Feller)

1. Bob Feller, interview with Rob Newell, July 2003.
2. John Sickels, *Bob Feller: Ace of the Greatest Generation* (Washington, D.C.: Brassey's, 2004), 104.
3. Bob Feller, telephone interview with Rob Newell, March 2000.
4. Sickels, *Bob Feller,* 265.
5. Feller interview, July 2003.
6. John Brown, telephone interview with Rob Newell, May 2004.
7. Bob Feller, *Strikeout Story* (New York: Grosset & Dunlap, 1947), 207.
8. Feller interview, July 2003.
9. Feller, *Strikeout Story,* 214.
10. Sickels, *Bob Feller,* 125.
11. Feller, *Strikeout Story,* 214.
12. Ibid., 216.
13. Ibid., 217.
14. Feller interview, July 2003.
15. Feller, telephone interview, March 2000.
16. Feller, *Strikeout Story,* 218.
17. Eddie Bockman, telephone interview with Rob Newell, April 2004.
18. Sickels, *Bob Feller,* 134.
19. Feller, telephone interview, March 2000.
20. Feller interview, July 2003.
21. In an interview in 1947 with the *Los Angeles Times,* Feller stated that he thought Robinson was a fine athlete but didn't have the baseball talent to play in the major leagues. "He couldn't hit an inside pitch to save his neck . . . if he were a white man, I doubt they would consider him big-league material," Feller was quoted as saying. His comments infuriated Robinson, and although Feller later admitted publicly that he had been wrong about Robinson's ability to play in the major leagues, his words triggered a rift between the two that continued for decades and resulted in charges of racism against Feller (Sickels, *Bob Feller,* 134).
22. Ibid., 277.
23. Feller interview, July 2003.
24. Ray Boone, telephone interview with Rob Newell, April 2004.
25. Feller interview, July 2003.

Chapter Nine—The Quiet Revolutionary (Hank Luisetti)

1. Michael Moran, "The Revolution Started with the Shot He Fired," *New York Times,* December 30, 1986, B-11.
2. Associated Press, "Hank Luisetti, 86, His One-Handed Shot Ruled," *Los Angeles Times,* December 22, 2002, B-12.
3. Moran, "Revolution Started."
4. Sam Goldaper, "Hank Luisetti, 86, Dominator of Basketball's One-Hander," *New York Times,* December 23, 2002, B-7.
5. Fimrite, "A Half Century Removed, World War II Seems but a Distant Thunder," *Sports Illustrated,* October 16, 1991.
6. Ibid.
7. Philip Pallette, *The Game Changer: How Hank Luisetti Revolutionized America's Great Indoor Game* (Bloomington, IN: AuthorHouse, 2005), 389.
8. Jack Laird, telephone interview with Rob Newell, May 2005.
9. Dave Newhouse, "Single-Handed Pioneer," *Oakland Tribune,* March 13, 1996, D-1.
10. Jeff Faraudo, "He Shot Basketball into the Modern Era," *Oakland Tribune,* November 17, 1999.

Chapter Ten—A Texas Hero (Jack Lummus)

1. Frank Golden, telephone interview with Rob Newell, March 2003.
2. George Franck, telephone interview with Rob Newell, March 2003.
3. "Giant Hero," *NBC Gameday.* Produced by Jim Bell and Pete Radovich Jr. Edited by Bill McCullough.
4. Ibid.
5. Pete Wright, telephone interview with Rob Newell, March 2003.
6. Jack Willis, telephone interview with Rob Newell, March 2003.
7. Wright, telephone interview.
8. Howard Conner, *The Spearhead: The World War II History of the 5th Marine Division* (Washington, D.C.: Infantry Journal Press, 1950), 1.
9. "Giant Hero."
10. John Antonelli, personal letter to Mrs. Laura Lummus, May 8, 1945.
11. "Giant Hero."
12. "Biography of Jack Lummus," available at http://www.jacklummus.com/Files/ Files_B/Biography_JackLummus.htm.
13. "Giant Hero."
14. Dr. Tom Brown, telephone interview with Rob Newell, March 2003.
15. "Giant Hero."
16. Mary Hartman, *Texas Granite: Story of a World War II Hero* (Dallas: Hendrick-Long, 1997), 199.
17. Brown, telephone interview.
18. "Giant Hero."
19. Brown, telephone interview.
20. "Giant Hero."
21. Hartman, *Texas Granite,* 210.

22. "Giant Hero."
23. Ibid.
24. "Christening MV 1st LT Jack Lummus," available at http://www.jacklummus.com/ Files/Files_C/christening_mps_1st_lt__jack_lummus.htm.

Chapter Eleven—Determination and Grace (Monte Irvin)

1. Steve Jacobson, "Monte Could Have Been 1st: Irvin Had Chance to Break Barrier," *Newsday,* March 3, 1997.
2. Monte Irvin, with James A. Riley, *Nice Guys Finish First* (New York: Carroll and Graf), 10.
3. Ibid.
4. Patricia and Frederick McKissack, *Black Diamond: The Story of Negro Baseball Leagues* (New York: Scholastic), 96.
5. Irvin, *Nice Guys,* 13.
6. Ibid.
7. McKissack, *Black Diamond,* 98.
8. Irvin, *Nice Guys,* 76.
9. Jack Lang, "Not Bitter, Just Grateful, Beams Shrine Bound Monte," *Sporting News,* February 24, 1973, 36.
10. Irvin, *Nice Guys,* 76.
11. Ibid., 95.
12. Ibid., 107.
13. Ibid., 101.
14. Jacobson, "Monte Could Have Been First."
15. Irvin, *Nice Guys,* 102.
16. Ibid.
17. Ibid., 103.
18. Clay Felker, "Irvin Tabbed as Most Underrated Star," *Sporting News,* October 3, 1951, 11.
19. Irvin, *Nice Guys,* 108.
20. Ibid., 104.
21. Felker, *Sporting News,* 11.
22. Irvin, *Nice Guys,* 103.
23. Ibid., 108.
24. Ibid., 124.
25. Ibid., 125.
27. Ibid., 123.
28. Dick Young and Jack Long, "Willie: Irvin Helped Me Make It," *New York Daily News,* January 24, 1979.
29. Ibid.
30. Transcript of National Baseball Hall of Fame induction ceremonies, August 6, 1973, Cooperstown, New York.
31. Ibid.
32. Irvin, *Nice Guys,* 235.

Chapter Twelve—A Lesson in Perseverance (Bert Shepard)

1. Bert Shepard, telephone interview with Rob Newell, October 2000.
2. John Shepard, telephone interview with Rob Newell, November 2000.
3. Bert Shepard, telephone interview.
4. Ibid.
5. Ibid.
6. Ibid.
7. Ibid.
8. Ibid.
9. John Shepard, telephone interview.
10. Ibid.
11. Quoted in Bill Gilbert, *They Also Served: Baseball and the Homefront, 1941–1945* (New York: Crown, 1992), 167.
12. Bert Shepard, telephone interview.
13. Buddy Lewis, telephone interview with Rob Newell, November 2000.
14. Ibid.
15. Bert Shepard, telephone interview.
16. Ibid.
17. Ibid.
18. John Shepard, telephone interview.
19. Ibid.
20. Bert Shepard, telephone interview.
21. Bill Gilbert, telephone interview with Rob Newell, November 2000.
22. Bert Shepard, telephone interview.

Chapter Thirteen—Just a Kid from the Neighborhood (Art Donovan)

1. Art Donovan, interview with Rob Newell, January 2005.
2. Art Donovan and Bob Drury, *Fatso: Football When Men Were Really Men* (New York: William Morrow, 1987), 95.
3. Donovan interview.
4. Donovan interview; Donovan, *Fatso,* 96.
5. Donovan, *Fatso,* 97.
6. Ibid.
7. Ibid., 98.
8. Ibid., 99.
9. Ibid.
10. Ibid., 100.
11. Donovan interview.
12. Ibid.
13. Jim Mutscheller, telephone interview with Rob Newell, February 2005.
14. Maureen Kilkullin, telephone interview with Rob Newell, February 2005.
15. Ibid.
16. Ordell Brasse, telephone interview with Rob Newell, February 2005.
17. Debbie Donovan, interview with Rob Newell, February 2005.

18. Ibid.
19. Art Donovan interview.

Chapter Fourteen—A Will to Live (Mario Tonelli)

1. Bryan Smith, "To Hell and Back," *Chicago Sun-Times,* February 3, 2002, 23.
2. Mike Isaacs, "The Greatest Tonelli of Them All," *Pioneer Press,* May 26, 1994.
3. John Lukacs, "To Hell and Back: 60 Years Ago, Notre Dame Star Tonelli Faced Horrors of Bataan, Refused to Die," USA Today, August 20, 2002, C-01.
4. Richard M. Gordon, "Bataan, Corregidor, and the Death March: In Retrospect," http://home.pacbell.net/fbaldie/In_Retrospect.html.
5. Alexander Wolff, "Tonelli's Run," *Sports Illustrated,* January 27, 2003, 76–83.
6. Ibid., 79.
7. Rob Lewis, "Nightmare of Bataan: From South Bend to Hell: Gridiron Star Endured Nightmare of Bataan," *American Legion Magazine.*
8. Lukacs, "To Hell and Back."
9. Lewis, "Nightmare of Bataan."
10. Joe Goddard, "What's Up with Motts Tonelli," *Chicago Sun-Times,* November 11, 2001, 106.
11. "The Fate of the POWS near War's End," http://history.acusd.edu/gen/st/~ehimchak/fate.html.
12. Tom Buck (as told to by Mario Tonelli), *LifeTimes,* August 1991.
13. Goddard, "What's Up with Motts Tonelli."
14. Lukacs, "To Hell and Back."
15. Buck, *LifeTimes,* August 1991.
16. Isaacs, "Greatest Tonelli of Them All."
17. Wolff, "Tonelli's Run."
18. B. Smith, "To Hell and Back."
19. Ibid.

Chapter Fifteen—Forever Changed (Cecil Travis, Lou Brissie, and Lefty Brewer)

1. Ted Williams, *Ted Williams: My Turn at Bat* (1969; New York: Simon & Schuster, 1988), 69.
2. Fimrite, *Sports Illustrated,* "A Half Century Removed, World War II Seems but a Distant Thunder," *Sports Illustrated,* October 16, 1991, 98.
3. Cecil Travis, telephone interview with Rob Newell, September 2000.
4. Fimrite, "Half Century Removed."
5. Ibid.
6. Travis, telephone interview.
7. Ibid.
8. Ibid.
9. Lou Brissie, telephone interview with Rob Newell, October 2000.
10. Ibid.
11. Bill Brewer, telephone interview with Rob Newell, October 2000.
12. Ibid.

13. Gary Bedingfield, *Baseball in World War II Europe* (Charleston, SC: Arcadia, 1999), 111.
14. Brewer, telephone interview.
15. Bedingfield, *Baseball in World War II Europe,* 113.

Epilogue: The Throwback (Pat Tillman)

1. Mike Wise and Josh White, "Ex-NFL Player Tillman Killed in Combat; Army Ranger Turned Down Millions to Serve His Country in Afghanistan," *Washington Post,* April 24, 2004, 1.
2. Gary Smith, "Code of Honor Throughout Tillman's Life," *Sports Illustrated,* May 5, 2004. Available at http://motherboard2.dnssys.com/discus/messages/5/20992.html ?1083358333.
3. Ibid.
4. Wise and White, "Ex-NFL Player Tillman," 1.
5. Ibid.

BIBLIOGRAPHY

Books

Baender, Paul, ed. *A Hero Perished: The Diary and Selected Letters of Nile Kinnick.* Iowa City: University of Iowa Press, 1991.

Bedingfield, Gary. *Baseball in World War II Europe.* Charleston, SC: Arcadia, 1999.

Bjarkman, Peter C. *The Biographical History of Basketball: More than 500 Portraits of the Most Significant On- and Off-Court Personalities of the Game's Past and Present.* Lincolnwood, IL: Masters Press, 2000.

Bloomfield, Gary. *Duty, Honor, Victory: America's Athletes in WWII.* Guilford, CT: Lyons Press, 2003.

Conner, Howard. *The Spearhead: The World War II History of the 5th Marine Division.* Washington, D.C.: Infantry Journal Press, 1950.

Donovan, Art, and Bob Drury. *Fatso: Football When Men Were Really Men.* New York: William Morrow, 1987.

Feller, Bob. *Strikeout Story.* New York: Grosset & Dunlap, 1947.

Fisher, Scott M. *The Ironmen.* Philadelphia: Xlibris, 2003.

Gilbert, Bill. *They Also Served: Baseball and the Homefront, 1941–1945.* New York: Crown, 1992.

Hartman, Mary. *Texas Granite: Story of a World War II Hero.* Dallas: Hendrick-Long, 1997.

Irvin, Monte, with James A. Riley. *Nice Guys Finish First.* New York: Carroll and Graf, 1996.

Landry, Tom. *Landry.* Grand Rapids, MI: Zondervan Books, 1990.

MacCambridge, Michael, ed. *ESPN Sports Century.* New York: Hyperion, 1999.

Marshall, William. *Baseball's Pivotal Era, 1945–1951.* Lexington: University Press of Kentucky, 1999.

McKissack, Patricia and Frederick. *Black Diamond: The Story of Negro Baseball Leagues.* New York: Scholastic, 1994.

Neft, David S., Richard M. Cohen, and Richard Korch. *The Complete History of Professional Football from 1892 to the Present,* 2nd ed. New York: St. Martin's, 1994.

Pallette, Philip. *The Game Changer: How Hank Luisetti Revolutionized America's Great Indoor Game.* Bloomington, IN: AuthorHouse, 2005.

Prime, Jim, and Bill Nowlin. *Ted Williams: The Pursuit of Perfection.* Champaign, IL: Sports Publishing, LLC, 2002.

Ramsay, Jack. *Dr. Jack's Leadership Lessons Learned from a Lifetime in Basketball.* Hoboken, NJ: Wiley, 2004.

Seidel, Michael. *Ted Williams: A Baseball Life.* Chicago: Contemporary Books, 1991.

Sickels, John. *Bob Feller: Ace of the Greatest Generation.* Washington, D.C.: Brassey's, 2004.

St. John, Bob. *Landry: The Legend and the Legacy.* Nashville, TN: Word Publishing, 2000.

Ward, Geoffrey C., and Ken Burns. *Baseball: An Illustrated History.* New York: Knopf, 1994.

Williams, Ted. *My Turn at Bat.* New York: Simon & Schuster, 1969, reprt. 1988.

Wooden, John, with Jack Tobin. *They Call Me Coach.* Chicago: Contemporary Books, 1972, reprt. 1988.

Magazines, Newspapers, Television, Other

Antonelli, John. Personal letter to Mrs. Laura Lummus, May 8, 1945.

Associated Press, "Hank Luisetti, 86, His One-Handed Shot Ruled." *Los Angeles Times,* December 22, 2002, B-12.

Associated Press. "Red Sox Ace to Get Training as Flier: Williams Asks No Deferment but May Not Be Called by Navy until Season's End—Passes His Tests Highly Rated as Seaman 2d Class—Says Finances Remove 3-A Reclassification Cause." *New York Times,* May 23, 1942, 17.

Associated Press. "Ted Williams, Near Solo State, Eager for Naval Flying Career: Red Sox Star Proves a Hard-Working Cadet in Civilian Pilot School at Amherst—Wins Praise of His Instructors." *New York Times,* December 1, 1942, 36.

Associated Press. "Williams Decides to Play One Season: Red Sox Batting Star Says He Will Enlist after Coming Baseball Campaign." *New York Times,* March 6, 1942, 26.

"Biography of Jack Lummus." Available at http://www.jacklummus.com/Files/Files_B /Biography_JackLummus.htm.

Buck, Tom. As told by Mario Tonelli. *LifeTimes 6,* no. 8, August 1991, 1.

Burris, Joe. "Glenn Pays Respects to Proud Fighter Pilot." *Boston Globe,* July 23, 2002, F-5.

"Christening MV 1st LT Jack Lummus." Available at http://www.jacklummus.com/Files/ Files_C/christening_mps_1st_lt__jack_lummus.htm.

"Coleman Humble Hero." *New York Times,* September 14, 1953.

Cushman, Tom. "Coleman Never Flinched When War's Shadow Loomed." *San Diego Union Tribune,* March 9, 2003, C4.

Davies, Frank. *Miami Herald,* Tropic section, May 26, 1996.

Drebinger, John. "Coleman to Open with Yanks." *New York Times,* April 14, 1951.

Faraudo, Jeff. "He Shot Basketball into the Modern Era." *Oakland Tribune,* November 17, 1999.

"The Fate of the POWS near War's End." Available at http://history.acusd.edu/gen/ st/~ehimchak/fate.html.

Felker, Clay. "Irvin Tabbed as Most Underrated Star." *Sporting News,* October 3, 1951, 11.

Fimrite, Ron. "A Half Century Removed, World War II Seems but a Distant Thunder." *Sports Illustrated,* October 16, 1991, 98.

———. "With the Wartime Death of the '39 Heisman Winner, America Lost a Leader." *Sports Illustrated,* August 31, 1987, 112. Available at http://iowa.scout.com/2/247034.html.

Flatter, Ron. "Everybody's All-American," September 11, 2003, espn.com, http://espn .go.com/classic/kinnick_nile.html.

"Giant Hero." *NBC Gameday.* Produced by Jim Bell and Pete Radovich Jr. Edited by Bill McCullough.

Goddard, Joe. "What's Up with Motts Tonelli." *Chicago Sun-Times,* November 11, 2001, 106.

Goldaper, Sam, "Hank Luisetti, 86, Dominator of Basketball's One-Hander." *New York Times,* December 23, 2002, B-7.

Gordon, Richard M. "Bataan, Corregidor, and the Death March: In Retrospect." Available at http://home.pacbell.net/fbaldie/In_Retrospect.html.

Greenwood, Chuck. "Around the Horn." *Sports Collectors Digest,* April 17, 1998, 50.

Isaacs, Mike. "The Greatest Tonelli of Them All." *Pioneer Press,* May 26, 1994.

Jacobson, Steve. "Monte Could Have Been 1st: Irvin Had Chance to Break Barrier." *Newsday,* March 3, 1997.

Lang, Jack. "Not Bitter, Just Grateful, Beams Shrine Bound Monte." *Sporting News,* February 24, 1973, 36.

Lewis, Rob. "Nightmare of Bataan: From South Bend to Hell: Gridiron Star Endured Nightmare of Bataan." *American Legion Magazine.*

Lucas, Jim. *World Telegram and Sun Saturday Magazine,* July 11, 1953, 4.

Lukacs, John. "To Hell and Back: 60 Years Ago, Notre Dame Star Tonelli Faced Horrors of Bataan, Refused to Die." *USA Today,* August 20, 2002, C-01.

McManis, Sam. "Jack Ramsay: In Addition to Being the Coach of the Portland Trail Blazers, He Has a Doctorate in Education and Likes to Compete in Triathlons." *Los Angeles Times,* May 5, 1985, Sports 3.

Michaelis, Vicki. "Ramsay Takes Lessons to Heat." *Palm Beach Post,* October 13, 1994, C-1.

Minutaglio, Bill. "Thrown for a Loss." *Sporting News,* February 21, 2000, 33.

Moran, Michael. "The Revolution Started with the Shot He Fired." *New York Times,* December 30, 1986, B-11.

Newhouse, Dave. "Single-Handed Pioneer." *Oakland Tribune,* March 13, 1996, D-1.

Papanek, John. "A Man Who Never Lets Down." *Sports Illustrated,* November 1, 1982, 80.

"Pension Fairness for NBA Pioneers," NBA statement during the hearing before the subcommittee on employer-employee relations. U.S. House of Representatives, July 15, 1998.

Smith, Bryan. "To Hell and Back." *Chicago Sun-Times,* February 3, 2002, 23.

Smith, Gary. "Code of Honor Throughout Tillman's Life." *Sports Illustrated,* May 3, 2004. Available at http://motherboard2.dnssys.com/discus/messages/5/20992.html ?1083358333.

"The Specialist." *Time* 50, No. 18, November 3, 1947, 76.

Transcript of National Baseball Hall of Fame induction ceremonies, August 6, 1973, Cooperstown, New York.

United Press International (wire). "Coleman Batting 1,000: Yankee Infielder on Successful Air Mission," February 4, 1952.

Williams, Joe. "Ted Williams and Coleman Get Raw Deal." *New York Times,* March 26, 1952.

Wise, Mike, and Josh White. "Ex-NFL Player Tillman Killed in Combat; Army Ranger Turned Down Millions to Serve His Country in Afghanistan." *Washington Post,* April 24, 2004, 1.

Wolff, Alexander. "Tonelli's Run." *Sports Illustrated,* January 27, 2003, 76–83.

Young, Dick, and Jack Long. "Willie: Irvin Helped Me Make It." *New York Daily News,* January 24, 1979.

Zacharias, Pat. "The Wolverines' Legendary Tom Harmon." *Detroit News.* Available at http://info.detnews.com/history/story/index.cfm?id=60&category=people.

Interviews

Aguilina, Bob. Telephone interview with Rob Newell, June 2003.

Bochy, Bruce. Interview with Rob Newell, May 2003.

Bockman, Eddie. Telephone interview with Rob Newell, April 2004.

Boone, Ray. Telephone interview with Rob Newell, April 2004.

Brasse, Ordell. Telephone interview with Rob Newell, February 2005.

Brewer, Bill. Telephone interview with Rob Newell, October 2000.

Brisse, Lou. Telephone interview with Rob Newell, October 2000.

Brown, Dr. Tom. Telephone interview with Rob Newell, March 2003.

Brown, John. Telephone interview with Rob Newell, May 2004.

Ceithmal, George. Interview with Rob Newell, October 2003.

Chappuis, Bob. Interview with Rob Newell, June 2003, November 2003.

Cole, Larry. Telephone interview with Rob Newell, July 2004.

Coleman, Jerry. Interview with Rob Newell, May 2003.

DiMaggio, Dom. Telephone interview with Rob Newell, June 2003.

Doerr, Bobby. Telephone interview with Rob Newell, June 2003.

Donovan, Art. Interview with Rob Newell, January 2005.

Donovan, Debbie. Interview with Rob Newell, February 2005.

Elliot, Chalmers. Interview with Rob Newell, October 2003.

Ezersky, John. Interview with Rob Newell, February 2003.

Feller, Bob. Interview with Rob Newell, July 2003.

Franck, George. Telephone interview with Rob Newell, March 2003.

Frye, George "Red." Interview with Rob Newell, July 2003.

Gilbert, Bill. Telephone interview with Rob Newell, November 2000.

Golden, Frank Telephone interview with Rob Newell, March 2003.

Isaacs, Neil. Interview with Rob Newell, February 2003.

Kilkullin, Maureen. Telephone interview with Rob Newell, February 2005.

Landry, Tom Jr. Telephone interview with Rob Newell, July 2004.

Lewis, Buddy. Telephone interview with Rob Newell, November 2000.

Lewis, D. D. Telephone interview with Rob Newell, June 2004.

Lightner, Ted. Interview with Rob Newell, May 2003.

Lund, Don. Interview with Rob Newell, October 2003.

Marcus, Dave. Interview with Rob Newell, May 2003.

McKay, Bob. Telephone interview with Rob Newell, September 2004.

Mutscheller, Jim. Telephone interview with Rob Newell, February 2005.

Noren, Irv. Telephone interview with Rob Newell, June 2003.

Palmer, Bud. Telephone interview with Rob Newell, February 2003.

Prasse, Erwin. Interview with Rob Newell, July 2003.

Ramsay, Dr. Jack. Telephone interview with Rob Newell, September 2004.

Ruscelli, Dr. Vince. Telephone interview with Rob Newell, February 2003.

Shepard, Bert. Telephone interview with Rob Newell, October 2000.

Shepard, John. Telephone interview with Rob Newell, November 2000.

Sweet, Bob. Telephone interview with Rob Newell, September 2004.

Tosheff, Alex. Telephone interview with Rob Newell, February 2003.

Tosheff, Bill. Interview with Rob Newell, January 2002.

Travis, Cecil. Telephone interview with Rob Newell, September 2000.

Vieau, Dale. Telephone interview with Rob Newell, February 2003.

Waters, Charlie. Telephone interview with Rob Newell, July 2004.

Willis, Jack. Telephone interview with Rob Newell, March 2003.

Wine, George. Interview with Rob Newell, June 2003.

Wright, Pete. Telephone interview with Rob Newell, March 2003.

INDEX

ABOUT THE AUTHOR

Rob Newell is a career Navy Public Affairs Officer and a lifelong sports fan. He and his wife, Mary, live in Springfield, Virginia, with their four children, Mary Kate, Sally, Robby, and Timmy.